Eve

C. E. Rowland

MNEMOSYNE
BOOKWORKS

Published by Mnemosyne Bookworks
MnemosyneBookworks@gmail.com

ISBN-13: 978-1-941159-05-7

We must be willing to let go of the life we planned so as to have the life that is waiting for us.

-Joseph Campbell

ONE

This was her third child, but they had called her an Eve since before the first one. Her name was Nasim.

It was her third labor, begun so recently that the midwife was still en route, and the only person standing next to her bed was Delia. She was trying to convince Nasim that she should meet the adoptive parents. "The Vice President, you know. It could be a useful connection."

Nasim was shaking her head so subtly that when Delia persisted Nasim thought that she hadn't noticed.

"If you ever wanted anything-"

Nasim held up her hand to silence Delia. "What could I ever want that he could give me? What could I *ever* ask for that I don't already have? All I want is to be freed from Eden, and he won't give me that."

A contraction.

Delia waited a minute, two minutes after it had ended. "Why not just shake their hands? It doesn't cost you anything; it could pay you back something."

"I've never met any of the parents. They really came all this way?"

"They always come," Delia said. "All of them come.

It's not a small thing to receive a child."

"Are you sure it's him? I thought they already had a boy." Maybe Delia wasn't sure. Maybe it wasn't him. Then she would let it go.

"He's important. Important people get more than they're entitled to. Sometimes important people grant others more than *they're* entitled to."

"Maybe I'll meet them afterwards," Nasim shrugged.

"You won't want to meet them afterwards. You'll be exhausted."

And Peter will be here by then, thought Nasim. *Peter won't even suggest it.*

The midwife arrived, a bag of supplies with her. "You doing okay, hon?" she asked. She was looking at her chart. The third child was never difficult, and the Eve was plenty young.

"Some water?" Nasim asked Delia, who understood that the topic was closed.

Seven hours later, it was finished. The child was born healthy, easily. Nasim had never asked its sex and never been told. She didn't touch it, didn't look at it. She held her hands over her ears as it cried, and some recently arrived attendant hurried it out of the room. The midwife waited through the afterbirth, her shoes kicked off and her feet savoring the luxury of the thick carpet. Afterwards she gathered the soiled birthing sheets and departed wordlessly.

Delia had left five hours earlier, and now only Peter remained. He switched off the bedside lamp, leaving them bathed in the silver light of the full moon. He slumped into an armchair near the head of the bed, then pulled a small package wrapped in brown paper from a drawer in the bedside table between them.

"For you," he said. "Because it's done again." After a pause, he added, "And we've been with you for six years. A little more, actually." He extended the package to Nasim, but she didn't take it.

Sweat still beaded on her upper lip, and her hair was damp with it.

"Get me a blanket?"

Peter left the package at her elbow and walked to the door halfway down the hall. He could just make her out still through the darkness, just see as she examined the paper, worked at the tape. In the closet he found a thin down blanket, the same one he had retrieved for her after the last child.

"Not that one," she said when he was close enough for her to make out its blue color. "Doesn't matter which, just not that one."

He turned back to retrieve a different blanket.

"It's beautiful," she said, switching the light back on. In her hand, she held a framed photograph, the brown paper folded and laid on her lap. The picture was an aerial view of a stand of trees, five hundred perhaps. It could have been in black and white, a sea of bare, tangled branches, but for the single tree at the center, its heavy bows decked in green. That tree was smaller than the rest or maybe just dwarfed by their sheer number; but it was alive, and the others were dead.

Peter's hand was waiting on a yellow quilt, but he didn't move. The closet door blocked their view of each other. "Do you know what that's from?"

He should know better than to ask a question when he knows the answer, Nasim thought. *Particularly today.* She clenched her jaw, shook her head.

"The ash borers. They came in shipping crates from

China and devoured every ash tree on this continent. That one was in an ash forest. Half a million trees, and just one left at the end." He took the blanket from the closet and closed its door. "Ash trees reproduced sexually, but that's the only one now."

Peter draped the blanket around her, concealing beneath it the halo of sweat already soaked into the clean sheets. No matter, he would change them again when she showered, or Delia would do it if her shift started before he had had the chance. He pulled a handkerchief from his pocket and wiped Nasim's brow with it.

"Thank you, Peter. That's all for tonight, I think."

"Of course." He turned to go but didn't. "May I ask, Nasim…?"

Nasim clenched her jaw again. Better to have Peter here than Delia, she reminded herself. Delia's sympathy only made her feel the pain more acutely, but Peter soaked it up, made it disappear. "Go ahead."

"Did you want to hold the child this time?"

"It's not my child, not mine to hold. It's easier to let go of something you've never had."

He waited for her to volunteer more, and when she didn't, he continued, "Don't you think it might give you some closure? Even knowing the gender of the child might help with... Weren't you curious?"

"I don't know, Peter. How could I not be? But curiosity is different from wanting to know."

"Maybe, though-"

"Thank you, Peter. That's all for tonight," she interrupted.

He touched the glass on the bedside table, touched the blue pill that he had laid next to it. "Ring if you need-"

"Thank you, Peter."

Two

The bullhorn squawked a few times before the man behind it mastered its operation. Cringing, he mouthed an apology to the man standing behind him before addressing the crowd, "We all know why we're here today." His brown hair was prematurely streaked with grey; his suit fit him well enough, though his tie was a bit old-fashioned. The bullhorn cut out for a few syllables before picking up again with his response to the blank expressions on the faces before him, "…support of Scott Davis's campaign to be your next Representative in Congress. So with no ado whatsoever, here's Scott!"

It wasn't a big event. Sixty people, maybe. Half what they had hoped, but the weather was foul, the wind whipping the intermittent rain, which, falling in March, meant everything would be frozen slick by nightfall. There was a smattering of applause. Was it the right time to begin the campaign? The balance of the calculus - an unknown candidate, the threat of burnout, a limited supply of cash, the extra time in the public eye - suggested it was, and Scott had declared his candidacy just the day before while chewing on the fear that they had left a variable out of their equation.

He seized the bullhorn from the man in front of him and

walked out to the edge of the stage. "Hello out there!" The applause strengthened momentarily, and he held up his hand for silence in case a photographer chose to freeze the moment for tomorrow's paper. "I can't tell you how happy I am that you all came out in spite of this awful weather. I know some of you are here for the cause I represent, but don't worry if you're not sure what that is because you'll know in about" - he looked at his watch - "three minutes."

It was the best speechwriter he could afford for now, but in spite of his skepticism, a murmur of humor ran through the crowd on cue.

"So what I'd like to do this afternoon is to introduce myself and my platform. Because I'm sure some of you are wondering, Who is Scott Davis, and what can he do for me?

"I grew up just down the road from here in M-----, went away for college, and came back after with my wife to raise my family in the very best place I know. That was the year the Plague hit." He looked at the woman standing across the stage from him, summoned the most earnest look he had, and shook his head the way the speechwriter had told him. There was an audible stir in the crowd, some uncomfortable shifting. "And my God if it wasn't the hardest decision my wife and I ever made to get those vaccines, to bring an end to our dreams of having a family." Eyes back on the crowd, though almost half the audience was sharing a pained moment with a spouse. As planned.

"Some people said it was an easy choice - the choice to live with the vaccine or die by the Plague. But I say it was a hard choice - the choice between living safely in a world with no future or risking one's own life to ensure that humanity would go on. If the odds of survival had been better, I think a lot of us would have taken that chance, a lot of us would have chosen the families we could have had, the future we could have had." Scott paused, nodded, and watched as his audience mirrored him.

"We spent more than five years thinking we were the last of mankind. Five years without a ray of hope, and then salvation: a new vaccine, one that no longer required us to make that choice. We could have protection from the Plague, and we could have our children, too. But there's a catch." He reminded himself that he should be pleased, not surprised, that the crowd was hanging on his words.

"We've now counted every woman who was willing to risk the Plague, every woman who was braver than I was, braver than my family was, braver than so many of us were." He said it, punctuated with his right arm, then dropped his hands to his side. "They are very few.

"In years past, we have called on soldiers to protect our freedom. We have leaned on civil servants - on firefighters and medics and police - to protect our lives. And now we look to these women to grant us a future.

"We have never faced a challenge as grave as this one. We could not go on as a country, as a nation, as a people but for these brave women. They are the heroes of this generation and of every generation to come." He didn't hit it right. The pause was too long, and the applause broke before he got out the next line, "Because they are the mothers of the future."

He let the clapping run for a five-count, then held up his hand for silence again. This time he was rewarded with a quick succession of flashes. One camera or more, he couldn't tell, but Alex would have counted them.

"So let's treat them like heroes!" It was the first departure from his solemn tempo, the first raising of his voice. Someone in the crowd whooped in reply, and Scott permitted a genuine smile to cross his face for the first time that day.

"Lock them up in cages!" It was a voice from somewhere in front of him. "Is that how you treat heroes? Breed them like animals?!"

Someone at the side of the stage dove into the crowd, towards the voice. The sudden silence was stunning and then broken again, "That's what he'll do to them!" Scott could see Alex now, could see that he was dragging the voice away. The people in the crowd shifted to let them pass. Some looked aghast from her to him; some eyed one or the other with doubt or confusion. The spell had been broken. Scott stumbled through a few more lines of his speech, but the tempo was off, and the crowd was dispersing; and he wasn't sure what he was supposed to do.

Alex found him shaking hands a few minutes later. "She gave me a card."

"Who is she?"

"Doesn't say a name."

"What then?"

"'Justice Always Prevails.'" He read off the white-on-black business card he was holding.

Scott shook another hand, grabbed another elbow, then turned to Alex. "A little melodramatic, don't you think?"

"It won't be hard to find out who she is. And if she's turning out this early in the game, we'll need to know everything about her."

Alex was right. It wasn't hard at all. The next morning, the photo of Scott, hand raised in the air, appeared on the front page of the *Post News*. The headline read, "Candidate Scott Davis Heckled by Anti-Eden Project Activist," and the activist was identified by name three lines into the story: Eleanore Biggs.

THREE

Nasim awoke in the late morning and groped, eyes closed, for the button at the side of her bed. She could hear the instantaneous response, the scraping of a chair pushed back from the dining table, the crunch in the pile of the carpet of her bedroom.

"Can you do something about the damn light?" She hadn't opened her eyes.

"Oh, windows aren't switched." Delia said it apologetically, and Nasim felt a twinge of remorse for snapping at Delia over something Peter had neglected.

Delia flipped a switch at each of the windows, turning the glass from transparent to opaque. Then, silhouetted in the bedroom doorway, she said, "Can I do anything else for you, or shall I let you get back to sleep?"

"I'm fine, Delia."

Nasim saw the silhouette hesitate. She could feel Delia's desire to ask - how the rest had gone, how she was doing.

"I'll tell you everything later," Nasim said.

Delia padded wordlessly back down the hall, and Nasim heard the scrape of the chair as she sat down again at the table.

"You and Peter both say you don't mind, but how can you not mind? Twelve hours every day, and not a single day off?" Nasim was curled up on the deep, burgundy couch in the living room of her coop. She forced herself to get out of bed every day now, even if she only made it as far as the couch. Delia sat beside her.

"Well, *you* never get a day off. And it's only temporary." Delia paused half a beat. "Besides, we both love you."

"I met him, you know. His name's Enzo," Nasim said.

"Oh! I didn't know you'd met him already. I didn't even know they had finished the profile matching. And? What did you think?" Delia's genuine interest was exaggerated, an attempt to veil her disappointment at having been kept in the dark. Peter must have been on duty when the new handler had stopped by, and why wouldn't he have told her? Why wouldn't Nasim have?

"He's a good match. He had some business - family, something - to take care of before he started, but he's moved here, I think."

"So it's all definite?"

Nasim nodded, "He's the one." She had asked Peter to keep it a secret. She had wanted to tell Delia, of course. In fact, she would have preferred that Delia have been the one present when Enzo had come so that the two of them could have shared a secret kept from Peter, but that hadn't been how it had transpired. So she had waited: Such a luxury to have a secret, to exercise this modicum of control. Such a rarity to be the one with the power.

Delia pried, "I have to know more."

"Why?"

"You know perfectly well why."

"Hoping for a little romance?" Nasim teased.

Delia flushed, "Well, no. Well. Yes. It's not so easy for us. It's not as though we can wander into town some evening for a date, you know?"

"What's stopping you? Other than the twelve hour shifts, obviously."

"Oh, I don't know. But even if we could, no one could ever understand what it's like to be a handler unless… well, unless they're a handler. And that's not a very big pool. At least not when you consider just the ones on this campus and then just the men."

"So what you're saying is…" and Nasim laughed.

"That I wouldn't *not* consider it under the right circumstances, which would obviously be if he's… uh…"

"Yes, Delia. He is. Very handsome. Tall and dark. Heartbreaking eyes."

"Is he?!"

"No. You of all people know-"

"That you didn't even look," Delia finished.

"But if that's what you want him to be, then what's stopping you from holding onto that image until the moment he gets here?" Nasim quipped.

"I didn't think you'd be so… cheerful today." Delia leaned into Nasim. "Six months of R&R before the next one."

"I know." Just by pointing it out, Delia had shattered the spell. The weight of the last days - and years - shattered the moment's respite as it fell back onto Nasim's shoulders.

"Was it awful?" Delia asked.

"Will you get me something from the kitchen, and I'll tell you about it." A question without a question's intonation.

"Mmm," Delia nodded. She retrieved a sheet of paper she had left on the round table that stood behind the couch, set with its four chairs into a bay of windows that looked out over manicured lawns and, beyond, thick woods bare with the season. "I called the kitchen earlier to find out what was freshest," she said, handing the note to Nasim. "I thought even you might need a real meal today."

"Trout. Extra brussel sprouts. Fried, though. Roasted, whatever. Not boiled. And make sure they don't give me any rice this time. They think because I'm 'ethnic' that I want rice with everything."

Delia swallowed the temptation to point out that Nasim had only once received an unrequested portion of rice. Instead, she picked up an old-fashioned phone, dialed the kitchen, then put on a heavy coat. "We'll be getting snow any day, I think," she said, before slipping out the door.

Nasim hadn't moved when Delia returned with a paper bag filled with boxes of food. Delia unpacked the bag onto the table and plated Nasim's food before unwrapping a sandwich she had brought back for herself. They both sat in silence on the couch watching curls of steam from Nasim's plate dissolve into the air. "Fork?" Nasim asked.

"Oh gosh, of course," Delia said, auditory filler while she retrieved a fork, knife, and napkin.

While they ate, Nasim began recounting the details of the night before. Then she fell into silence, and handed her half-cleared plate back to Delia. "Not hungry anymore."

FOUR

The breadth of Eleanore Biggs's shoulders was exaggerated by the cut of her suit jacket, cinched narrow at her waist. She was tall, her hands large even in proportion to the rest of her, and her grip was firm, though the severity of her pale blue eyes regularly inspired flaccid handshakes from others. She was, at the moment, fixing her short hair - a few blind ruffles from both hands - and when she finished, she turned to Sam.

"I'd say that went well."

Sam nodded in agreement. "We certainly have their attention. And I've no doubt we'll share the headlines tomorrow."

"Did you contact *The Star*?"

"And the *Post News*. They'll both be keeping an eye open for us in the future. They asked for a quote for the story."

"And?"

"I told them we'd give them an exclusive if they call tomorrow. We don't want to be buried in the fifth paragraph of Davis's article."

"I don't disagree," Eleanore said.

They were sitting in a large outbuilding at the edge of Eleanore's estate, off an access road that came in a back gate that no one but Sam ever used. The room was too cold; Eleanore picked up a heavy silk scarf rumpled on the table and wrapped it around her neck, pacing the length of the room as she did. Sam sat at the table, still wearing a thick winter coat, hands in pockets. At the other end of the room was a substantial mahogany desk, a black leather chair behind it. They hadn't had need of the building for years, and the dust on the desk made the wood dull in spite of the bright overhead lights.

"Do we have an in at the Davis campaign?" Sam asked.

"Money buys a lot of things, and an in is one of them. We'll know his schedule better than he does. And I daresay what I've allocated for that line item will buy us a good deal more information than that."

"Are we bringing in anyone else?"

"Only peripherally, I think."

"Like old times," Sam smiled. "We should develop our materials."

"I'll have the groundskeeper come down tomorrow and get the boiler running. And someone to clean." Eleanore was leaning against the desk now and tracing patterns in the dust with her gloved hand. "We can get to work in earnest tomorrow evening."

Sam rose and poured a drink from a tumbler on a table in the corner. "Want one?"

"Thanks."

"Give me a sense of the scope you're envisioning," Sam said, pouring a second glass.

"You know the really sickening thing about crises like the Plague? The thing that gets me the most? The unjustified sense of national cohesiveness it spawns. President with low approval ratings? Bomb your second biggest city, blame a terrorist, and you'll be more popular than FDR. Crash the stock market, blame Chinese hackers, you're fucking JFK. And what comes after? The ability to govern on the basis of meaningful debate goes out the window. Politics is a game of contention, and what the Plague has left us with is a bunch of idiots like Scott Davis and Celia Pederson, who agree on every point of every issue except the Eden Project. Well, if the Eden Project is what people are going to care about this year, then I suppose that's what we'll care about, too."

"Mm."

"You've seen the polls, of course?"

"Last I saw, half the population hadn't heard of the Eden Project, and the other half was split down the center. Fifty percent wouldn't give up free choice to save their own mothers, and fifty percent can't stand the thought of leaving the future of the free world - the whole world - in the hands of a bunch of immigrants who were too poor to get hold of a fifty dollar vaccine."

"Do you have a sense of the number of people, of women we're talking about?"

"Not off the top of my head."

"Five hundred million people in the country; figure conservatively twenty percent of those are women of child-bearing age. The vaccination rate was close to 90%. Among the unvaccinated, the infection rate was almost a hundred percent, and among those, fatality rate was-"

"Eighty percent."

"That leaves two million fertile women."

"Less than half a percent of the population," Sam sighed.

"Since the new vaccine came out, all anyone wants to

talk about is how to move forward. And of course the only way to move forward is with the cooperation of the those women. Or, in the right political climate, without their cooperation. This election decides it. But I'm sure I don't have to tell you that if you've so much as looked at a campaign ad this year."

"Not a position I envy those women. How many of them were hold-outs against the first vaccination campaign? Do you know?"

"What, the women who wanted this role? The women who rolled the dice so they could have children?"

"Yeah."

Eleanore shook her head. "I don't know. Maybe a tenth of them, probably fewer."

"What's the demographic of the rest?"

"Poor. Young. Most don't speak English. In a word, exploitable."

Sam topped off both drinks before returning to the seat at the table. "It's a good fight to fight."

"Well, it's the only fight we've got, so it's a good thing it's a good one."

FIVE

It was the first time since the day Peter and Delia arrived that more than two places had been set at the round table behind Nasim's deep, red couch. She had called the kitchen a week before to ask about having a waiter sent, about the nice flatware, about alcohol, which, given the nature of her vocation, was never available without special dispensation. A man had shown up half an hour beforehand with a cart of covered plates, chilled bottles, and an elegant table cloth that he busied himself with. It seldom occurred to Nasim anymore how strange it would have once seemed to watch someone work without offering to help.

By the time Peter and Delia arrived - Delia having gone to change into something nicer because there were so rarely special occasions and Peter not yet on duty - the table was set, the cart of food tucked out of sight in the kitchenette; and the waiter stood at attention just far enough from the table as to be unobtrusive. They had walked in together, a half-knock on the doorframe honoring the special occasion, and they all felt silly when Nasim tried to take the coats that they were already hanging in the closet themselves.

Nasim ushered them wordlessly towards the couch and

then looked from them to the waiter and back while Peter and Delia exchanged glances, their own silence inspired by Nasim's pantomime. When the waiter stepped forward and asked what they would drink, Nasim's excitement bubbled over. "I hope it's okay. I wanted to do something special, and I didn't know what; and I hope that... that this is okay."

It was Peter who said, "Nasim, of course it's going to be won-"

But she interrupted him, "After all you've both done for me, it's something for you, you know. For the three of us, really. Because, as Peter pointed out, it's been more than six years now. And because you've both done so much more than I could have asked. Always, you have, but especially since Cath left you've really had no choice. So it's for us. To celebrate us." She had stumbled over the name. Cath. It stuck in her throat every time. She wondered if she could ever say it enough times for the repetition to erode the scar.

Delia clapped her hands together, "That's the sweetest thing, Nasim."

They took their first round of drinks in the living room and then moved to the table, where course after course materialized from the hidden cart, all kept hot or cold by some magic that Nasim never thought to wonder about.

Their conversation was intimate and easy. Delia and Peter had both been matched to Nasim through a battery of personality tests and psychological profiles, their innate qualities constituting the bulk of their qualification for the position. The intent had been to find handlers who would remain with their Eves for all twelve pregnancies, and even the bureaucrats executing the Eden Project had understood that the intimacy in the relationship required greater compatibility than most marriages. At the beginning, without the benefit of the data the Project would generate and with the need to screen millions of applicants in just a few months, the psychologists had made too many compromises in the balance between the compatibility of the handler to the Eve and the other qualities that had been written into the manual, loyalty to the program not least among those. The resulting attrition of forty percent of the first-selected handlers had been the project's most significant failure.

Her tongue loosened by two glasses of wine, her tiny dessert spoon quivering halfway between plate and mouth, Nasim said, "I've never told either of you about my brother." The spontaneous revelation made her heart pound.

Delia and Peter looked at her in puzzlement. She had talked about her parents and about a sister, younger by two years, who outlived her parents only to succumb to the Plague weeks before the release of the new vaccine. But she had never mentioned a brother.

"He was four years older than I was. His name was Abbas. When my father developed the symptoms, my mother sent him away so he wouldn't infect us, and two days later, she had the symptoms, too, and went after him. When she left, she told Abbas that he was the protector now. That's what he did for two years. He protected us. And when his time came, if he had seen me, I know he would have told me the same thing: my turn to be the protector." The story trailed off, and Nasim dragged her spoon across her plate, absently tracing out patterns while she waited for the tingle of nerves that the sudden divulgence had provoked to subside. When she finally looked up, she found both Peter and Delia regarding her in silence. Nasim could see the list of questions accumulating behind Delia's eyes; they would be cast one by one until she had filled in all the blanks. With Peter, though, Nasim was never as sure.

"I'm sorry," Nasim said. "I think I've spoiled the mood." She pushed her piece of cheesecake, marred by her spoon but still untasted, into the center of the table and looked at the waiter, as though he could absolve her.

"No, no," Delia said. "That's a lovely thing to share."

Peter's eyes settled on Delia. He had always assumed that he could have been matched to almost anyone, that his protective nature would have suited him to any Eve, but then he had never known about Abbas, about the role, well-defined already, that he had been picked to play. Delia, he had always thought, had something harder to match. The things about her that drew Nasim could have easily put off other people, but the fact that they seemed made for each other, whereas he seemed made for anyone, had forged a much deeper bond between them than he could have hoped to share with Nasim. Or that was what he had thought.

Six

The Davis campaign headquarters were in a space that had in the last three years served as a nail salon, a financial planner's office, and a florist, with ample time spent vacant between each failed tenant. Alex had pushed for a smaller place closer to the center of the city, but Scott didn't think they would manage to fit even the handful of volunteers they mustered every Saturday afternoon into a space any more tiny than this one. The press he had gotten thanks to Eleanore's heckling, though, had finally given him enough name recognition that the donations were flowing. Not fast, not easily, but there was a steady trickle of money out of something other than his own bank account. Just enough to afford an office on the first floor of one of the low buildings from which downtown proper was visible, just enough to afford "Washington Avenue" in the address, even if it was seven blocks east of where anyone wanted to be.

At the first sign of their turn in fortunes, Alex had begun packing, and Scott, stumbling in that morning after a late campaign event with an open bar, had been distraught to find his campaign manager taping up a fifth box. But for a day and a half now all anyone had done was pack or load boxes into the two cars that were shuttling back and forth between here and their much more respectable new headquarters in downtown proper. And Scott? Scott was on the phone, talking to anyone who would pick up. And the only thing he talked about was Eden.

Alex waved his hand in front of Scott's glazed eyes, then mouthed, "Lunch when you're done," and held up a grease-stained paper bag. Scott nodded in reply, breaking the cadence of his spiel for just long enough that the person at the other end could be heard to say, "Thanks, I'll give it some thought," before the line went dead.

Scott shrugged, "I wasn't going to get anything out of him anyway." He tore open the paper bag on the empty desk in front of him, revealing a fat burger sitting atop a pile of fries. "We've got to stop eating this crap."

"I'll let you know when the budget allows for anything other than crap," Alex replied.

"Have you fed the troops?"

"Always before the general."

"Good."

Both cars had just departed, leaving the two of them alone, the silence around them unusual and welcome.

After a few bites, Alex said, "We've done some digging on the Biggs woman."

"Can we not call her 'the Biggs woman,' please?" Then he added before Alex could reply, "And this whole lunch thing was a ploy to get me to talk about her, wasn't it?"

"Biggs. Champion of leftist sympathy causes. Lots of money. No family. It's a hobby or something. But she's been under the radar for a while, not a peep in almost a decade. Apparently, a lot of people assumed she'd died."

"So she's not from the Pedersen camp?"

"Nope. Works for herself. Has an associate. Sam

somebody. Couldn't find anything out without a last name, couldn't find a last name. It's not clear if this person is hired help or as… 'idealistic' as Biggs."

"That's really it, though? The Eden Project is really the beginning and end of their involvement?"

"It's the beginning and end of us, Scott. That's what this whole election is about."

"You know, I really think… Look, I know it's the most important issue. Hands down. But I don't think this is enough to get me elected. The man I was just talking to, he wanted to hear about economic policies-"

"There are no economic policies anymore. There's one. One policy, no contention. I promise you, Scott, whatever people ask you on the phone, whatever they bring up in town hall meetings, whatever they tell you when you shake their hands, there is only one issue. The Eden Project is the only thing up for grabs, it's *the* difference between you and Pedersen. And I know I don't have to remind you that this is the only election we have to win this thing. Lose this time, and there is no Eden."

Scott looked for a napkin to wipe the grease off his hands, then rubbed them on his jeans. "Jesus, Alex. You really think when it comes down to it, people like Pedersen would vote humanity out of a future? You think they believe the shit they're selling? That a voluntary program is going to save us from fucking extinction?"

"They believe it."

"It's a rhetorical question."

"I don't care if it's rhetorical. Stop asking it. I know you feel like you're the small-time nobody in this race, but the Eden tide is rising, and it's going to take you with it. No doubts, no questions, no questions that could even remotely be construed as doubts. Embrace the fucking platform."

C. E. Rowland

"I live the fucking platform, Alex. We *have* to win this. Christ. Can you imagine what this country would look like in fifty years if we didn't? You ever been to a ghost town?"

"We're not going to lose, Scott. That's the point. We can't lose."

"Just answer the question. It wasn't rhetorical."

"No."

"Well they're creepy. Fifty years from now, Chicago'ould be a ghost city. Four million people reduced to, what, maybe four thousand? The tragedy they'd write." Scott's lips had curled in distaste.

"Scott. Look at me." The sneer disappeared as Scott's eyes focused. "We're on the right side of this issue. No one is going to vote humanity into extinction. The issue is going to win; we're going to win. End of story."

Scott took the first bite of his hamburger. "I've heard there's already a black market. That women are selling their bodies for ten grand a go. They get a genetic sample from each of the buyers, and the one whose swimmers get there first get the kid for an additional 'donation' upwards of 90k. Makes me sick. Sick that they're doing it. Sick that anyone is participating."

Alex shook his head.

"Let's find an Eve for our side. Bring a little humanity to the issue. Get me someone young, attractive. Good story. Someone that reminds people of their daughter. Get me one of those, and we'll show them the kind of respect these women deserve, the kind of protection they're entitled to. Can you get me one of those, Alex?"

Alex was already nodding. "This, Scott, is how candidates with downtown headquarters think."

SEVEN

DECEMBER 13, 2070

Enzo sat in a plain wooden chair in a windowless room. Across the table from him was a man in an identical chair. Over their heads hung a naked light bulb, motionless, its shoulders covered in a thick layer of dust.

The man pushed a manila folder across the table to Enzo. "It's protocol, you understand. You may feel as though you've been through all this before, but we're going to do it again."

Enzo nodded in reply.

"Please open the folder, and read the first page."

Enzo complied. The type was large and bold, but he could see the corner of the sheet underneath, where the print was miniscule.

"Yes, okay," he said.

"You finished?"

"I've finished."

"So you understand that your first allegiance is to the state, and your second allegiance is to your Eve."

"Yes, I understand."

"And you understand that as far as we're concerned, there can be no conflict of interest in those loyalties because what is best for the state is always in accordance with what is best for the Eve."

Enzo nodded.

"I need a verbal confirmation."

"I understand."

"Next page, please."

Enzo flipped to the next page, the one with tiny print running from edge to edge, and began to read. The man stood and paced the room slowly, then stopped in front of the mirror on the wall opposite Enzo.

"Finished," stated Enzo after an appropriate length of time, although he hadn't read more than the first few sentences.

"Sign at the bottom."

"Finished," said Enzo, halfway through his signature.

"I wish to emphasize this point with you, Mr. Aseno," the man said, thumping his index finger onto the page. "No fraternization. Period."

"Yes, sir."

"You understand that when I say fraternization what I mean is-"

"Yes, sir. I understand," Enzo interrupted.

"Please read the remaining documents and sign where indicated. I'll be back in a few minutes."

The man let himself through the door behind him. On one wall of the small office it concealed was a one-way mirror through which a woman sitting at the desk watched Enzo. The man took a position at the window, and the woman shifted her gaze to him, dressed in a cheap suit, his fingernails bitten to the quick.

"What do you think of him?" he asked the woman.

"You're the one doing the primary assessment. What do *you* think of him?" She was smartly dressed in a black suit, her legs crossed under the desk and one shoe dangling off her foot. She held a pen in front of her, an index finger on either end.

"I think he's going to sleep with her."

"Well." She watched him; he watched Enzo.

He turned suddenly to face her, the rubber of his sole squeaking as he swiveled. "I'm almost certain of it. Their matching is… the way their relationship will develop… it's almost inevitable. But there's nothing in the data - in the *numbers* - that contraindicates him. He's not only the best match we've found for her, he's the only one."

"We could start over."

"We can't start over," he sighed.

"If we didn't have him, we'd have had to start over."

"But we do have him. She won't have a substitute in, and we can't keep the other two working twelve hour shifts. We can't afford to have one of them leave. We can't start over. Besides, he's a fantastic match. Most Eves never get one this good." He sank his weight into one leg, then the other, back and forth. He pulled at his tie, the looseness of which betrayed the number of times he had made the same gesture already that day.

"He's signing the papers, isn't he?" the woman asked.

"They all sign the papers. In two weeks, the papers won't mean anything to him."

"You want to know what I think?"

"Please," he said.

"I think there are worse things than a little romance to pass fifteen years of solitude."

He ran his hand down his forehead and over his eyes, pushed out a big sigh. "You're not wrong. But if things didn't work out-"

"People survive. Besides, you already said it, they're a

wonderful match. Most people never meet that person. Lucky Eve gets him delivered to her doorstep."

"But-"

She interrupted him, "Look, we're hiring him to be a handler, and if something else evolves, well then at least we knew it was a possibility."

"But that's exactly the problem! My professional opinion is that it's not just a possibility - it's *likely* - that they'll wind up fucking."

"Eric," her patience was waning, "our attrition rate for recruits from the first year is at almost forty percent. From the second year, it's twenty-five. And after that, it's five. It's not a perfect process, but it's a hell of a lot better than it used to be, and that's not because of your professional opinion or mine, it's because of the numbers. You listen to the numbers. You write your report with the numbers. You make your recommendation with the numbers. If he quits, maybe you'll get yelled at. If he quits after he sleeps with her, you'll definitely get yelled at. And then you'll point to the numbers, and you'll say you did everything you could."

He nodded, rubbing his temple with his right hand.

"Also," she said, "you can put the fear of God and Country in him."

He glanced out the window to see that Enzo had closed the manila envelope, that he was sliding it back and forth across the table. As Eric reached for the door, the woman added, "You'll never be certain about the first one. It gets easier."

"Mr. Aseno," Eric announced as he passed through the door.

"Yes, I finished. I've signed them all."

"One more time, Mr. Aseno, I shall remind you of the enormous responsibility that you are assuming. The Eves are the only plug left in the chasm of extinction," he cleared his throat and rubbed the sweat from one palm to the other. "And you will be exclusively responsible for one such individual for eight hours every day from now until the end of her reproductivity. I cannot sufficiently impress upon you the gravity of the commitment you make here today. Although you aren't legally bound to remain in your Eve's service through the end, you should feel both morally and patriotically compelled to do so. This is not a job, Mr. Aseno. This is a profession. It is a career. And it is the one that we anticipate you will practice until your Eve's retirement. Is that clear?"

"Yes, sir."

Eric gestured towards the door through which Enzo had entered the room. Enzo stood, the legs of his chair scraping the silence.

"And Mr. Aseno?"

"Yes?"

"You understand that should you choose to leave this job, we have means of... of preventing other lines of employment."

"Yes, sir."

When Eric returned to the office, the woman looked amused. "Plugging the chasm of extinction?" she asked.

"I know, I know. Otherwise?"

"Otherwise, not bad."

"He'll never find out that I made up the last bit, will he?"

"Not if he never leaves."

EIGHT

"What we really need is to bring one of these poor girls into this," Sam said, chair tipping dangerously back, feet propped on the table. Eleanore was sitting behind the desk. The room was warm this time, the dust gone, though the musty smell persisted. A more substantial bar had appeared near the glass doors that they used to come and go. There was another door separated from this main space that was intended as the entrance. Back that way was a bedroom, too, from when this building had served some long-forgotten purpose.

"Not just any of these poor girls, Sam. Davis has been trying to recruit one for his campaign. The first one threw a salad at him."

"And the second?"

"They've only just gotten hold of her. She's thinking it over."

"The first, then."

"I have her details here. I trust you'll relish the thrill of the hunt."

Sam smiled, "If you've got her details, it won't be much of a hunt."

"I've had her address redacted for your pursuing pleasure." The page she slid across her desk, far beyond Sam's field of vision, did indeed had several lines blacked out. The origin of the information and the reason for the redaction - in which Eleanore had had no part - were left unspoken.

"What's her name?" Sam asked.

"Nasim Karami."

"What's her story?"

"This is why there's the goddamn sheet of paper, Sam." Eleanore's comment was only partly in jest. Their relationship was older and more intimate than any other in either of their lives, but it retained the hierarchy that had existed since Eleanore had hired Sam for their first cause.

"So I'll bring her in." Sam's feet thudded from the table to the floor, and Sam stood to retrieve the piece of paper, held it up to the light to look for text printed under the thick black lines but found none.

"Given her response to Davis, I would guess that a simple outline of our platform would be enough to coax her to our side, but please do have a back up plan. These girls aren't easy to come by."

The following morning, Sam was sitting in a car idling outside the housing complex where Nasim lived in a two bedroom apartment with four older women. The one who answered the door, who pulled it open as far as the chain would allow, studied Sam with eyes so dark they were almost black. She let the door fall closed, let it hang on its latch while calling into the apartment behind her, "Nasim, someone to see you." A few seconds later, the scratch of the chain being released, and the door opened just enough for a girl, maybe fifteen, slender and green-eyed, to peer through.

"I want to talk to you about the Eden Project. About the other side of it, the side that's trying to stop Scott Davis." Sam waited for a reaction. The girl's eyes narrowed, and the door closed a few inches, concealing what little of her body Sam had been able to see behind it.

"How did you find me?"

"Just some old tricks. Don't worry, there's no legion of reporters outside, if that's what you're thinking."

"That's not what I was thinking. Who did you say you were?"

"My name's Sam. I work for a woman named Eleanore Biggs. You might have heard of her? She's a prominent critic of the Eden Project. She'd very much like to talk to you."

Nasim finally opened the door wide enough that Sam could see all of her. She was dressed in cheap clothes that hung on her narrow frame, and her long, dark hair was coiled in a knot. Sam wasn't sure whether she was beautiful, but her features - the aquiline nose, the gauntness of her face, those eyes - were striking.

She was equally sizing up Sam, the close-cropped, lusterless brown hair and narrow face with high cheekbones, the long-sleeved cotton shirt and ill-fitting khaki work pants and heavy boots.

"What's her name again?"

"Eleanore Biggs."

"Where does she want to talk to me?"

"I talk to you first. If you like what I have to say, then she talks to you."

She shook her head as though she were going to decline, but instead she said, "Okay." The door fell closed, and she reappeared wearing shoes and a jacket a moment later. "Where?"

"You eaten lunch?" It was too early for lunch, but Sam figured she would be hungry, whether she had had breakfast or not. Nasim shook her head, her eyes watching her own feet as they carried her down the stairs.

The place Sam took her was expensive in Nasim's eyes but not fancy. "Order anything," Sam suggested. "Ms. Biggs is paying."

The conversation, perforated by silence, consisted of Sam's questions and Nasim's monosyllabic answers. She would only look at Sam for as long as it took to reply, and then her eyes returned to her plate or the waiter or the napkin she was worrying. It wasn't until she had finished and Sam had suggested that they order dessert - an offer that elicited a glimmer of excitement from Nasim - that Sam broached the topic of their business together.

"You of all people must understand what's at stake with the Eden Project for, uh, a certain portion of the population. That's what we're trying to make voters see. That what some people perceive to be a national need doesn't trump the rights, the liberty of a minority, no matter how small."

Nasim nodded, though she hadn't thought much about it before. She had only recently heard of the idea, and, in fact, the notion had only come into existence two months earlier after the new vaccine, the one without sterility as a side effect, had been released. Within a few days of that, a well-dressed man in a black SUV had come knocking on her door and, upon confirming her identity, had nodded to the man and woman hanging back behind him. They had barged into the apartment, and one brusquely rolled up Nasim's sleeve while the other prepared a syringe. They had given no explanation and had requested no consent. They had seventeen to do that day, names from a list that Nasim was disquieted to know existed, and would have another twenty the following day. Within three weeks of the vaccine's release, every woman who had not been rendered sterile by the old vaccine had been dosed with the new one.

Almost immediately, people began to view the newly vaccinated women in a different light, part suspicion, part wonder. The first mention of their duty to reproduce and then the first talk of making that duty compulsory followed in short order.

Nasim had been unaware of the developments until Davis's campaign manager had offered to take her to lunch. Davis had been waiting when they arrived. He had been tentative in the introduction, uncertain how to proceed, but that hesitation disappeared as he launched into his talking points. He wasted no time in explaining to Nasim that her body, by virtue of its fertility, now had a duty to society, an unfortunate burden for which she would be amply rewarded. The waiter had just brought the starter salads when Nasim finally began to hear through the euphemisms that Davis used. The moment she was certain - that this man was suggesting that she ought to be required to grow children for other people because she had had the misfortune not to be vaccinated earlier - she launched her salad at the candidate and took off running.

By the time she ate her last bite of carrot cake, Nasim had agreed - quietly at first and then more emphatically as she realized that these people could protect her from the likes of Scott Davis - to join Sam and Eleanore and their cause.

"Your cause," Sam corrected her.

NINE

Enzo's first shift started at midnight, and having no sense of the protocol, he rang the doorbell. Down the hall from her bedroom Nasim could hear the false-whisper of Delia's anger.

"What are you thinking!? You're five minutes early. If you had had a little patience, I would have met you on my way out the door and explained the freaking protocol. Which is that we don't ring the bell in the middle of the night! Who rings a bell in the middle of the night!? What kind of person?" Delia's voice sank below the threshold of distinguishable words, but Nasim could hear the babble of conversation for several more minutes.

Nasim sat on the edge of her bed, straining to hear the words from living room, to discern whether Enzo's voice was offering any defense. Her toes curled into the deep carpet, silver in the ambient light because the moon was full, and full moons made Nasim want the windows transparent at night. She listened through the silence after the words had faded, trying to make out the closing door. Delia must have left by now. Nasim grabbed the thick, white bathrobe that hung from a hook on her bathroom door and, cinching it closed, wandered into the living room, where the yellow light from the lamp beside the couch made her squint.

Enzo was seated on the couch, knees on elbows, head in his hands, black curls poking out between his fingers. He sensed her there before she said anything, his head snapping up an instant before he stood. His mouth was half open, but whatever he might have intended to say remained unspoken. Instead he studied her with nearly black eyes under thick eyebrows. He was small, not much taller than Nasim, and his thin face, sharpened by his narrow nose, gave his whole frame a slight appearance. Nasim wondered whether his skin was dark or just tan and whether Delia would agree that he was handsome.

"Don't worry about Delia," Nasim offered, and when it became clear that he still had nothing to say, she continued, "There aren't many new handlers, so everyone forgets what it's like not knowing the protocols. You'll be fine, though."

"I have no doubt."

It wasn't the response she was expecting. "I wasn't suggesting you did. I just thought that maybe in your silence you might be wondering…" The feeling of speaking to a stranger, the discomfort of not knowing what to say felt so foreign now that she only ever spoke to Peter or Delia. She couldn't find the words to finish the sentence.

"It's easier to ask what I'm thinking than to guess it." His tone was sharp, his demeanor, aloof, not at all like he had been at the meeting where she had approved his hire.

"It would be," she said. A bubble of anxiety threatened to displace her annoyance. She waited to see if he would say anything more, and when nothing came, she moved past Enzo, and sank into the couch next to where he had been sitting. "I get up around six. I'll ring the bell to call you. Your room is down the hall on the left. Mine is at the end of the hall. I don't mind if you sleep while you're on duty, but you might bring a change of clothes to sleep in. I don't want to wait for you to dress every time I need something."

Enzo was still standing, his hands clasped behind his back. He nodded when Nasim finished speaking.

"And I do expect you to speak when spoken to." She wasn't sure whether she had said it as a rebuke - to his silence or his earlier sharpness - or whether it was an awkward attempt at levity. Delia or Peter would have known which.

"Of course."

"And occasionally without having to be spoken to." This time it was a rebuke, for his failure to understand her earlier intention or for making her feel so uncomfortable in her own living room at an hour when she would usually be asleep.

"Yes."

"I'm going back to bed," she said. If Delia were there she would say something reassuring. That however he might seem in this moment, Enzo had passed the same tests the others had, that she would almost certainly grow to like him. *Almost* certainly, Nasim imagined herself countering. She reflexively placed her hand on her belly and instead felt the emptiness inside her. "Remind me to call the postpartum nurse tomorrow," she said as the wave of loss passed through her.

Enzo nodded. He saw the flash of pain on her face, the way her posture crumpled, and he wanted to reach out, touch her arm; but instead he said, "I'm sorry I woke you. It won't happen again."

He watched her walk down the hall, her white bathrobe seeming to float after her bare feet had blended into the darkness.

TEN

APRIL 19, 2062

"I've found one," Alex whispered as he passed Scott, who was leaning over the desk of a volunteer-turned-employee adjusting a few details in the plan for the campaign event three days hence.

"Better be better than the last one," Scott turned and spoke after him, loud enough to bridge the gap of four desks that Alex, in a hurry, had already crossed.

Scott found them in the lounge, an area that had probably once served as an executive office. Scott, though, had preferred to have his desk at the hub of the activity, so this space had been fitted with a couple of couches someone had brought in from a disused basement, and Alex had purchased a small refrigerator and microwave for the space. It wasn't uncommon for Scott to stay the night there, sleeping on the couch and foraging through his staff's leftovers for dinner.

She was much older than the last one, maybe a little over thirty. She was slightly overweight, her hips were wide, and her breasts were heavy. Whereas the other one had been nervous, this woman was all warmth and strength. She was seated on the smaller of the two couches, and she half-rose to shake his hand.

"I'm Ruth."

Scott looked to Alex for a more thorough introduction. "Ms. Clayborn opted out of the vaccine in order to preserve her opportunity to have children." Scott's head rolled back in relief as he leaned his weight into the door jamb. He had heard that such women existed, of course, but that there was one now seated in his lounge bordered on the miraculous.

"Ruth. May I call you Ruth?" He didn't wait for her to reply before adding, "Please, call me Scott. We like to keep things friendly around the office. Why don't you tell me a bit about… your decision."

"Well, I… I don't know. I always knew that I would be a mother. It's how I thought of myself, really. Not a thing I was willing to give up, Plague or not."

"So you weighed your chances-"

"No, it wouldn't have mattered. Eighty percent mortality, ninety-nine percent. God put on this Earth to make children, and if He had decided to take me before I had any, then He would have had His reasons."

"And the Eden Project…"

"The most important thing humanity will ever do, as far as I'm concerned. This is our chance, you know? Last century, what did we spend our resources on? War, terror, politics that spawned more terror. The greatest minds came up with the atom bomb, the independent minds came up with the suicide bomb."

"But with the structure and support-"

"And the resources and the good will of the government and the people, we have this chance to be better than we've ever aspired to be before, to do things out of selflessness and love. The women like me, yes, but also everyone who supports the Project. The infrastructure that supports the women, the people who adopt the children, the politicians who direct the funds, the taxpayers who supply them. Every person in this country will be measurably responsible for our salvation from this Plague."

Scott nodded, his eyes betraying incredulity. He wondered if Alex had dragged this woman in off the street and coached her, if this was a practical joke, but Alex was looking inordinately pleased with himself.

"What about," Alex prompted for Scott's benefit, "what about the people who oppose the Eden Project?"

Ruth's forehead crumpled, and she shook her head. "I don't even know what to say about those misanthropes. What's their game?" She looked at Scott as thought he might have some answer. "Can they really desire the end of civilization? They want to see it all fall apart, want to walk empty streets, to die alone on an empty planet? Is that it?"

"Some would say," Scott offered, "that their issue with the Project is in the degree of choice that the women have."

"What higher calling is there!? What more could a person want at this moment in time than to be the mother of humanity? And that's not an easy task without the support the Project puts in place. Those people who say it's a matter of choice, well without the Project, what choice do I have? I could have one, maybe two children and support them, *maybe*. And I'm one of the lucky ones: the economic reality is that without the Project, most Eves don't have a choice. Most of them don't have families left. They're young. They're overwhelmingly unemployed. How are they going to have children? Healthy children, children who are raised in stable families, children to build the future? How will they raise those children, how will *we* raise those children but for the help the Project promises?"

"Has Alex filled you in on what exactly we're asking

from you?"

"He's given me a general sense. Appearances at a few campaign stops. A few minutes of speaking."

"Maybe a couple of advertisements," Alex added.

"And you're in for all that? Of course we'll pay you as a consultant."

"Oh, no." For a moment it wasn't clear to either man what she disagreed with. "I couldn't accept any payment. This is my cause. I should be the one paying you for all the fight you're bringing to it."

Scott looked at Alex again, a crooked smile on his face, head shaking in a slow sweep of disbelief.

"I think I speak for everyone at this campaign," Alex said, rising from his seat to shake Ruth's hand again, "when I say that we couldn't be happier to have you with us."

"Absolutely," Scott echoed.

ELEVEN

When Peter arrived at eight the following morning to relieve Enzo, he found the latter looking tired and disheveled. "Did you not sleep last night?"

"Of course, I did," Enzo said, not entirely untruthfully. He had fallen asleep on the couch sometime after five. He hadn't known that he would be permitted to sleep and so had drunk several cups of coffee before arriving too early at Nasim's door. He had been furious with himself over the poor first impression he had made with Delia (and, no doubt, Delia would have told Peter as well), furious with Delia for berating him when a simple explanation would have sufficed and for doing so loudly enough to keep Nasim from falling back to sleep, which is what he suspected would have happened if Delia had kept her voice down. He had no way of knowing that Nasim had had every intention of greeting him but had drifted off while waiting for him to arrive. With the caffeine preventing him from sleeping, he had spent most of the night stewing.

Nasim would normally have rung as soon as she awoke, but he was a stranger and didn't know the protocol, besides. And he had been so unpleasant. So she instead started the shower herself, though she couldn't find the supply of fresh washcloths from which Delia or Peter would have drawn. She kept looking over her shoulder, straining to hear over the sound of the shower, positive that he wouldn't take the initiative to show up without having been summoned but terrified that he might. And, although she had remembered to place her towel on the heater, she forgot to switch it on, so it was cold when she got out. Her clothes, usually laid out while she showered, were in drawers she never opened, and by the time she had managed to find everything for herself, Peter had already arrived.

"Nasim," he said instead of knocking to announce his presence in her room.

Upon seeing his face, Nasim burst into tears. In reply, Peter wrapped his arms around her. She leaned into him, her forehead resting on his warm neck. When the sobs had subsided, he pulled a handkerchief from his pocket, blotting the tears from her face with it and then handing it to her to wipe her nose. "I've called the postpartum nurse," he said. "She'll be 'round in half an hour."

Nasim nodded.

"And Delia and I will work with Enzo. It's a difficult situation for him and for you and for us. Remember what it was like when Delia and I started? You and Cath knew each other; she knew exactly what you wanted. You probably didn't even realize you'd developed expectations that we would fail to meet. It didn't take that long to figure things out. But that's not your concern. Delia and I will handle it." Peter placed his hand on Nasim's chin and lifted her face so she was looking at him. "But first the postpartum nurse, okay?"

The nurse was late, but she had remembered the medical kit that she sometimes left at the clinic. The consultation was brief, and she handed Peter a bottle of tiny, sweet pills with the instructions, "Twice a day until they've run out." Afterwards, Peter retrieved the breakfast order he had called in and set one of the green tablets and one of the usual blue ones beside the place he set for Nasim. He set a second place for himself while she ate.

When he sat down, picking at the muffin he had brought back from the kitchen, Nasim began, "I had forgotten what it's like to talk to someone who doesn't know me."

"How was it?"

"Horrible."

"He won't not know you for long. Then it won't be so bad, eh?"

"Maybe it was horrible because he was horrible." She tried to voice it as an accusation, but Peter could hear the worry in her tone.

"How could they match a horrible person to a person like you?" It was too easy for Peter to make her smile, she thought. She ought to be allowed to sulk every once in a while.

"You and Delia will really-"

"Of course, we will. She told me about last night."

"She didn't tell you what happened after she left."

"Well, given that you didn't ring for his this morning, I assume it was awful?"

"It was! I went out to talk to him. He hardly said anything back. Just enough for me to know that he's arrogant and inconsiderate and unapologetic. Well, mostly unapologetic."

"Nasim," Peter said and waited until she looked at him to continue, "Arrogant, inconsiderate, unapologetic people are the first ones to get booted in the screening process. So either this country has run out of potential handlers, or what you saw was just a nervous man who was embarrassed at having made a mistake in his first minute on the job. Why don't you forget about last night? You'll have a thousand more with him to overwrite that memory."

Nasim pushed her breakfast around her plate. Never, never did Peter just let her complain. There always had to be a solution. Delia, now she would be empathetic.

When she finished eating, Nasim pushed her plate away. "Come sit with me when you're finished?" she asked. Then she moved to the couch and grabbed the reader that was lying on the table, flipping through for something more entertaining than what she had been reading the day before. When Peter had finished clearing the table, he sat next to her on the couch with his own reader. She leaned into him, propping a pillow on his shoulder for her head. "Do you think," she asked after they had read awhile, "that they'd let me get a pet?"

"Aren't we your pets?"

TWELVE

"What they're talking about is using people - human beings! - as breeding animals." Eleanore was sitting behind her great desk, her arms spread wide across its empty expanse, her hands clenched in fists.

"But don't you think," Nasim said, "that if we all just sat down together, surely we could make them realize...? They must realize. Anyone with any humanity would see... The injustice, the..." Her voice wavered, while her eyes scanned the room again before returning to the floor in front of her feet. The fact that there were no words to convey her horror, didn't that in itself guarantee the righteousness of their side? Nasim looked up for a moment to glance wide-eyed from Eleanore to Sam, who was pacing the the room without a discernible pattern, then her eyes returned to her own feet. Sam said nothing, and Eleanore began to shake her head.

"It could seem that way, Nasim, but a public battle is what we need. A private conversation to convert one person costs too much. Imagine it takes an hour, and at the end we have no better than a fifty percent chance that we've actually changed the man's mind. How many hours would it take for any impact to be felt at all? Just in this campaign, the number is inconceivable. Ten thousand would be barely a dent, even if we changed the mind of every person we talked to, but that would take the three of us from now until well past election day. When we hold the debate in public, though, we might change ten thousand minds in one evening."

"But if we could change Scott Davis's mind, then we could use his support-"

"If we change his mind, we remove the issue from this election. He can't run against Celia Pederson without this issue. There aren't any other differences between them."

Nasim looked to Sam, hoping to find support there, but Sam was looking elsewhere - anywhere other than at her - and was still pacing. "But then whoever was elected would be on our side, and isn't that-"

"Public minds, Nasim. We need pressure from public minds, and the only way we get that is a public fight. We need spectacle and drama. We win by having a national conversation, not by ensuring one solitary district."

Sam finally took a seat at the table opposite Nasim, Eleanore still visible over Sam's shoulder. "This isn't the most intuitive path, and it's not the path of least resistance; but this is the one that's going to work, Nasim. This is what Eleanore and I do. We champion causes, and we've been doing it longer than you've been alive. We can win this fight with your help, but we can only work together if you trust our methods."

Nasim nodded, the quiver of her heart in her throat subsiding with her acquiescence. She had surprised herself when she had disagreed with Eleanore, and it had surprised her even more that she hadn't been cowed by Eleanore's first retort.

When Nasim had left, Sam turned to Eleanore. "Not the fighter we'd hope for."

"I suppose they're not in it for the thrill." Eleanore swirled the half finger of whiskey remaining in her glass, then held it up to Sam, "Well, cheers regardless. We'll have our thrill."

Sam spread out a rolled sheet of paper vellum that covered half the table. Eleanore drained her glass, then drew in close to study the diagrams drawn in black ink, bulleted text, and lone sentences that spidered across every inch. This was Sam's skill, a plan laid forth on paper, drawn with an old fountain pen. She had hired Sam on the recommendation of an activist friend - the best details you'll ever see on a plan, the friend had said - but the first time Sam had unrolled such a document, Eleanore had nearly snorted her whiskey through her nose. She had expected animated holograms at a minimum and would have been more pleased with a virtual reality display. Yet before her was nothing but a sheet of nearly transparent paper scribbled over with lines of inconstant weight.

Now, though, she loved these plans, the fine pen strokes and the smooth paper. A painstaking map of the venue, places to stand marked for any number of scenarios, and, from each of those points grew the many foreseeable contingencies. Talking points sprouted from each branch in space or time, a living map of every outcome. Eleanore saw their path now as Sam did, not downward, passive to the force of gravity, but as an upward thrust, a conscious choice at each juncture that led ultimately to the conclusion of their own design. She traced one such path across the paper, then a second.

"The event is in two days, their rally at the VFW," Sam said. "I promised her we'd just be observing this time. She looked horrified at the thought of anything more than that."

"She's coming back tomorrow, though?"

Sam nodded.

"I'll talk her through it," Eleanore said.

"Through…?"

"What it'll be like."

"You don't need me here?"

"No, I think maybe it would be good for the two of us to spend some time together." Eleanore looked from the plan to Sam. "Oh, don't look so worried. I'm not going to try to push her into something she's not ready for. I want to put her at ease, not bully her into submission. She's right, after all: conversation can be a powerful tool. Anyhow, she'll be less guarded if there's only one other person, and I know she'd be more comfortable around you, but she needs to trust me, too. We've got months to go. I'm patient enough. She's valuable enough. Tell her to come to the main house."

Sam nodded and traced an index finger across the opposite palm, the invisible line a reminder to call Nasim in the morning.

"We'll be fast friends by the time the day is over. Does she drink coffee?"

"Tea," Sam replied.

"Oh, so much better." Though it was late, Eleanore picked up the phone on her desk and called up to the house, ordering an assortment of teas and pastries for the following day. "We'll get her hooked on the fight, Sam. Don't you worry."

"If that's your plan," Sam replied, "who am I to worry?"

THIRTEEN

DECEMBER 15, 2070

Delia found them still on the couch, Nasim having fallen asleep with her head rolling off the pillow onto Peter's shoulder. Neither Delia nor Peter ever waited in the hall for the other to exit as she had told Enzo to do the night before, but didn't she feel that Enzo ought to be letting himself into Nasim's coop, either; and ringing the doorbell was out of the question. She closed the door quietly behind her, and Peter mouthed that he would stay a few minutes longer. When after half an hour, Nasim was still not awake, he placed his free hand on her cheek.

Nasim sensed Delia moving through the space behind the couch. "Time," she said, and the time appeared projected on the wall before her. "Oh, Peter, you should have woken me earlier." Part apology, part accusation.

When Peter left, Delia took his place. "You look like you haven't moved all day."

"What gives it away?"

"You're about a foot into the couch." It was feather-stuffed, and the cushions gave an inch or two an hour. "Could I tempt you with a walk? It was a nice day, and it's still pretty warm out."

"I can't tell you how much I would rather sit here."

"Then don't tell me. Just come. We don't have to go for long. It's getting dark soon, anyhow."

Nasim failed to find any words of argument and shrugged. She struggled to push her body, still off balance from the sudden change in it, out of the deep cushions, but Delia took her arm and pulled her free. She let Delia find a coat suited to the temperature, a red peacoat - which of her handlers could have thought she would like that? - that she almost refused. But Delia was brisk in her movements and had Nasim buttoned into the coat and bedecked with scarf and hat before any protests were uttered.

They went out the glass door: Nasim always avoided the hallway outside her coop, it's fluorescent lights and industrial carpet and the scars on the walls that no one had ever touched up, all reminders that this was an institution rather than her home. The weather was perfect for mid-December, the radiant heat from the setting sun glowed against their faces while the cold air just showed their breath. The woods where they often went were a quarter mile across well-kept grass criss-crossed by paved paths that they never used. They went slowly and without talking until they reached one of the dirt tracks through the trees. The underbrush had been burned in the fall, and the woods were so open that the path was barely visible, but habit kept them on it.

"So we've all met Enzo now," Nasim said.

"We have," Delia agreed. "And I have to say that he hasn't made a good impression. Ringing the bell in the middle of the night."

"It was worse than that. I got up," catching Delia's look, she added, "not because he woke me - I was going to get up regardless. But there he is sitting on my couch, and he doesn't even say hello. Doesn't say a word, in fact. Just stares at me, and then when he finally does open his mouth, all that comes out is, 'I'm an arrogant asshole.'" She spoke the last part in the way she might give a voice to a dog, comical and un-human.

"He didn't!" Delia sounded delighted. "To you?!"

"He did!"

"What about this morning?"

"I didn't see him."

"He didn't help you?"

"I didn't ring."

"Nasim, why didn't you ring for him?"

"Well…" She didn't want to admit that the thought of being naked in front of him made her uncomfortable, didn't know herself whether to feel embarrassed by her shyness or whether the discomfort arose from her hatred that her body was treated as some clinical thing.

"Well, regardless, I can't believe he didn't come by on his own to make himself useful."

"I don't know. It might be a lot to ask on the first day, for him to know what to do without my telling him." She wrung her hands at the memory of the worry he might appear without having been summoned.

"Not at all! It's his job to take care of you, just as much as it's my job or Peter's. If he didn't know what to do, he should have asked you, not skulked around like some-"

"I really wasn't bothered about it this morning, but last night-"

"And he knows what you've just been through! He knows it's not even been a week! Surely they told him."

"But he can't possibly understand. I doubt he's ever met a woman who's just given birth."

"Well, I don't like any of it. Not how he was to me last

night. Not how he was to you. Not how he handled this morning. I wouldn't be surprised if the matcher who set this up was fired tomorrow."

"It was only his first day, though. He was probably mortified to have woken me up and just didn't know how to handle himself."

"That's what all that training is for. He's not supposed to come here to learn; he's supposed to *know.*"

"That might make it even worse, though. All the training and then messing up in your first minute."

Delia stopped walking. They had come to a lake. If it was a cold winter, it might freeze thick enough to skate on, but there wasn't any sign of ice yet. "You sound like you're defending him."

Nasim sat down on a log, fallen this summer, its branches still clutching dead leaves, and she watched the colors of the sunset through the dead woods. "I guess I am," she admitted. "Peter's fault, I think."

FOURTEEN

Alex had scheduled a meeting with Scott several days earlier only to appear with a tailor in tow. Over Scott's objections, Alex had raised his voice just enough to be heard, "It doesn't matter how busy you are. If you don't look the part, you won't win the seat, so everything is going to wait for this man." He had been right, of course.

In a dank bathroom in the basement of the VFW, Alex held the new suit in one hand, a tie he had picked in the other. Scott stripped off his jeans, one leg falling onto the wet tile in spite of his effort to prevent just that. He stood on his shoes, polished this morning, to keep his socks dry and pulled on the new pants. The jacket he shrugged over a white shirt.

"You sure I need this?" he asked, pointing to the tie.

"You want to look like a professional or a fucking amateur?"

When they were back out in the hall, he paused so that Alex could remedy the mess he had made with the tie.

"Teeth okay?" he asked.

Alex grunted in reply.

"Has Ruth arrived yet?"

"She's around somewhere. Alyssa is looking after her wardrobe for now. Maybe not the best long-term choice."

The staging area was exposed, so though it was the first he had seen of Ruth since their conversation in the lounge, Scott said nothing, only took her hand in his - half handshake, half clasp of reassurance - and gave a warm smile in case anyone was watching. He was anxious. This was the first time he had brought in someone he didn't know, someone without a track record, and if speaking in his own voice was finally starting to feel natural, giving someone else his message to ferry for him was not at all.

They walked onto the stage together, Scott and Ruth and Alex following behind. Scott wished again that he had pushed Ellen harder to come. It would have been better for her to introduce Ruth. But what was the expression, *If wishes were...* something?

The middle of a failing marriage was the worst place from which to be campaigning as the defender of families. Not failing, per se, he reminded himself, though the stress of the campaign gave him even less time to do whatever it was Ellen wanted him to. And children, the lack of children, had dissolved so many relationships around them in the last few years. A tremor running through every young couple, the loss of their imagined child felt as some fraction of the loss of a living child; and while some couples leaned on each other, others found less and less reason to stay together. She hadn't said it, not yet, but Scott felt it deep between them and couldn't tell yet whether it would pull them together or apart.

Still mired in his thoughts of Ellen, he spoke only a few lines of his script before introducing Ruth. Alex had planted enough people in the crowd to turn uncertainty about the politicization of one woman's vaccination choice into thunderous applause, and by the time Ruth turned the audience back over to Scott, a chant - his name - had started up, probably begun by one of Alex's people. Scott let it run.

When he finally raised his hand for silence, Scott's thoughts were still stuck on Ellen. Maybe if she were here, maybe if she felt this energy, it would do something for them. He wasn't sure what, exactly.

Afraid he would squander the energy of the crowd, Scott only spoke a few words to them before stepping down to shake hands and look earnest and appear interested in the problems that people dumped on him. Everyone had something. Could they really not see how inconsequential their issues were compared to *the* issue? A half percent change in sales tax, a minute alteration to farm subsidies, a threatened change to zoning laws; he had given up trying to explain that Congress had no authority in matters that were legislated by the states. Inheritance tax laws. That was the one that really goaded him. Were there truly people so habituated to selfishness that they worried about heirs they couldn't have? Scott had mastered the smile, though, the one that made people feel singled-out, important, and he doled it out generously to everyone who took his hand or offered a problem.

When Scott finally made the door an hour later, Alex was waiting to clap him on the back.

"I hope you got Ruth out without any trouble," Scott said.

"Are you kidding? She's the belle of the ball and loving every minute of it. She's still in there talking."

"Jesus."

"Jesus, she's incredible? Or Jesus, we've never had a crowd like that?"

"I don't know. Just, Jesus."

It was a scene that Scott's eventual political allies, running their own races in their own districts, would be replicating within weeks, but with Ruth, Alex had put them well ahead. Given his budget and the size of his congressional district, being at the forefront of anything was remarkable, and the attention that this was about to bring to his campaign, attention that would rapidly be buoying his bottom line, would be so far beyond the scope of what Scott had imagined just two weeks earlier.

When he made it home that night after a meet-and-greet at a dessert shop and a few handshakes exchanged at a local pub, Ellen was waiting. And she was smiling. "I saw the news. You're all over."

"It was a great day. I wish you could have been there." As he said it, he heard the accusation, unintended, and added, "But, of course, I know it was important-"

"I wish I could have been there," she interrupted. "Maybe tomorrow I can come."

Fifteen

Enzo was surprised to find Nasim still awake when he slipped into her coop at midnight. It was the second time that he had drawn the night shift and the first time he had found Nasim still up for it. She was painting her nails, and Peter was looking amused. To Enzo he said, "I don't know what's happened to our Nasim, but someone vain has taken her place" before retrieving his coat.

"Listen, I was thinking," said Nasim as the door closed behind Peter, "and Peter already thinks it's a good idea, so you have to agree; and it won't be your fault if it's awful. It'll be his fault. We'll blame him together."

It hadn't ever been like the first day again. On the second night, Nasim had been sound asleep. He had brought shorts and a shirt to sleep in and had woken to her bell at six in the morning. He had respectfully averted his eyes while doing the things that Peter had instructed him to do. Turn on the shower. Retrieve a clean washcloth. Turn on the towel heater. Set out her clothes for the day, underwear from this drawer, shirt from another. Jeans most days and a tee-shirt; she would let him know if there was a deviation. There was no trace of the annoyance he had evoked in her two nights before. As the week wore on, she gave brief instructions - the shower should be hotter, black underwear postpartum and during her period - but most of them came from Peter when the two men met during Delia's shift. Soon the passage of time had begun to alleviate his embarrassment over that first night, and Enzo had started to smile more easily and speak more freely.

The second week, he had drawn the morning shift, and in the weeks that followed Nasim grew certain of the suitability of the match. He was easy to talk to now that he talked, and he laughed too hard at his own jokes, which he told ceaselessly. Nasim loved the texture of his charm, feigned arrogance, equally feigned self-deprecation. Enzo was just as impressed with her, the depth of her humor, the wit that betrayed a sharp intelligence in spite the stereotype that accompanied her unasked-for profession.

"Enzo?"

He returned to the present moment, to Nasim painting her toenails late at night in a bright yellow room bathed in the glow of her favorite lamp. She loved color and light, and every room was painted brightly and lit by lamps that burned incandescent bulbs, nearly impossible to procure anymore. And yet the lamps were always on, little suns she kept burning for her own joy.

"And what are my fair lady's thoughts for which I can give approval but assume no blame... upon inevitable failure?" he teased.

He sank into the couch next to her, and the movement caused her to miss her nail and paint the toe instead. When he laughed, she took the brush to his nose, leaving a pink stripe down its bridge before he had a chance to respond.

"Take it back, or I'll turn your whole nose pink," she threatened.

"Take what back, your royal painintheass?"

"All of it. Laughing at me, calling me names, your disparaging comments about my brilliant idea."

"I do, my liege. I rescind it all." She tried to land another brush stroke on him while he held her wrists to deflect her hands. She gave in eventually, breathless from the exertion and from laughing, and slumped back into her own crater in the red couch. "Now tell me, what's this idea?"

"Well, now it's got all this attention, it's going to sound silly. It was just supposed to be a line or two exchanged at the beginning of the scene, and now it's got all the pressure of a major plot element."

"Then you'll have to wait up for me again tomorrow and tell me then."

"But I can't wait that long," she insisted.

"Then you should tell me in the morning. You can shout it to me while you're in the shower and I'm rifling through your undies."

"Don't joke about that, Enzo." Her tone hadn't changed, but he could already tell when something said in jest was meant in earnest.

"Then I guess you'll have to tell me now, and then we'll have to go on talking for hours and hours so it's only occupied the relative first few lines of our extended scene."

"You're ridiculous, you know that? Why don't you just tell me it doesn't matter?"

"If I did… I'd be lying," he smirked.

She managed in a quick stroke to leave a trail of pink across his cheek and emitted such a squeal of delight that she clapped her hands over her mouth in embarrassment, streaking nail polish across her own face with the motion. When they had finished laughing, she finally said, "I think we ought to all have dinner together on Sunday nights. When you draw for your shifts for the week. You're all here anyhow. You could stay a little longer."

"As you wish," Enzo said, bowing low from his seated position.

"That's from some old movie, isn't it?"

"Have you seen it?" he asked.

"No."

"Well, we'll have to rectify that. I'll see if we can get it for tomorrow night. You bring the popcorn, I'll bring the flicks."

"We could check right now, you know?" She grabbed her reader from beside the couch and began to thumb through, but he took it from her hand.

"*You* bring the popcorn, and *I'll* bring the the flicks. Besides, it's way past your bedtime, m'lady. If you expect to be up at ungodly o'clock tomorrow morning, you'd better rest those sweet eyes."

"Fine." Under her breath she whispered, "Computer, play the movie famous for the line 'As you wish.'"

Projected on the wall across from the couch, an ancient-looking video game appeared. Baseball in five colors and countable pixels, the first scene of *The Princess Bride*.

"You're impossible, you know that?" Enzo said.

Nasim leaned her head against his shoulder and began watching but was soon asleep.

SIXTEEN

OCTOBER 8, 2062

Perhaps because they couldn't vote, neither of her parents had ever instructed Nasim in civic engagement, and they had certainly never attended any political rallies that she knew of. In fact, though she had never been conscious of it, Nasim's parents had kept themselves and their children well clear of crowds, their unvaccinated status making every handshake a potential portent of death. So it was with great anxiety that she now found herself thrust into the midst of this crowd, people pressed up against her on all sides. Sam had her by the wrist and was dragging her through the bodies. When the hand slipped for a moment, she had frozen in panic, and Sam had had to come back for her, the current of the mob having separated them even in those brief instants.

Signs thrust overhead, shaken in anger and in excitement, pulsed with the rhythm of the crowd. And in that rhythm, too, were that chants that flared up, first sporadically behind or ahead of her and then, gaining force, washing around her, swallowing her up. All of it timed to a fast heartbeat, reverberating through her until she couldn't tell whether it was the motion or the sound or her own self that she felt pounding in her chest.

The rest of the din, too, was oppressive. In the lulls between chants, in the pockets where they hadn't caught yet, conversations were shouted over the real shouting, back and forth across the barricade that separated them from the other side, from the people who wanted to snatch away her freedom.

They were headed for a podium somewhere at the front that she had seen when they were still far enough back, but now, pressed into the scrum of people, the visible landmark was swallowed up; and in the moment that she and Sam lost contact, any sense of orientation that Nasim had had disappeared. Sam pulled her onward, though, grip tighter than before so she wouldn't slip away so easily.

It was the densest, loudest part of the crowd that they finally broke through, falling into a line of police in riot gear that stood between the people and the stage. The stage with the podium where she was expected.

The riot gear was what really frightened her. Sam had told her about the crowd ahead of time, though the warning had been insufficient. And about what would happen on the podium. She didn't have to say anything. Someone else was speaking, like all the other times. She was just the object, the poor child. Eleanore had said it - Eleanore said things that surprised Nasim sometimes - that it was good she was so thin because it made her look younger than she was. To be the showpiece, the face, wasn't so intimidating, even in front of a crowd this size. They wouldn't feel the sweat on her palms, wouldn't hear the quake in her voice. But the riot police, their shields raised in a plexiglass wall against the crowd that had moments before spit her out, the same shields that in miniature guarded their faces, what were they there for? And the batons that hung at their sides, the ones that some of them rested their free hands on. On their belts, too, they had canisters with hairpin triggers, some of them had three or four, and all of them had a gas mask that hung behind, the goggles staring dully at Nasim, Janus faces to mind the people on the podium while the brute force faced forward.

They had been waiting for her on the stage, the speech held until she could be there to stand, slender-hipped and fearful, in evidence. When they reached the stairs, she climbed warily, in spite of the hands waving her up. Sam had let go of her wrist the moment before, and the slackness in it was mirrored in a lightness in her head but whether from the noise or the crowd or the fear or just the stairs, she wasn't sure. But the blood returned to both her hand and her head a moment later, as she stood where they pushed her, next to the podium, next to the speaker.

She tried to listen to the words, spoken ostensibly for her own benefit, about freedom and choice and the opposites of those things - oppression, and the word 'slavery' was mentioned once. But though the chanting had quieted, it hadn't ceased, and carried from the back of the crowd she could still feel the tattoo of a heartbeat, echoed in the thrusting of the signs that she could now read. *Freedom, Not Eden! Women ≠ Broodmares!* And the single word: *Choice!* And she could see the barricade now, waist-high concrete things to the right of the stage and not as distant as she would have expected. They disappeared into the flux of people, but she could see the line they made stretching back to where the crowd thinned, and there the barriers picked up again.

On the other side of the barrier, the rhythm was different, and that crowd responded to the beginning of the speech by redoubling its jeers and raising fists into the air.

Some of the eyes on that side looked through Nasim, while others ogled her hungrily.

She didn't see the moment that provoked it, but the riot police, as a single unit, pulled out their clubs. Several of them, too, seamlessly transferred a can of tear gas into the free hand of the arm holding the shield wall in place. The crowd, the speaker, the human wall - all paused now for a moment, measuring each other - and then a single person, his movement amplified by the stillness around him, vaulted over the barricade, from that side to this.

In that instant, the peace was shattered. The two factions swept into each other, struggling against each other, and the riot police moved forward, towards the fighting but separated from it by the people who had not yet reached it and by those who were trying to escape it. From Nasim's place on the podium, she saw them draw no distinction, these men and women with their masks hanging behind them. They pressed forward, into packed bodies that had nowhere to move, their clubs making room for them where there was none. With a shout from one that was echoed back by the others, they as a unit slipped their second faces from their belts and with a fluid motion clipped them into the helmets they wore. It took less than a second, but Nasim already felt Sam's hand around her wrist, pulling her back towards the stairs. Now in quick succession she witnessed as every fifth officer lobbed a canister into the crowd and in a wave outward from where each one landed, the fighting turned to panic, the shouting to screaming, the press forward into a panicked search for escape.

SEVENTEEN

"I just can't believe that they could have matched such an arrogant jackass to *you*. I mean, I've heard that some of the Eves are... kind of bitchy. But you're the sweetest thing that's ever lived, Nasim, and he's... a douchebag." Nasim loved the way Delia struggled to insult people, struggled even to find the words. Her upbringing had left her full of judgement but with few enough ways to express it. Enzo had not yet overcome his poor first impression in Delia's eyes, and Nasim wondered whether Enzo might be harboring a similarly poor opinion of Delia for her humiliation of him on that first night.

"I don't know that you've given him quite the chance he deserves. He's not *horrible*."

Delia opened her mouth, but no words came out.

"You don't have to like him, though," Nasim preempted. "You can think whatever you want of him. I'm just saying," Nasim said, a smile creeping across her lips, "that you were the one hoping for someone tall, dark, and handsome, and he might not be tall, but-"

"Oh, that's not even fair! I wasn't hoping for a handsome jerk. They all are, though, aren't they? All the handsome ones?"

Nasim's smile disappeared. "I wouldn't really know."

"No, of course not. I didn't mean... I wasn't thinking, Nasim."

They were walking again, through the woods, on their way back from the lake. A pair of squirrels darted across the path in front of them and then paused their preoccupation with each other to chastise the two women.

Nasim tried to contain the darkness that had been stirred by Delia's words. Why did a single reminder of the life she was missing rouse such bitterness in her? And the comfort she tried to offer herself - that at least she had allies in Delia and Peter and now Enzo - was always immediately followed by the remembrance that the allegiance of these 'friends' was really to the system that enslaved her. *Too complicated*, Nasim thought, as her mind retraced the familiar pattern again, etching the scar one layer deeper. *My river,* she remembered. Her father used to call it that, the serenity of a clear stream that was marred by a single footprint in its mud bottom; one disturbance, and the pristine water became murky. No force but time could restore it. Every day that she practiced patience, he promised her, would be like adding a pebble to the stream. Eventually the mud bottom would be covered, and nothing would disturb the clarity of the water. *I haven't practiced at all.*

"Oh, Nasim." Delia paused, and the squirrels redoubled their scolding. "Nasim, look at me. I'm sorry, okay? Do you forgive me? I won't talk about it anymore, about handsome men and love and that." Delia's eyes were brown, lighter than Enzo's. Her long hair was tied up in a knot, the wisps that escaped, the color of flax and the rest, the color of mud. A deep worry line etched her forehead.

"You can still talk about 'love and that,'" Nasim said,

her arms limp at her sides while Delia's hands clutched her shoulders. She didn't want to explain about the river, the way the turmoil billowed up in her from just one misstep. She didn't want to think about the complexity of her relationship with her handlers. She looked away to interrupt the earnestness between them, turned her body to free herself from Delia's hands, and continued walking. "So you don't care for Enzo?" Nasim's steered her thoughts back to him. Even just thinking about him made things feel simpler. *The water's still clear upstream,* she imagined he might say, and though she would tell him that the analogy didn't work that way, maybe he would still be right.

"Well, he's a total know-it-all, for one," Delia said, falling into step behind Nasim. "And I'm sure half the stuff he says he's making up. But there are all these suckers who don't see through the façade, you know? They just drink it up. All the things he says, this persona he projects."

"Who, though?" Nasim wondered aloud. Was she one of these suckers, drawn in by an act? She saw nothing disingenuous in him, just some playfulness that sometimes masked the underlying sincerity. And the energy he possessed, too, the ebullience that was beginning to surface, a love of life that Nasim didn't think had survived the Plague.

"Everyone. The other handlers, the nurses, even the cooks in the kitchen. I can't tell you the number of people - women, really - who have come up to me in the last couple of weeks and told me how lucky I am to be working with him. And, I mean, Christ, it's not even fair to say that it's the women; it's everyone. Everyone loves Enzo."

Everyone loves Enzo, Nasim thought.

Delia went on, "I don't know what it is about him. I could walk around with a smile plastered on my face all the time, too, and always, always have to have something to say about everything. What do people see in that? It's plastic. It's narcissistic."

Enzo loves life, Nasim thought, *And everyone wishes that they, too, loved life. So instead they love Enzo and his easy, infectious laugh.*

"Think about this, Nasim. Do you really want him hanging around for the next decade of your life?"

"Delia!" Nasim was truly surprised, "I'm not going to get him fired!"

"No, no, I'm not saying you should. I'm just saying you should think about it. God knows you have to deal with him infinitely more than I do. Is that really someone you want to have responsible for... for you?"

"Delia," Nasim said reproachfully.

"I just think that if for any reason you decided that it wasn't going to work out, a few words to the person in charge of the match would, you know, fix it. Because I know they don't want you to go through what you went through with Cath a second time."

Nasim heard it in Delia's voice: the concern was genuine, not petty. "Delia, really, I don't think he's nearly as bad as you think. I know he made a horrible first impression, and, yes, he's a bit arrogant, and maybe he is a know-it-all." *Stringing along a bunch of unwitting victims like me,* she added in thought. "Anyways, you don't have to like him. And you don't even have to interact with him all that much. But I was thinking of having the three of you to dinner on Sunday nights. You know, when you draw shifts?" She had waited this long hoping that Delia would forget her dislike of Enzo, but seeing no improvement she had finally grown impatient. "Would you come if I did that? You wouldn't have to, obviously."

"Of course I'd come if you wanted me to."

EIGHTEEN

"You're not listening to me!"

"I am listening to you! You're not looking at the fucking numbers!"

"You're not fucking listening to me about what the fucking numbers mean!"

Scott threw his hands up in the air, "Well then tell me what the fucking numbers mean!"

Alex was across from him, his arms spread wide bracing himself against the table. They had walked into the break room moments earlier, slamming the door behind them; but the walls were thin, and the argument was obvious, and the staff outside who would have strained to hear what was being said heard well enough without straining.

"The fucking numbers mean that we're going to fucking win!" Alex shouted.

"The fucking numbers say that we're fucking behind."

"Christ!" Alex brought his hands up and slammed them both back onto the table. Then he took a breath, his eyes fixed on his own white knuckles. "You," he said, poorly masking his frustration, "are *the candidate* for the Eden Project. The Eden Project is polling at 55%. You're going to win."

"I'm *the candidate*, and I'm 15% behind the issue. Forty fucking percent, Alex. Tell me how I'm going to win when four weeks from now, 40% of the people in this district are going to cast their ballots for me. In what world is that winning?"

"People are going to walk into that booth, and they're going to vote on the only issue there is. Your issue wins, you win."

"And this explains why I'm polling at 40% how?"

"Six months ago you were a fucking nobody, Scott, and you were running against Celia fucking Pederson. Jesus, two months ago you were still a fucking nobody, and the Project was polling at 42%. Pederson had the issue and the name recognition, and you were on your way to unemployment. This week, you have the issue, and you've got I don't even know how many times more press coverage. If you're not at 50% within four weeks, I'll fucking resign."

"You won't need to resign, you'll be fucking fired," Scott said, but the anger had gone out of his voice.

"And one more thing," Alex began, still annoyed at Scott's moment of doubt. "You think any of Pederson's supposed supporters who don't like her stance on the Project are going to show up to the polls? If the election were today, I'd give you good odds of winning with the numbers where they are."

A smile crept onto Scott's face. "So we're going to win?"

"Christ, Scott, if you don't believe it, how are they going to believe it?" Alex pointed through Scott and the door behind him at the volunteers who had only in the last minute given up trying to make out the voices from the break room. His contact with the table broken, Alex's posture relaxed, and he sank into the ratty armchair behind him. "You're a piece of work, you know that?"

Scott fell onto the couch and threw his legs over one of the arms. "You say that like you're peaches and sunshine to work with."

"A few more weeks, and then we can dial back until the work really begins in January. Don't let the wear start to show now."

They sat in silence for a few minutes, then Scott asked, "Ruth's coming to the thing tomorrow?"

Alex nodded. "And Ellen?"

"Things have been so much better. I think that first day with Ruth she finally realized that what we're fighting for could actually deliver a baby into her arms. In the not-too-distant future. Every time she asks me how an event went, every time she offers to come to one, that's what she's got on her mind. "

"And that your odds of getting one as Mr. And Mrs. Congressman are infinitely better than your odds as Mr. And Mrs. Davis?"

"I don't think that hurts, either," Scott admitted.

"Whatever helps."

When they left the break room, Scott announced that he was ordering pizza for the lot of them and stuffed $200 into the hands of one of the volunteers with instructions to buy beer. "Because," he had said, "we're going to win." It was the same sentiment he echoed an hour later to many more ears when the pizza boxes were spread out across the stacks of paper that covered their shared desks and the beer was floating in a sink of icy water in the break room.

"Another day," he announced, "another percentage point in the polls." The new numbers had come in just ten minutes earlier.

"Plus or minus three," someone in the back said. The comment was dismissed with a grumble from the other volunteers, though it had been well-intentioned.

"*And*," Scott interrupted the stir, "our pet issue is up another two points. With this kind of momentum, we can't lose. So this," he hoisted a beer and a slice of pizza into the air, "is the first celebration of the people who are making this a reality." When the only response he received was a few nods from the heads in front of him, he shouted, "*You*, folks. This is our first celebration of *you*."

The high spirits of the afternoon dissipated most of the anxiety that had settled after the earlier argument, and when Ruth arrived that evening to cold pizza and warm beer, she felt no trace of it lingering. The three of them planted themselves in the break room with a printed schedule. "Four weeks," Alex said. "Ruth, double check all these dates. You're with Scott for every event you can make it to. And we have three to four events a day. It's all about maximizing visibility and drawing media coverage. We're doing everything from town hall meetings to soup kitchens to barber shops to…"

"I don't have anything else," Ruth shrugged. "I don't see why I couldn't do them all."

"That's our girl," Scott smiled and then added, "We're going to win this. I can feel it. And the victory… it's that much sweeter for being on the right side of this issue."

"It's a mystery to me that they sleep at night," Ruth said, looking past Scott in the direction of Celia Pederson's campaign headquarters.

NINETEEN

Delia did come to dinner. She was on duty during, so short of skulking in her bedroom, she had little choice. Peter and Enzo had walked over together from the handlers' apartments and together entered the coop, where they were greeted by the smell of roasted garlic and something savory - meats or mushrooms - and rosemary.

Almost anything Nasim could want was hers for the asking. Poor compensation, she thought, for the use of her body as an incubator, and she almost never requested anything. But what difference did it make? No one noticed her silent protest; no one cared that she sacrificed the paltry benefits she earned in exchange for her misery. So she had called the kitchen and ordered dinner for the four of them and a waiter to serve, and afterwards she had asked Delia to call a gardener about having the grass beyond her glass doors replaced with flowers in the spring. There were other Eves who asked for more, but Nasim couldn't think of anything else.

With Delia that afternoon, she had watched a blanket of snow falling, and she had told Delia to call for hot cider to be brought before dinner. That's what they had been drinking when Peter and Enzo arrived, stomping their boots before they pulled them off, Peter balancing by the door and Enzo sitting on the patch of tile just inside the living room, his feet hanging over the threshold into the hall. Their coats hung in the closet, the men joined the women at the table and poured themselves mugs of cider from the carafe on the table's lazy Susan. The waiter, who stood discretely in the kitchen, in view but unnoticed, emerged with cheese and crackers and a platter of grapes and tangerines and wedges of grapefruit pulp, the skin peeled off each piece.

As they ate, twilight was slowly swallowed up by dusk, and by the main course, their faces were half-bathed in white moonlight reflected off snow and half-lit by the orange glow from the fireplace. Nasim had hoped that the evening's atmosphere would be easy and comfortable, but she had worried that her intimacy with Enzo would only underscore the distance that hadn't yet been bridged between Enzo and the two other handlers. But digging in to the meat, a rib roast carved among potatoes mashed in cream and onions, they couldn't help but laugh together and talk together.

Knowing her fondness for sweets, Enzo had called the kitchen that afternoon and added to the poached pears a request for spiced molasses cookies. When the waiter brought them out after the pears, Nasim looked at each of her handlers, trying to guess who was responsible, and said, "I think someone must be missing their cookies because they aren't ours."

"They are, though," Enzo smiled. "My grandmother's secret recipe - or it was secret until I shared it with the kitchen staff."

"You should have said. I would have saved room," Nasim said, trying the gauge the likelihood that she could eat even another bite without unpleasant consequences.

Enzo just smiled some more and said, "It doesn't matter." He took one for himself, and Peter's hand hovered over the table, halfway committed to taking one of his own. Delia's face, though, had gone sour.

"You really have to make a contribution to everything, don't you, Enzo?" Delia asked. The venom in her voice seized the attention of the others, paralyzed any camaraderie that might have been growing.

Peter, his voice too soft, asked, "What do you mean, Delia?"

She hesitated, almost shook her head that she had meant nothing, but then she said, "This is Nasim's dinner, her plan, her invitation. It's just the sort of thing Enzo would do to change the menu. Even with this dinner, even with Nasim, Enzo usurps the conversation; Enzo gets the last word. Typically rude. Typically inconsiderate. Just…" She looked at the others, assessing their faces without really caring what she read there.

Before Delia could render her final pronouncement or Enzo could reply, Nasim intervened. "Delia, it's okay. I don't mind about the cookies. I'd have one if I weren't full, but I am; so it makes no difference one way or the other." Turning to Enzo, she added, "It's just a gesture of good will. Towards me, towards all of us."

Peter began to nod, his hand finally reaching out to take a cookie, and Delia snapped her gaze in his direction. "I would have thought you, at least, would see through all this. Here and with everyone else, it's all the same story. Enzo wags his junk in everyone's face, and everyone mistakes it for fucking flowers."

Peter had let the cookie fall to his plate when Delia's eyes had struck him. He said nothing. Nasim he could disarm so easily, but Delia didn't respond the same way.

Enzo pushed his seat back as though he were going to get up from the table. "Delia, wherever you've picked up this absurd notion of me, I suggest you put it back. I had no *intentions* this evening beyond bringing cookies. It's not a manipulation, not a statement, not anything but cookies."

"There's a context for everything, Enzo," Delia spat. "And you've provided ample context for anyone with their eyes open." She looked through Nasim and Peter as she rose from her chair and, without another word, retreated to the handlers' bedroom.

Peter waited a moment, then cleared his throat and excused himself from the table to retrieve the straws, a spoon, a dessert fork, and a dinner fork, their handles indistinguishable. He and Enzo drew silently for their shifts for the following week, and Peter handed the leftover spoon to Nasim, as though that was her lot. Only after was the silence broken by Enzo, who said to Nasim, "I have to get some things sorted before I'm on duty. Thank you for…" he motioned towards the table. "And I'm sorry about…" He motioned towards the table again. Nasim nodded.

Once Enzo had left, Peter took Nasim into a warm embrace and whispered, "It was wonderful, and you were lovely; and don't feel otherwise."

TWENTY

"Three broken arms, six concussions, thirteen needed stitches, and more black eyes and bruises than we could count. And," Sam drew out the word and the anticipation behind it, "I found the woman who got hit in the head with the tear gas canister."

"And?" Eleanore asked, pulling her feet off her desk so that she could lean forward.

"She agreed to be interviewed. On camera."

Eleanore clapped her hands in delight. "How does she look?"

"Like someone smacked her over the head with a can of tear gas," Sam laughed. "Stitches on her forehead where the impact split the skin and a nasty rainbow of bruise across most of her face."

"And you've got a taker?" Eleanore was shaking her head, her grin uncontained.

"Reporter will be here at four-thirty to set up. And our lovely face said she could get here by three so we could do some coaching."

"Sam," she said. "Sam." After the pleasure had steeped a few moments, she added, "You can't give me just the good news. What about the counter-protest? What did they get out of the riot?"

Here Sam's face finally lit up. "Nothing."

"Nothing?"

"Not a broken bone. Not so much as a stitch, from what I could ascertain. They probably accrued some bruises, but as far as I know, they're not pursuing anything."

"Nothing," Eleanore repeated. "Incredible."

She poured herself a drink and then joined Sam at the table, where the plan lay unrolled, tight script in cobalt ink spidering across the cream paper. It was anchored at its four corners by sachets of sand the same deep blue as the ink.

"I didn't know whether you wanted me to call Nasim in for this."

"I don't think so. We'll save her for tomorrow." Eleanore traced her finger through the web of action before her. "She hasn't turned out quite as I'd hoped. It's too bad she doesn't have a better name. We ought to have done something about that. She's the right face, you know. But what American family falls in love with someone named Nasim?"

Sam nodded. "Ruth, on the other hand?"

"Oh, Christ. Ruth's… something else. If 'Nasim' had been 'Emily,' no one would be talking about Ruth. In the court of public opinion, innocence is worth an order of magnitude more than matronly-ness."

"But foreigners don't hold a candle to Americans."

"You couldn't tell her from a Texan by looking. I thought that would be enough for a face, but…"

"But even a face needs a name."

Today's face was named Laura, and the bruises that covered it were black, with a rainbow of yellow and green that bled around the edges and sickened her skin all the way to her neck. The effect was so off-putting - and so much more so than even the day before - that Sam cancelled the make-up artist who had been hired to make Laura camera-ready. Eleanore and Sam walked her through the questions the reporter would likely ask, suggested a certain phraseology here and there, offered some points to work into her responses that would bolster public perception of the cause she was fighting for, the cause that had earned her this mistreatment at the hands of people whose actions had been sanctioned by her own elected representatives.

The reporter was local, but the face was right, and the syndicates had picked it up by early evening. It was broadcast and streamed and printed the following morning, and by late the next day, the numbers betrayed an uptick of support for them for the first time since summer. Two days later, the several points' lead the Eden Project had held had dissolved back into the margin of error of most of the surveys.

In that time, Laura's bruises only traveled, the black diluting into a puddle of purples and blues as it seeped down the side of her face. Sam touched base with her before some of the interviews, requests for which had been flooding in since the first evening, but Eleanore stayed away. They couldn't risk the perception that Laura was Eleanore's puppet - or worse, that she was Eleanore's creation, bruises and all - particularly given their good fortune in Laura's eloquence and the ease with which she handled the camera.

Instead, Eleanore shifted her attention back to Nasim, who, in spite of her name, remained the asset of far greater potential value, untapped though it remained.

"I want you to wear jeans at the next event," Eleanore told Nasim, who was sitting in Sam's usual spot at the table and looking skeptical.

"I've just been wearing the clothes that Sam's bought."

"I know, but I want you to wear some of your own clothes. What you're wearing right now, for example."

Nasim looked at the faded t-shirt that hung on her and the worn jeans. Most of the pants she had were hand-me-downs from the other women she lived with, but these were one of the pairs she had from before. Her skin was just starting to show through where the horizontal fibers at the knees has begun to split apart. She had always been thin but never quite as thin as she was now, so the belt that held them up was cinched too tight, and the way they hung in the back was unflattering. "These?"

"Those."

"But don't these just make me look…"

"American." "Poor?" They both spoke at the same time.

"The problem is your name."

"My name?" Nasim had preferred talking to Sam from the beginning. Eleanore intimidated with her big house and her imposing desk and rich clothes and with her bluntness. Nasim kept hoping Sam would walk in and interrupt this, take it over, say the things that Sam said.

"Voters don't relate to people named 'Nasim.' They don't have children named 'Nasim.' They don't *want* to have children named 'Nasim,' and they don't particularly care if someone named 'Nasim' has children for them."

Nasim fixed her green eyes on her hands, folded on the table in front of her.

"We just need to remind them that you're not so very different from them. You may not have been vaccinated when the rest of us were, you may have had 'ethnic' parents, but we're all struggling now, and you're no different in that respect."

TWENTY-ONE

Days with Peter sometimes dragged on, but evenings Nasim always enjoyed. He was good for reading, especially when she asked him, as she was doing ever more often now, to read the same book that she was. They sat on the couch together or he on the couch and she lying in the thick carpet in front of the fireplace, her upper lip beaded with sweat from the heat of it, and after a while, one would remark to the other that the protagonist was spoiled or the antagonist too evil or the plot dull, and they would while away hours in digression.

The winter had been long this year, with a storm in mid-April that froze the crocuses, but spring was impatient now, skipping over the days when the forties felt warm, plowing into mid-eighties and warm evenings as though summer had already begun. The windows were open and the glass door, and the lengthening evenings lit the room. Those things would usually have brought Nasim a sense of relief, quelling her longing for light and heavy rains and thunder and crickets. On this evening, though, Nasim found herself stuck half a page into the seventh chapter, unable to focus on the sentence that she had been rereading for a number of minutes that she had lost track of and equally unable to find joy in long rays of red sunlight that were licking at her feet through the open door. She was propped on her elbows, a paper and ink relic spread in front of her, her toes wiggled into the carpet.

"Peter." She looked up to where he was lying stretched out across the couch. His book was projected onto the ceiling, and he finished the sentence he was on before he rolled his head to face her.

"Nasim."

She waited a long time, not sure what she wanted to say. "I'm sick of reading."

"Worried?"

She nodded, scrunching up her face to dam the unexpected tears welling up. She glanced behind her, where a workman, taking advantage of the fair weather, was replacing her windows for different ones, but he was oblivious to their conversation. Peter rolled off the couch and adopted the same pose she was in. "Less worried than last time?"

She shook her head, tucking her chin into her chest, and a few tears squeezed from her eyes, dissolving into the carpet. Peter sidled up next to her until their shoulders touched, and she leaned her weight into his. The Protector.

There was nothing difficult about insemination. It had taken naturally three times already, and there was no reason to think that it wouldn't again. The doctors were good at it, even better now than they used to be. Five minutes in the stirrups at the moment they had determined, a needle-less syringe that they always showed her but she never felt. *In vitro* fertilization was a later resort, one that she had not yet experienced and the threat of which terrified her.

"Do you want me to be there? I can come even if I'm

not on duty. If you want." It was the first time Peter had offered, the first time anyone had suggested over-riding the schedule that was determined by two forks and a spoon. Nasim had never really thought about the fact that the shifts could be altered or the people moved, that that lay in her power.

Nasim tried to smile at Peter. She glanced at the workman again, hoped he was nearly finished. "I know it's not so bad. It's just the weight of it, of the whole thing. And that's the moment it begins again. Back to step one."

"Each time, though, you're one iteration closer to the end. You don't have to tell me now. The offer stands, redeemable any time. And for anything. Okay?" He waited long enough to see her nod and then added, "Besides, I still haven't figured out what to do with all my free time now that I'm not working twelve hour shifts anymore."

Nasim's gaze was fixed on the book on the floor in front of her, though she wasn't reading, and she hoped that Peter wouldn't go back to his book. He didn't.

"All finished here," the man's voice startled her. It was the first he'd spoken to her. She said nothing, and he nodded his head and left with his tools.

"Peter," she eventually broke the comfortable silence, "what do you think of Enzo?"

"I don't need to think of Enzo very much."

"Really, I want to know."

Peter paused in reflection. "It seems to me that he's growing to love you as much as Delia and I do. And that's what matters most in this line of work."

"You don't like him?"

"I do like him, as a matter of fact. But I don't think you should be overly concerned with whether your handlers like each other. What do *you* think of him?"

"I think he's wonderful."

"Well then."

"It's just with Delia…"

"I'm sure you haven't had to ask Delia her opinion of Enzo."

"She sees something in him, something off about him. That no one else seems to see. So who's wrong about him? Delia or everyone?"

Peter leaned back, his eyes idling over the book that was still projected overhead, though the words were in the wrong orientation now. A better computer would have corrected that automatically. "Does it matter? Delia sees something in him that she doesn't like. Maybe everyone else sees the same in him but likes those qualities. It doesn't have to be a matter of intrigue and ulterior motives. So long as you like him, so long as he performs adequately as a handler - not just the job, but the role, too - then I think it's fine. Don't you?"

"You don't think there's something there, something bad, that I'm not seeing and that she is?"

"Relax, Nasim. You have years to find out who he is, and I can promise he's not a psychopath, if that's what you're worried about. Just figure it out, the two of you, one step at a time. People are too complex to view through anyone's filter but our own."

Nasim nodded. After a long silence, Peter muttered, "Computer, reorient," and both of them returned to the words in front of them.

TWENTY-TWO

NOVEMBER 4, 2062

The final seventy-two hours of the campaign included only a few minutes of sleep for any of them. Scott and Ruth had split up to double the ground that they could cover, and Ellen was out, too, though mostly with Scott. Alex bounced back and forth, struggling to keep pace with the schedule he had drawn up for them.

They had all started in the northwest corner of the district and worked their way across and south. Ruth was waylaid at a shopping mall by a handful of women who longed to be pushing strollers when she ought to have been on her way to a grocery store, and Scott was running early because the deli where his third stop was planned had been flooded overnight by a water main break. The tempo of their stops might be mismatched - and the meet-ups that had been sprinkled through the days impossible - but their purpose, Alex reminded them every time he caught up to one or the other, was singular: coax voters to the polls.

"I don't know, Alex," Scott said, his hands gripping the steering wheel and his foot playing with the brake pedal as he waited for the light to change. Scott's driver was following behind Alex's car, but Scott hated not driving and so had insisted on this opportunity. When the light turned, he floored the gas. "What are we doing here? What's the handshake-to-vote conversion rate?"

"That's an irrelevant question. We're playing at the margins, Scott. It doesn't matter how many hands you shake, as long as you shake the one that gets you the office. Besides, what's a few more hours after the number we've already put in?"

"Do you have any new numbers?"

"You asked me that two hours ago."

"Well?" Scott persisted.

"Don't you think if I had new numbers I would have led with that?"

"Christ, Alex. Sometimes just answer the fucking question."

"I have no new numbers."

"Tell me again about the last ones."

Alex started to object, but they were nearing their next destination, and he could see no advantage to subjecting potential voters to an angry Scott. "You're down a half point as of yesterday. But a half point, that's statistically irrelevant; the margins are plus/minus four."

"And."

"And the Eden Program is back up to fifty-one for, forty-four against. That's as definitive as we were ever going to see it after Biggs started dressing their girl like a hobo."

Scott accelerated into the parking lot, a few feet free of traffic, before he punched the brake and sent Alex lurching forward in his seat.

"We're not where I hoped we'd be, Scott. But our odds of winning are as good as Pederson's - better than Pederson's, if you ask me - and today might be the day you shake the right hand. Leave her running," he added, as Scott reached for the keys. "I'm going to drive back to meet up with Ruth."

When they met late that night at Scott's campaign headquarters to debrief, Alex was carrying three plastic bags stuffed with paper carry-out boxes of Chinese food.

"No rest for the weary," he said, unpacking the bags. The volunteers had left a few hours earlier, the stragglers packing up when the ten o'clock cutoff for the last phone calls had passed. The three of them hadn't bothered with the lights as they had come in, and only now did Ruth turn on a lamp in the break room. The low angle of the light hollowed out their eyes and left them all looking so bleak that Alex considered switching it off again for morale.

They finished up so late that they didn't bother to go home. Ruth slept on the couch, and Scott hung over the end of the loveseat, while Alex found a corner sufficiently distant to muffle the grating of Scott's snoring.

The following morning, they did it again. Diners and hairdressers and churches and coffee shops and pharmacies. The bars where men were watching the game, the Sunday afternoon knitting circles where women no longer made booties and tiny hats. When they weren't conferring with Alex between stops, Ruth and Scott were on the phone. They called their most vocal supporters to pull them into the final press. They called total strangers to discuss the single issue. They called headquarters to spur on the volunteers. And then they got out of their cars and shook more hands and patted more backs and gritted out a few more smiles.

When Alex met Scott for the fourth time that day, he came with news, "New numbers."

"And?"

"You're up three quarters of a point since the last

numbers." He saw the lag in Scott's processing. "Which," he added before Scott could respond, "is obviously well within the margin of error. It's really no different from the position we were in yesterday except that-"

"Except that we're ahead."

"We *may* be ahead," Alex corrected.

"For the first time." Regardless of the reality, Scott's smile was insuppressible. "We're ahead."

Alex let him have a moment before insisting, "We're in a dead heat."

They worked late into that night again, again convening with carry-out a few hours after the last volunteers had left.

"One more day," Ruth sighed.

"Well…" Ruth and Scott both glared at Alex, but he was too tired to care. "There is the matter of Tuesday."

Ruth shook her head. "I'll give you gentlemen tomorrow, but that's all I have in me." It wasn't, though. They slept there again Monday night and were woken Tuesday morning by the arrival of the second-to-last shift of volunteers.

"I think I'll start with a coffee shop," Ruth said before disappearing into the office where they had all hung changes of clothes.

"Just don't do anything stupid today, Scott. Like stumbling into the buffer area around a polling place," Alex offered before he, too, disappeared to pick up his lucky cufflinks, which he only ever removed from their box on days like this. Didn't want the luck to run out.

Scott splashed some cold water over his face and made a pot of coffee while he waited for Ruth to vacate the office so he, too, could change. "Last day," he whispered to himself.

TWENTY-THREE

June 2, 2071

It was Enzo who was on duty the morning of the appointment. He arrived while she was in the shower and laid out her clothes for the day on her bed, then, one foot on the tile of the bathroom and one foot dug into the carpet in Nasim's bedroom, leaned up against the doorjamb, the back of his head resting on the wood frame. Steam fogged the glass door of the shower, but drops of water washed it away so that the blur of Nasim's smooth back and slender hips were rendered clear in vertical streaks.

"There was a message. They want you there at 11:30."

"Was it really worth ruining my shower to tell me that?"

"Would have kept, I guess." He listened to the sound of the water running, then, "While you're captive…"

"Mm?"

"Should we talk about the fact that your phone is a relic?" He laughed. "I mean, why on earth don't we just use the computer?"

"I had it disabled."

"Disabled for calling?"

"I don't know. Just seemed like it made it too easy for them to hear me all the time. And see me."

"You don't think they can do that anyhow?"

"I don't like to think about it."

"But how did you even get that ancient thing?"

"Came with the place."

Enzo snorted. "They built these fancy coops from the ground up, and they installed a hard-wired phone system?"

She turned the water off and opened the door. She didn't understand the fluttery feeling in her stomach when she saw him lately, the way her ears burned when he teased her, the way she blushed at nothing when he was around. She didn't understand why she had been sleeping poorly, why when her mind wandered during the late night hours that she waited to fall back to sleep it was to thoughts of Enzo and to imaginings of the things they might one day do together.

"Maybe they had some phones left over from a contract last century." A cloud of steam escaped from the confines of the shower where she stood, dripping and waiting. Enzo eased his weight off the doorframe and pulled Nasim's towel off the heater, reaching around her to drape it over her shoulders.

"Do you think they would give me heated floors if I asked?"

"Christ, Nasim, isn't it hot enough in here for you?"

She flushed a deep crimson but smiled in reply, loving the cool tile on the soles of her hot feet as she padded to the sink. When she was half dry, she dropped her towel to the floor, and Enzo replaced it with her thick bathrobe, as soft and bleach-white as the towels. From the vanity, she took a small bottle of some expensive serum and emptied half of it into the palm of her left hand. She rubbed it brusquely onto her belly, scrubbing it into the stretch marks that became more pronounced with each pregnancy.

"Nasim," Enzo said with a gentle scold, "let me do it." He pulled her hand away from her reddening flesh and took the bottle from beside the sink. Kneeling in front of her, he traced each line back and forth until the sheen of the liquid had disappeared into her skin. She felt a tingle all the way into her spine each time he touched her. When he had finished, he hopped up and folded her bathrobe over itself, cinching the belt before he returned to his place hovering at the door.

Insemination took place at the clinic, a half mile across the grounds. Enzo walked with her arm in his, the slight resistance he felt betraying her dragging feet. "We shouldn't be late," he said. "You don't want to miss the window and have it not take." But Nasim only dragged her feet more, immune to the smell of summer around her.

The office was plain, a drab waiting room with only four chairs and a heavy desk dwarfing the bespectacled receptionist. She ticked off Nasim's name as soon as they entered, and either their entrance or the receptionist's action prompted someone to emerge from the door behind the desk before they had even had a chance to sit. In the beginning there had been other Eves in the waiting room sometimes. But Nasim had once heard a woman screaming from one of the other exam rooms, and, either intentionally or by happenstance, she had never again encountered another Eve at the clinic.

They were escorted to one of the rooms, the same one in which all her other appointments had taken place. The silent escort left them, and Nasim changed into the thin robe that hung on the door, handing her own clothes to Enzo to hold. He sat on a chair in the corner of the tiny room, just a few inches from where Nasim's foot rested in the stirrup of the examination table.

The moment she was changed and seated, the door opened, and a doctor entered carrying a cooler no larger than a novel. Enzo's attention was focused on the doctor until Nasim caught his eye with wiggling toes. She motioned for him to come closer, to stand beside her, then clasped his hand tightly in hers.

"You know the routine well enough." Half statement, half question, and Nasim nodded in affirmation. The doctor opened the cooler and drew out a vial and syringe as he continued, "Do you have any questions?" It was her right to ask about the donor. Eves almost always asked the first time, though Nasim hadn't. Almost no one asked the second time.

Nasim shook her head and squeezed Enzo's hand tighter. He could see her eyes turning liquid, so he placed his other hand on her shoulder.

When the doctor left the room no more than two minutes later, the tears began to run. Enzo wiped a few away, but she swatted at his hand. "Help me dress," she said, shedding the robe in a pile on the floor. For a moment he stood paralyzed. "Help me dress," she repeated.

They walked back in silence. Enzo tried once to hold her arm, but her body stiffened at his touch. She followed him, though, when he walked into the door at the end of the building and down the hallway instead of taking the path outside to her glass door. Nasim hadn't been through there in more than a year. The light over her door was out, and a long, black streak marred the wall across from her entrance.

In the time it took Enzo to untie his shoes, Nasim had disappeared into her bedroom. He found her lying on the floor on the far side of her bed, half curled and facing the deepest corner of her coop.

"Nasim," he whispered, "Nasim."

Her body shook with a stifled sob and then a second before returning to perfect stillness.

Enzo eased himself between the side of the bed and Nasim's back, wrapping his arm around her and cradling her body in his. Once more, he whispered, "Nasim."

TWENTY-FOUR

"I didn't really think we'd be out today," Nasim said to break the silence in the car. Sam was driving the two of them to a rally. "I mean, obviously, if there's a rally… I just didn't think there would be today." When Sam still offered no explanation, she continued, "You know? I would have thought maybe *yesterday*."

Sam finally stirred from silence, "It's typical. Since they made Election Day a holiday to increase voter turnout. It's the day even apathetic people have time to go to a rally. Your parents never took you?"

Nasim shook her head. Her fingers were absently playing with the frayed edge at the inseam of her jeans. "They never really took us anywhere. I can't even remember going out to eat."

"Who's 'us'?"

"Oh, me and my brother and sister. I guess I never told you about them?"

"I guess I never asked."

"They… uh… they didn't survive. That's about right, you know? There were five of us. My parents and me and them, and I'm the only one who made it. I mean, I never got sick or anything. But anyways…eighty percent."

"Did they die before your parents?" Sam asked.

"No, after. My brother, he was older. He took care of us when Mom went into quarantine. And then when she didn't come back, Abbas just kept at it until he disappeared one day, too. We didn't know where he was until we got the call from the hospital a week later that he hadn't made it. That was… not so long ago. And then my sister. Last November. Two more months, and she would have… well, she would have been on her way to the rally with us." Nasim's jaw was clenched, but she had learned how to hold her grief in. "Eleanore would have liked her better than me, anyways."

"I don't…" Sam didn't know how to respond to any of it. "How old were you when your parents…?"

"Twelve."

"Eleanore does like you, you know. That's just… it's not the level that she interacts with people on. So it might seem sometimes like she doesn't like you, but she does."

"It's okay, Sam. I don't really mind," she said, her voice barely audible.

Sam waited until the action seemed unrelated to the conversation, then turned on the radio loud enough to listen to but low enough to talk over.

"Abbas was sixteen, though," Nasim said after a few miles. "So he really was old enough to take care of us. It's not as though we were… there was food on the table every night. And we had an aunt who helped as much as she could, but her husband didn't want… they already had kids." The babble of the radio sounded more urgent for a few moments, and Nasim waited, not sure where Sam's attention was directed. "You shouldn't feel sorry for me," she finally said.

Sam groped for a reply and finally settled on, "No one

has had an easy time of it. But you've had more than your share. I don't feel sorry for you. But I'm sorry it's something you've had to live through."

They drove the remaining thirty miles with just the radio talking.

The crowd at the rally was at least half as large again as the last one, but the passion of the other group was diluted here. The signs swayed back and forth in a gentle wash, and the chants ran out of sync with the signs and even, at times, with each other. There was no podium, and the people who might have populated a counter-protest were instead at their own rally on the other side of the city.

"We're just shaking hands," Sam said in answer to Nasim's unasked question. "Every hand you shake, that's a person who's more likely to vote. And in this crowd, that means they're voting for Pederson. And for you."

They recognized her when she entered the crowd, these people, these allies. Some of them knew her name. All of them knew her face, and all of them knew that it would be the face worn by the next generation if they lost. They pressed around her, reached out to touch her. Just a girl. "Fifteen," she heard someone whisper, though it wasn't true anymore. She had turned sixteen last month.

"Have you voted?" she heard Sam asking the people as they passed through her sphere, and she was startled by the number who said, "Not yet." If they were here, didn't that mean they cared? If they cared, didn't that mean they should have voted already? "On our way there now," some said.

Some of them wanted to talk, wanted to tell her how brave she was, as though bravery had something to do with losing your parents or with surviving the Plague unvaccinated. Some of them shook their heads as they shook her hand. Maybe she reminded them of someone they had lost; or maybe it was because she was too young, a child who would bear children; or maybe it was because they already knew that she had lost. But she pushed the last thought from her mind and smiled at them and said, begged, "Please vote."

They stayed late into the afternoon, Nasim having long since lost any sense of time in the blur of faces that passed by her. Her throat was parched from her plea, her cheeks ached from trying to smile, though she wondered how much it instead resembled the terrified grimace that it really was. Maybe if she had had Scott Davis's smile things would be easier. Sometimes she wondered if people rallied to him for his smile, if their indifference to her was because of hers. Sam's phone rang, though, and suddenly she was being led away, back to the car.

"Enough's enough," Sam said. "We're going to watch the results come in at Eleanore's. In the big house. I've got a change of clothes waiting for you there, if you don't mind."

"I don't mind," Nasim said, relieved that she wouldn't have to mingle in this sad uniform that set her just another degree apart from everyone else.

"You did great."

Nasim shrugged.

"Really. The whole thing. All of it. We've done everything we could do. You've done everything."

TWENTY-FIVE

Nasim had felt a migraine coming on, so though she had grown into the habit of staying up until Enzo left when he had the evening shift, she had turned in early. When Enzo and Delia crossed paths at the door, he smiled and wished her a pleasant night.

"She didn't stay up with you?"

"Not feeling well. If I were in her shoes, I don't know that I'd ever be feeling well."

"How do you mean?" Delia asked.

"It's quite a thing she's asked to do. And surely none of us can pretend she's doing it by choice. Don't you wonder about the justice of... all of this?" He implicated everything with a wave of his hands.

"Do I wonder?" There was anger in her voice. "Of course I don't wonder. This is my life, Enzo. I've given the whole thing to the Project, as much as Nasim has, and-"

"Don't compare what you do by choice to what she does by-"

"We're all serving, Enzo. I'm not saying what I do is equal to what she does, but I'm here for her every day from now until she leaves here. You don't think I do that because it's a fat paycheck, do you? You don't think that's why Peter's here, do you?"

"Not at all," Enzo hung in the doorway, his back to the hall. Delia squeezed one shoe in her hand, her knuckles white. The other was still on her foot.

"What are you doing here, Enzo? If you don't believe in this, why are you here?"

"I do believe in this. I'm here because I believe in it. Because I believe that we need the children. But this place! The horrors of this place. You know why they replaced the window panes with safety glass? You heard about the Eve who smashed a window so she could slit her wrist with the glass?"

"Keep your voice down!"

"But, Delia, you can see the pain she's in, can't you?"

"I… I love her so much, Enzo, and the implication that you care about her more than I do…" Her face betrayed her seething anger even more than her voice did. "You couldn't be more wrong. But that doesn't change that the right thing-"

"The 'right thing'? The thing that makes her suffer?"

"It's not our position to decide what is right and what isn't. It's an argument that was settled years ago by people better qualified than you or I. Those people decided that the right thing was to preserve the future of humanity. I agreed with them. I agree with them now. The cause is bigger than any person. *Humanity* is bigger than any person, Enzo."

"Of course," he sneered. "Sound logic when you're subjecting unwilling women to this… this institutional rape?"

"How dare you! How dare you compare what we do here to some crime perpetrated in dark alleys! If you don't like it, leave. And do it now, not in a year, not in five. She doesn't deserve to go through that again."

"But what would leaving solve, Delia? How would that help Nasim?"

"'Nasim, Nasim.' Why don't you seem to be able to grasp that this is about a lot more than just Nasim?"

"Because... because our humanity. Look at her, and tell me what's left of our humanity? If this is how we save it, if this is a price we're willing to pay, are we worth saving?" He turned on his heel and disappeared into the hallway, the door falling shut behind him.

Delia sat for a long time on the edge of her bed. No one became a handler without believing in the Eden Project. That was the selection criterion. A personality test matched the applicant to an Eve, and an interrogator - a team of them, sometimes - ascertained in three hundred different ways that the applicant *believed* in the Project. They had questions that got the truth out indirectly, of course, but they just asked, too. *How do you feel about the Project? How did you vote?* They asked once just as a person sitting across the table. They asked again in a polygraph and again after that liquid that no one liked the smell of. They asked a final time with the electrodes that some people said let them see your thoughts, but no one really knew if that was true; and if they had been able to see her thoughts, they oughtn't to have had to ask her the questions, Delia thought.

There were the things they didn't ask, though, that might have been more telling than their blunt questions and their thousand-question surveys that were supposed to root out the sentiments that even she was unaware of. They ought, she thought, to have asked what she would do when her Eve pulled her one way and the Project pulled her the other. Maybe it wouldn't have told them anything; it might have told her something.

Enzo laid it out as though it were something simple. The Project or Nasim. But how could it be a choice between them when Nasim was necessary to the Project, and the Project was necessary to everyone?

It had been so much easier in the beginning. She might have heard that it had been difficult to coax the first child from Nasim's arms, but someone else had been there to do it; she hadn't even seen. And if Nasim was melancholy, there were postpartum hormones that precipitated that; and plenty of people, all sorts of people, felt the apathy that Nasim described.

And besides, it wasn't a choice between the Project and Nasim; it was a choice between the future and Nasim. How could one life ever be worth more than the sum of the future?

And Enzo. Arrogant, self-righteous, and sure. Enzo, who couldn't keep an opinion to himself, who had to know everything about everything. Enzo - who in less than a year had relinquished his loyalty to the cause that he, too, would have had to swear an oath to - *he* had figured everything out. *He* had picked Nasim with a certainty that smacked of accusation.

Nasim or the future. How could she pick people who weren't yet born, just soulless single cells, over the person she loved more than anyone she had ever known?

They ought to have asked her what she would do about the conflict. But they never asked anyone that question.

TWENTY-SIX

Alex had had the foresight to hire a caterer. And somehow he had also arranged for a number of televisions that were now mounted around the main room of the office. The desks had all been pushed to the outside walls and covered with white table cloths and blue bunting, and they were piled high with food.

When Scott, Alex, and Ruth stumbled in together, their eyes bloodshot, it was to cheering from the volunteers who had assembled to watch the returns. The polling places were still hours from closing; Pederson was ahead, but the counties that were reporting had been expected to go for her. Numbers from their counties had only just started coming in, and every time an update flashed up on the screen, a cheer drowned out the reporter announcing another incremental gain for Scott.

Alex, though, had seen disappointment in rooms more optimistic than this one. He retreated to the break room, slumped onto the couch, and closed his eyes. *This is the last one*, he promised himself. It was the same promise he had made at the end of the last campaign, but that loss had driven him to try again. A win tonight, and he was done with campaigns: an office job on Scott's staff, someone else could handle re-election. A loss and... why think about it?

Scott, who a few minutes before had been too exhausted to climb the single flight of stairs, had already found himself a place in the heart of the room, at the center of the bodies. The energy he drew out of a crowd of supporters didn't even compare to this, to the high from these people who had given him loyalty for nothing. Not for promises, not for handshakes, not for feigned compassion. Hours and faith and love, and they had never asked for anything in return. And now they cheered him on, so dedicated that they celebrated his success as their own. So he clinked his beer bottle with that of each person there, and drank a swig to the health of every single one of them. And when the numbers flashed on the screen, he hooted and cheered and stomped his feet with them and never once looked at the margin of error on the exit polls.

Ellen was there, too. She sat next to Alex for a while, and they said nothing but felt each other's relief; and she shadowed Scott for a while, though she shrank away when he joined in the shouting.

The hungriest person in the room, though, was Ruth. She studied the maps on the peripheries of the screens, the contested races in every corner of the country. She tallied the wins against the losses and saw the picture emerging: if the outcome in this room remained uncertain - and it was obvious to her, if not to anyone else, that it still was - her outcome was nearly assured. Five more contested races they had to win, out of the twenty or more that remained in play. Five more to know with certainty that the Eden Project would begin. Even without those five, there was a chance. There were people in mismatched races whose ambivalence had been more visible than they meant it to be, who perhaps leaned one way but could win without the issue; they might yet be pulled to the right side for a price. But five more, and those people wouldn't matter.

The polls closed at midnight, part of the same voting reform that had made Election Day a holiday, but even with the automated counting, there was still a lag in reporting. These were the moments that Alex hated most. Someone must already know the outcome. Someone saw the final numbers the moment the polls closed, yet all the media had were their half-reporting precincts. He had wondered more than once whether it had been built into the voting reform, room for manipulation, an hour's time to change the algorithm to a more favorable outcome.

The caterers had already been out twice to restock the bar, and when it ran dry a third time, they hadn't been able to find an open store from which to resupply. The numbers that crept further and further in Scott's favor were so intoxicating, though, that no one noticed the fading buzz.

By one o'clock, four more races had been called in Ruth's favor. Every crumb of the food had disappeared. The champagne, intended for the moment of celebration, had been discovered in the refrigerator of the break room, popped, and drunk. A momentary convergence of too much excitement and fatigue and anxiety had lulled the room into a quiet that suddenly made Scott feel as though the reporters, a different one on each screen, were shouting some discordant message at him.

And then a number flashed. The final tally. All precincts reporting. Davis: 49.6%, Pederson: 49.1%. The count was narrower than he would have supposed. She had had votes hidden somewhere in one of his counties. But the margins were irrelevant to the outcome; he had seized his victory.

Someone smashed an empty beer bottle against the side

of a desk, but even the sound of shattering glass was lost in the uproar from the people surrounding Scott. A couple of them tried to hoist him onto their shoulders, but they stumbled and fell and laughed instead. Hands reached for him to clap him on the back and found whatever they could, his face, his chest. He looked around for Ellen, who was there, smiling and nodding and shell-shocked, and he pulled her to him, through a bubble of people around him that didn't want to part.

TWENTY-SEVEN

When the fourth child was born, Enzo wept. He had hated the thing, resented what it was leaching from her - nourishment and happiness - but he had also loved it because it was a life that she had grown. So many times they sat side by side on the couch, and Nasim had taken his hand and placed it on her belly, and he had felt the thing struggling inside her.

The labor had begun at the end of Enzo's shift, and he had wanted to stay; but Nasim had clenched her teeth and shaken her head, and he had felt relieved after all when Peter arrived. But the moment the child had come, he had felt it, a visceral thing that bubbled up from his stomach and became the vomit splattered across his shoes. He found himself back outside Nasim's coop, his hand braced against the wall of the fluorescent-lit hall, when the door opened. The nurse was carrying the child, swaddled in a thick wrap. She looked at Enzo suspiciously.

"What is it?" he asked, his eyes fixed on the bundle.

"A boy," the nurse replied. She moved past him, shielding the child from Enzo with her body.

Enzo slumped to his knees when she was out of sight,

his forehead pressed against the wall that separated him from Nasim's bedroom.

Peter emerged from Nasim's coop not long after and found Enzo, now sitting with his back to the wall, looking pale and clammy.

"What are you doing here?" Peter asked.

Enzo answered slowly, searching for an excuse as the first few words came out. "I didn't know if she would need me."

"She will in eight hours. Delia has this shift." He said it matter-of-factly, as though it were a perfectly normal thing to have forgotten.

"She's not here yet." Enzo felt disoriented, hungover, but he didn't think he could have missed Delia's walking by him.

"She came in through the glass door. Didn't want to run into the child if it was still here."

Enzo nodded.

They stayed there in silence for a few moments, Enzo still sitting, his head rolled back against the wall. Finally he said, "There's just nothing I can do for her. It's worse… it's the worst form of slavery what they're doing to her. And we're supposed to watch it happen. We're supposed to…" He trailed off.

The buzzing of the lights was deafening to him.

Peter answered him, "We're supposed to make life bearable for her. We're supposed to be strong for her. We're supposed to make her strong."

"What have you ever done to make her strong?"

It wasn't the question Peter had expected. What *had* he done to make her strong? He had only ever tried to be kind and gentle and shield her from what harm he could. He had pushed her to take the blue pills because they promised to make her happier. But he had never done anything that he could offer up in answer to Enzo's question.

"You should get some rest," he finally said to Enzo. "Her pain is more important than yours. She'll need you in eight hours."

Over the next days, Enzo held Nasim through her own tears, and he ensured, when the green pills arrived to supplement the blue ones, that she had one when it was due. He held her hand and touched her face, and when she stepped out of the shower, he tried not to stare at her now-shrunken belly.

"You're too good to me," Nasim said one afternoon. They were watching a movie, one of the old ones that he liked. She had been so tired the past week that she hadn't noticed the butterflies in her stomach; only today had she felt them again as she had edged closer to him, and she had wondered, too, if he could feel the hammering of her heart. But if he had noticed, he had said nothing, and they had both been drawn into the distraction of the movie. An hour or more in, Enzo's arm had fallen asleep, and it was his repositioning himself that had stirred Nasim to speak.

"Too good to you? How so?" he asked.

"You rub my feet." She bit her lip and cocked her head at a coy angle.

"Do you want me to rub your feet?"

"Only if you're offering."

He extricated his awakening arm from behind her and pulled himself out of the couch. He walked to the phone and ordered a plate of cookies, then settling on the floor in front of her, Enzo took a foot in his hand and began to massage it.

"Those aren't for me, I hope. I only just managed to lose eight pounds." Nasim tried to smile but couldn't.

"They're for whoever eats them," Enzo shrugged.

A knock at the door half an hour later found Enzo still seated on the floor, though the massage had ended some time before. Their attention had wandered between the movie that was still playing and some threads of idle conversation that they had woven together haphazardly, and the interruption was welcome. They had both forgotten about the cookies, which Enzo transported from the door to the table at the end of the couch.

"What makes you think I want cookies today?" she asked him, a note of criticism in her voice.

"I don't know, Nasim. Misguided attempt to console you with things that you otherwise enjoy? It must be... I can't even imagine how difficult it is for you. In a kinder world, he would have been yours, but-"

"Who?"

"The child."

Nasim sprang up, her face contorted by sudden anger. Enzo froze, his palms unconsciously turned towards her. "Never," she hissed at him. "Never!" she shouted, and she grabbed for the first thing in reach, the plate of cookies. Turning on her heels, she hurled it into the glass door. The plate shattered, and the chunks of warm, broken cookies streaked across the glass and decorated a path across the floor from her to there. "Never, never tell me that!"

He was already on his knees cleaning up the mess, the shards of ceramic and the still-molten chocolate staining the white carpet, with hands that he didn't realize were trembling. Not knowing what had set her off, he knew even less what to reply. She broke the silence again, "I don't deserve that! I don't deserve to have to know!"

Enzo heard the door to her bedroom slam. He cleaned what he could, his pulse pounding in his ears. He called a janitor to get the stains out of the carpet, then wavered a few moments, his hand still resting on the phone and his eyes fixed on the flashing colon in the time projected on the wall. Peter would be here any minute, so Enzo slunk to the door to await his replacement.

"I've done something," Enzo said, when Peter opened the door. "But I don't know what. I said something, and she threw a plate."

Peter's tone lacked judgement. "What did you say?"

"Just that if the world were more just, he would have been-"

"He." Peter said.

"The boy. The child."

"She doesn't want to know. She hates knowing the gender."

"But how could I have known?"

"You know now," Peter shrugged. "It's kinder to shield her from some things. It's part of the job."

Pacing her room, Nasim counted out her losses on her fingers. Chronologically: father, mother, brother, sister, aunt, friend, daughter, infant, infant, a son. Too many already to risk another, she reminded herself again. She had already tried to forbid herself from loving him, tried to scare herself off with a shadow of warning from the mother she resurrected in her mind. *A pointless love. An unrequitable love. An invitation for grief, for loss without having ever first profited the gain. Is this the story you want to write?* She had dredged up the fear that Enzo was no more than a set of eyes to watch her, a set of ears to listen, a pair of lips to inform, just a medium to carry out the will of the Project. The tightening in her chest when she saw the walls around her, when she felt the kick in her belly, that relic of terror she had known at sixteen when she had been matriculated into this slavery, Enzo was a part of that, she reminded herself. And now she added to it all the anger she felt in this moment, the adrenaline that was coursing through the tips of her fingers, sent there by the heart she could hear pounding in her ears. Another reason not to love him.

TWENTY-EIGHT

"It was the best fight we've had," Eleanore said to the three dozen drawn faces around her. She was subdued but smiling, a glass of champagne in one hand and the knife that had rung it still held in the other. "And it's fitting that Davis's race be the deciding one, the tipping point."

Most of the two hundred people who had started the evening in her house had left in the hours before, some because they were there socially, no skin in the game, and some because they had seen the way the numbers were pointing and held little hope for a last-minute reversal. They had known what Ruth knew - and what Eleanore knew, too - that there was a vote or two in some of the less competitive races that could be bought after tonight, just enough margin of error that the Eden Project could squeak through even without a clear victory tonight.

But the Eden Project had its clear victory, and they had their loss, no matter how they spun the numbers. By election results, by popular vote, by House race or Senate: all the tallies gave the same outcome. It was by no more than a few percentage points - and in many cases by no more than a few fractions of one - but a loss nevertheless.

By quarter to two, Sam and Eleanore were the only people left in the ballroom. Their bar had never risked running dry, a testament to Sam's planning rather than the appetites of the guests, and Sam poured two drinks from what remained.

"If the election had been two weeks from now or two weeks ago, it might have gone the other way," Sam offered.

Eleanore shrugged. "If wishes were… whatever that expression is." She turned off the last projection that was still talking and leaned against the wall, her eyes fixed on the gilded ceiling twenty-five feet overhead.

"Nasim's still here somewhere. I'll find her and take her home."

"Sam, this has been too much fun. What a fight!" She shivered in satisfaction. "I want you to find something else for us. Our next project. It doesn't have to have the visibility of this one. Obviously," she continued, "there's not going to be another issue like this for years. But that doesn't mean we can't dabble."

Sam had sunk to the floor, back propped up against the legs of one of the tables the caterers had brought. *Chairs next time.* Sam marked a palm with the opposite index finger, an imagined line to serve as a reminder. *Lots of chairs.* "I'm sure we'll find something."

"It's been so long," Eleanore said after a while, "that I can't even think. Everything we used to do was settled ages ago. The immigration issues and the animal stuff. And the wars, of course. Ooh, for a good war."

Sam stood and repeated, "I'm going to find Nasim and take her home," before disappearing into one of the anterooms. Nasim was in the third one Sam checked, lying on a chaise lounge. She was staring at the wall across from her, though when Sam entered her eyes fixed instead on the movement.

"You want to go home or just sleep here for the night?"

"What are we going to do, Sam?"

"There aren't many times in life that question's irrelevant, but this is one of them. We've already done all we were going to do. Now we go to sleep, and one morning you'll wake up, and they'll have a plan for you. They'll tell you what to do, and you'll do it."

"But there's still… it's not *finished* yet. There's no law yet. We can still-"

"The fight's over, Nasim. I'm sorry."

Nasim's eyes drifted back to the wall opposite her.

"Do you want to stay here tonight? Or do you want me to take you home?" Sam repeated.

"How can this be the end? This isn't how it was supposed to end. And it's not over!" Nasim's green eyes burned into Sam again. "How can you say that it is when there's so much more you could do?"

"It's not fair, Nasim. It's no more fair than the Plague taking your your parents, taking any of the people it took. It's no more fair than the vaccine taking away everyone's opportunity to have children. But the outcome is obvious now. It's not a matter of what you or I want. It's not a matter of what Davis wants, either. Everyone cast a ballot today. And we didn't win."

"I didn't cast a ballot!" Nasim shouted. "It's *my* life, Sam. My *life.* And everyone got to vote but me." Desperation cracked her voice, but she bit back the tears that threatened.

Sam shrugged. "That it's not fair doesn't change the outcome." When Nasim gave no reply, Sam repeated, "Do you want to stay here, or do you want me to take you home?"

Nasim rolled over, turning her back to Sam, her face inches from the orange wall behind her. She studied the stipples and cracks in the plaster until she was confident that Sam had left and then closed her eyes and let her exhaustion carry her not into sleep but into some other state of passive consciousness that had replaced sleep in the past weeks. Someone laid a blanket over her some time later and though she wanted to draw it tighter around her, she didn't want to betray that she was awake or break her own stillness. So she lay there, feeling a lick of cold air leak in every time her chest rose, and let her body sleep while her mind marched on.

TWENTY-NINE

November 4, 2072

"There's a thing I've done. It seemed right at the time – has seemed right all along – but I realize now that it's not." Peter was sitting across the round dining table from Nasim, his hands clasped in earnestness. "That's not quite how I meant to say it."

He had teased Delia so many times for the way that she rehearsed the things she would say, practiced how the words came out, how the pauses fit in, how the cadence matched the intonation. Now he wished he had done it. Enzo's question had haunted him for the better part of a year - *What have you ever done to make her strong?* – and he had spent a good deal more time asking it of himself than answering it. *Not enough,* was the only conclusion he seemed able to reach. And finally, *It's within my power to do more – or to try.* He had formulated some idea of what that might entail – opportunities to nurture her curiosity, a more deliberate selection in the books that they read together. Perhaps, he had told himself, he might be more honest with her one day, tell her the things that he shielded her from now. But sitting at the table across from Nasim's puzzled expression, he wondered whether any of it ought to be said aloud.

"No, I think it's not at all what I meant to say. I'd really... I'd just been thinking about the books that we read together. And I think maybe I've done you a disservice in what I've steered you towards. There are far more interesting things, and I've..." Would she want to know that he had figured her too fragile for so much great literature, that he had thought its darkness would reverberate too strongly in her? Or that he had known she would lack the education to appreciate it to its full potential? There was no condescension in his actions – had wanted to protect her, wanted to keep her entertained – but he could think of no translation into words that preserved the integrity of his intentions.

But she laughed. "That's all? You're sitting across from me stone-faced and pale, and what you're here to confess is that you haven't made the best reading recommendations? Well, do better next time." She waited to see if he had anything further to divulge, and when she decided that he didn't, she stood up from the table. "Will you build me a fire?" she asked.

"Yes." He took a moment to relish the relief at her having broken off the conversation so abruptly. "I could show you how. If you'd like."

"Why would I need to know how?"

"It's not a question of need. It's one of desire. I love building fires, Nasim. Maybe you would love it, too. Maybe you would hate it, and then we'd all know another thing about the world: Nasim loves fires, but she hates starting them."

She considered while she dug her toes into the deep carpet. "Show me."

Fifteen minutes later, a fire crackling in front of them, Nasim asked, "What will we read next?"

"I don't know yet. I'll make up a list. That's half the problem, you know, that I just come up with something off the top of my head and then later think that something else would have been much better; but by the next day I've forgotten it again."

"So then what are we doing with the rest of the afternoon?"

"You're full of questions."

"You should be full of answers," she chastised.

Peter shrugged, "Perhaps that's a question that *you* have an answer to, though."

Nasim peered into the fire. "S'mores, I think."

Peter called the kitchen and returned to his usual spot next to Nasim on the floor in front of the fire. "And do you suppose," she asked, "that they'd let me make a fire outside? In the woods, where Delia and I walk sometimes? It might be nice to do it there."

"We could build a fire ring tomorrow. I don't think they'll notice."

"And what about now? Couldn't we just go now?"

"We could," Peter laughed, "but maybe it's better saved for tomorrow. Aren't we about to have s'mores?" She didn't reply right away, and Peter goaded himself to start, "There's one more thing, Nasim." These things that he had kept from her – no, shielded her from – they had weighed on him for as long as he could remember. Surely she was better off not knowing, but how could he espouse that view, really, when truth ought to be preeminent? And what had been a long and slow deliberation in his mind had, in the last weeks and the last few hours especially, started to feel increasingly urgent. Finally he had decided that Nasim herself was the one best equipped to resolve the question: "I don't always tell you everything. I don't lie to you, not ever, but sometimes my omissions feel… no better than lies. I've only ever done it to spare you from knowing things that I thought would needlessly hurt you. But I've never asked you if that's how you would want it. Is it? Is that how you want it?"

It was odd to hear Peter with uncertainty in his voice. Nasim chewed her lip, and a deep line appeared across her brow before she responded, "I always want you to tell me. Always."

"Are you sure? Some of them are awful, Nasim."

"Tell me one."

He wished that he could remember anything other than the most horrible examples, but wracking his mind turned up nothing else. "Do you remember the Eve who used to live next door, and one day she vanished; and I told you she was on bed rest?"

"Of course."

"It was true, in a sense. She had tried to end her pregnancy, so they-"

"How?" Nasim interrupted. "How did she try to end it?"

"She…" *Should I really tell her?* "She ripped one of the filaments out of her toaster oven. And used that. Tried."

Nasim was looking into the fire. She nodded, "And then?"

"And then they restrained her so that she couldn't do herself any more harm. Bound her to her bed, called it 'bed rest.'" It hurt him more to tell her than it had to hear about it.

Nasim's lip twitched just once. "For how long?"

"For the five months of her pregnancy that remained."

The silence between them stretched for minutes, punctuated by the occasional pop from the fire.

"I always want you to tell me," Nasim finally said.

THIRTY

Scott would have liked to sleep later, had planned to, in fact, but the phone had rung early and Ellen had answered it before he had managed to stop her. He had expected a reporter, but instead someone asked him to hold for... he didn't catch the name, and when he asked, he had already been transferred to silence on the other end of the line. His moment of indecision about whether he ought to hang up or wait ran too long, and suddenly there was someone shouting, "Scottie!" in his ear.

"Who is this?" he asked, rolling out of bed, resigned now to getting up.

"Jesus, Scottie - Is that what you go by? - Archie Soren." Soren, House Majority Leader. He had run unopposed in his own district, had dismissed the question of the Eden Project so many times that it was unclear whether he had ever taken a side. Alex had been one of probably hundreds of people who had trolled through all the archived interviews in the hopes of gleaning from them some sentiment, but he - and everyone else - had come up empty.

"Archer Soren?" Scott clarified. *Is calling me?*

"'Archie' to my friends. Listen, these are unusual times,

and you're an unusual man in an unusual position. First, because you're a nobody who beat an incumbent who was a household name. And second, because you're a nobody who's got something I want. Let me rephrase. You *were* a nobody until you beat an incumbent with a household name and found yourself in possession of something I want. So I'm going to do you a solid, and you're going to do me one back."

Scott was waiting for a lull in the conversation, something to respond to. His feet were cold, and he was regretting having gotten out of bed. The lull didn't arrive, though, and the regret did nothing to warm his feet.

"I'm going to bring you into the legislative process for the Eden Project. I want you to consult on it until you get to Washington. Hell, I want you to come to Washington until you get to Washington. Because we're starting on this right now. It might not pass until after the new year, but then, it might not be ready for a vote until after the new year. The point is, we're moving on this. Now. So that's what I'm giving you. And what you're giving me is Ruth. We'll doll her up a little - she's not the best face for the movement - but Christ, somehow she *became* the face of your movement. And I want her here. Lots of photo ops, interviews, whatever. If she can do it in Wisconsin, she can do it for the whole damn country. I've got to go, but someone will be in touch."

The line went dead. Scott looked around his bedroom, hoping to find some audience for his reaction, someone, if nothing else, to affirm the reality of what had just taken place.

Affirmation, though, waited until that afternoon, when the promised 'someone' got in touch. In the interim, Scott had called Alex to report the morning's unusual phone call.

They had met at a bagel shop, where Scott had relished that he no longer felt compelled to introduce himself to everyone, to shake hands with everyone, to smile at everyone. Alex had taken apart his sandwich, peeling off the lox and capers to eat before the bagel, while he listened to Scott's story.

"Well," he offered when Scott had finished, "it is your pet issue."

"It's everyone's pet issue. It's *the* pet issue."

"And you have Ruth."

"Yeah, what am I supposed to do with that? She's not a commodity I can trade."

"She's a little like a commodity you can trade. You know that if you asked her if she was interested, she would be. Whether you ask is on you, so whether she goes is on you."

Scott sighed, "So much for our break until January," but his grin betrayed his real sentiment.

So when he received the second call that afternoon, he answered it with the news that Ruth had already agreed to move to Washington, to be the face of the movement, with the condition that she been brought into the legislative process as a consultant to the consultant, a request that Scott hadn't foreseen but the advantage of which he recognized. At the other end, they were already assembling their team and planned to begin in earnest the following Monday. The sooner he could be there, the better. The woman on the phone reiterated that point, the second time leaving firmly planted the implication that a leadership role in the group would be difficult to wrest away from anyone who might assume it in his absence.

By the end of the day, Scott, Ruth, and Alex were packing. They had booked flights for Saturday and had found a guesthouse to stay in for a while. Ellen was less eager to move, though she found little enough appeal in staying behind alone, so she had suggested that she do the more serious packing - the packing for their move into a second home - while Scott lived out of a suitcase and hunted for something permanent.

When he fell into bed that night, it was to a different state of exhaustion than in the wee hours of the morning before. Finally, action. Finally, movement towards something tangible. To this point, everything had been a losable battle, but now what stood between himself and his objective was simple persistence. The Eden Project was guaranteed and, with it, the future of the country. And with his new position would likely come the perk that he hoped would save his marriage: a child.

THIRTY-ONE

"You've been so quiet lately," Nasim said.

"Have I?" Enzo asked without much question in his voice.

"Well, why?" Her hands migrated unconsciously to her belly, where the fifth child had begun to grow.

Enzo delayed his answer, hoping some distraction might arise and spare his having to reply. Eventually he said, "I guess I've been thinking about things. Old things. Places I've been." He groped for something more, but that was all he could invent.

"Tell me about your favorite one," she instructed.

Enzo buried his other thoughts. "I lived in Washington for a little while. Not long at all, actually. It was right before I came here."

"I thought you were in Utah before you came here."

"Sort of, I was. My family was. It was complicated. I was in the process of moving to Washington – I had a place but my things hadn't arrived yet – when my brother got sick. So I had my things sent to Utah instead and spent the next few weeks going back and forth, and then I came here. I went through all the logistics of moving there and then only spent a couple of weeks in the state. But it was beautiful. It was where I wanted to be. When I got there, it was like coming home for the first time, you know?"

"You've never told me about it." She made no effort to mask her disappointment.

"I barely lived there. It didn't seem important."

"But if that's what you've been thinking about, then it must be at least a little important."

"I suppose." They were sitting on the couch leaning up against each other. Enzo shifted so that Nasim couldn't see his face.

"Will you dream with me?" she asked him.

"About what?"

"About the things that we can have in the future. I want to see this place you're homesick for."

"It's not that important…"

"Indulge me," she pushed.

"Okay," he sighed, "you can see it."

"No, I want you to *show* it to me. I want to see it *with* you. That's an important part of this dream."

He pulled himself back to the moment again, "Okay, we'll go see it. Together. Just the two of us?"

"Just the two of us," Nasim affirmed.

"Do you want to stay there awhile?"

"We should. To get the feeling of the place, you know."

"Maybe a cabin in the woods," Enzo said. "Because that's what's beautiful about it. The woods and the mountains that loom over them. They're a different kind of mountain, you know. It's not like the Rockies; it's not some big wall of rock. There's just the one enormous peak, and then way off in the distance another one by itself. Because they're volcanic," he clarified.

"A cabin in the woods," Nasim agreed. "In the shadow

of the volcanoes."

Enzo laughed, "It sounds funny when you say it like that. It's not like... like being in Hawai'i or Pompeii or something. It doesn't *feel* that volcanic. It's just beautiful."

"Well, however you want to say it. I want a dog. This is an important addition. A brown one with floppy ears. But I've never had one, so I don't know how to take care of them. Do you know?"

"Even in this fantasy you don't know how to take care of a dog?" Enzo couldn't help but crack a smile.

"That's not how the fantasy works, Enzo. It needs a basis in reality. That's what makes it compelling." She said it as a point of fact, as though there were only this one way to spin a dream–world and she were surprised that she should have to explain something so elementary to him.

"Okay, I can take care of the dog."

Nasim pushed her body closer to Enzo's and laid her head on his shoulder. They sat in silence for a long time. She didn't feel butterflies anymore, but she still thought about him in the middle of the night. Her waking reveries were more defined now – dreams of being with Enzo long into the future, of a time when they would be unimpeded by the changing of shifts and the cycle of inseminations and births and the Project more generally. They would just be – the two of them – in whatever fantasy she was building of late.

"I've never seen mountains," Nasim finally said. "Not the volcanic kind or the other kind."

"You haven't?" He didn't know whether it was more surprising to him that he didn't know that about her or that a human – any human – could have lived so much of life without seeing a mountain.

"You know I've never been out of the Midwest."

"Yeah... I did know that. I guess I had never thought through the implications. They're... I suppose they're not so different from what you see in pictures. But they make you feel... small. Not in a bad way, though. Maybe small's not the right word. They give perspective. Something so grand, so enormous, your problems can't be very big when you're faced with that." He paused, "I don't think I'm saying this quite right."

"I'll understand when you show them to me."

Nasim listened to Enzo's breathing in the silence that followed and felt the rise and fall of his chest.

He marveled that she could think about a future while imprisoned in this present. To her, maybe it was an escape, but to Enzo it only underscored the inequity. The theory of it had been so reasonable: It wasn't any different from conscription, and that hadn't been so terrible a thing, or no one thought seemed to think so a century removed from the last time it had been exercised. But it felt different. To ask a man to die for his country. To force a child into a woman's womb for her country.

"You've gone all serious again," she said.

"You'll see how beautiful the mountains are, and you'll understand," he replied.

THIRTY-TWO

Nasim called Alex on Thursday afternoon and through gritted teeth apologized for her position in the opposition and suggested that she might be able to help them achieve the most humane eventuality, to which Alex said, "Honey, the day that fifteen-year-olds who can't keep their salads to themselves help write legislation is the day I retire." He was laughing too hard to hear her say, "But I'm sixteen."

"Twelve sounds like a reasonable number to me. You figure nine months of pregnancy, six months in between. It's not as though they're going to be nursing, so that's six months of total recuperation. They're done at, what, thirty-five? And then we take care of them for the rest of their lives? What a life. You give us fifteen years, and we'll give you everything your heart desires from now until the day you die. Are you sure people aren't going to balk at this?" It was a week after Nasim's call in a conference room somewhere in Washington.

"We want to paint these women as heroes. Which means we have to treat them like heroes. They do their duty for the country; we do our duty towards them."

"Twelve, though? That might be fifteen years of service in a perfect world, but in the real world-"

"Two years into the program, our doctors are going to know everything about every one of these women-"

"It's not unrealistic to think that we'll have 85% success rates with artificial insemination in women we've been monitoring this closely for a number of years. I would recommend, though, that guidelines be put into place on when IVF becomes appropriate. Say, after four failed attempts at artificial insemination."

"But you absolutely must take into consideration how long the woman has been monitored. Four attempts for the first try, yes, but by the third or four pregnancy, we should only need one or two tries before IVF is indicated."

"And, of course, once IVF *is* indicated, it would be advisable to simply continue that course of treatment. Eggs will only need to be harvested once, and there's no reason not to continue to use them once the woman's body has already been subjected to the stress."

"To the question of multiple births, now..."

"Multiple births should count towards the twelve. Twelve children, not twelve pregnancies."

"I don't agree. They'll all push for IVF to improve their odds of multiples so they finish more quickly, and that's not in the best interest of producing the healthiest children. Twelve pregnancies, not twelve children."

"But we've already discussed that miscarriages don't count towards the total, and that was at your insistence, as I recall. Your inconsistency-"

"Twelve *full term* pregnancies. I'm not in the business of incentivizing women - particularly *these* women - to take unnecessary risks. We can't reward miscarriages, and we can't reward multiple births."

"Gentlemen, we would appreciate an opportunity to revisit your opinions on these, ahem, medical matters once you've had a chance to discuss among yourselves. As to the politics, there are still several items that I'd like to hear about before wrapping up for the day. Specifically, what are our thoughts on adoption eligibility?"

"Anyone ought to be eligible to adopt. Why that should be a question for this committee-"

"That anyone ought to be eligible doesn't aid in the selection of couples who receive-"

"Already the assumption that only couples-"

"We're not pouring billions of dollars into this project to send these children off to live with just anyone!"

"So what then?"

"I think if we look at this from an analytical perspective, it's obvious we'll need to identify the metrics that optimize a child's chances for success. If we have a hundred homes with two parents clamoring for children, why select the home in which there's only one parent?"

"And if there are a hundred wealthy households, are you going to similarly cut out the middle class because you want to 'optimize-'"

"Okay, well clearly this a point we're going to need to revisit. We're not looking for the answers, here, folks. We're still trying to identify the questions, okay?"

"Well obvious follow-on to that question: What's the source of the paternal genetic material? Are we going to allow adoptive fathers to be... well, genetic fathers?"

"Absolutely. We need to maximize genetic diversity or we're going to be dealing with a whole different set of issues in a hundred years."

"Although, there are certain genetic elements that we won't want to propagate. In a way, this is a chance to eradicate anything from Huntington's to Alzheimer's. So there ought to be a screening process at the very least."

"And some sort of donor pool for couples who are otherwise eligible but who fail the genetic screening process?"

"If we're already eliminating adoptive parents for socioeconomic reasons, I don't see why we shouldn't hold genetics to the same standard. Unless we're *all* here in the interest of giving children to the rich and powerful?"

"Not to mention that your donor pool is going to turn into a eugenics experiment in about a day. You can screen everyone out of eligibility. I'm willing to bet 80% of the people in this room have corrected vision!"

"Please, please. Let's retain some civility. This is a dialogue. We're not passing laws today."

"We've had no discussion of the kind of infrastructure we imagine. Are these women going to be living in their own homes? What kind of services are they going to be provided with? Beyond medical care, of course."

"Allow me to offer a suggestion here, gentlemen, as I'm the only one among you who will be directly affected."

"By all means, Ruth, go ahead."

"Living in the general population isn't going to be good for morale. In either direction. It will make the public feel like we're getting special treatment while we look like 'the woman next door,' and it'll be a daily reminder to any of the women who feel... stripped of their rights. What you want are private apartments isolated from the-"

"That won't make it feel like a prison?"

"Well, I recommend that you not make it feel like a prison. I'd suggest more of a resort atmosphere. There ought to be people on hand. Not on call, mind you, on hand. Twenty-four hours a day. I'll let you think up all the reasons that's necessary; there are more than a few. And you'll be wanting for a name for us. I suggest you call us 'Eves.'"

THIRTY-THREE

"I have a surprise for you," Peter said. "Two surprises, but maybe I'll save one."

"You can't do that! You can't tell me there are two and then give me one. How can I enjoy the first one if I'm wondering what the second one is?"

"You need to learn to live in the moment, Nasim."

"The moment sucks," she teased. "Unless it happens that I'm getting a surprise. Then it's not so bad."

Peter sighed, "Well it'll take a while for all of it to come in, but the first part arrives today. They're books. A hundred, to be precise. From a list put together by someone far wiser than I am. And a bookcase to put them in; that seemed like a good idea." After several months spent feeling inept for his inability to develop a better reading list, he had finally remembered that entire curricula had been developed in the area.

Nasim beamed. "You did that for me?"

Peter glanced away to hide a flash of pity – that she should be grateful for someone to provide even the resources for her to educate herself – and of shame that it had taken him so long to do something so simple for her. "I can't promise that I'll have anything insightful to say about them, but if you'd like to, we can read them together and talk about them." For himself, he had gotten the digital copies, not wanting to answer questions about why an Eve should need two paper copies of a hundred old books.

"Of course we will! I can't tell you how excited I am!" He could see her chewing on another thought. Finally she asked, "What's the other surprise?"

"Are you sure you don't want to save it for another day?"

"What good would that do me?"

"I don't know, maybe you would—"

"Just tell me, Peter," she interrupted.

"Okay. I got a pass. For the two of us to go into town."

Nasim's expression turned cautious. "For what?"

"Not for anything in particular. Just to see. Just because I thought you might want to."

"Peter," she rubbed her sleeve self–consciously over her eyes, "I can't imagine anything better."

Again, he looked away, embarrassed by her gratitude for something that cost him nothing, not even much effort. "It's... I don't know what you expect, Nasim, but it might not be that."

"I don't care what it is, I just want to see. I haven't seen the real world in a decade. I know you almost never leave, but that's different from not being able to."

"It's not going to look like the world you left," he warned. He wondered whether he had made a mistake.

"When can we go?"

"I don't have the pass yet." Responding to her immediate look of concern, "I promise it's coming. It's been approved. They just haven't delivered the actual piece of paper yet."

"So as soon as it comes?"

"If you want. There are other considerations. We could wait for nice weather or a weekend or something, or we can just go."

Nasim sat awhile in silence, "I'll think about it. About what I'd like best. But, Peter?"

"Mm?"

She threw her arms around his neck. "Thank you so much!"

An hour later, a knock on the door announced the arrival of the bookcase and the first box of books. Nasim directed the two men delivering it to put it against the east wall of her bedroom, then the north wall, then decided it would be better in the living room beside the fireplace, and finally next to the sliding door in the space that was somewhat dining room, somewhat living room. They hurried out the door once they had gotten it settled there, fearful that she might change her mind again. Then she and Peter sat on the floor in front of it and unboxed the books, Nasim turning each one over to read its back cover before deciding on a shelf.

"Should we arrange them alphabetically, do you think?" she asked Peter.

"That's a perfectly good way to do it."

"By author, probably. Although it doesn't do any good to have all the anonymous stuff lumped together, so maybe alphabetically by title? Oh! Is there some order we ought to read them in? Maybe we should arrange in that order."

Her excitement was endearing. "We could read them chronologically, but I don't know how long it'll be before we have them all. We might get held up waiting for the first to arrive."

"Well, so we could read them in any order, but maybe we should arrange the chronologically. Then they'll be with their... their book peers. You know what I mean, right? That it would place them in the right context. Eventually, once I'd read enough of them."

"Sure."

"But I guess the geographic context counts, too, right?" she asked, running her fingers over the cover of the *The Idiot*.

"Also, yes."

She ultimately arranged them by the color of their spine, as much a concession to her own indecision as it was to aesthetics. This first box was small, only filling half of one shelf, but she nevertheless stood proudly in front of her collection, lovingly touching them and picking out this book or that one to scan – for the third or fourth time – everything that was printed on the cover.

"Which shall we start with?" Peter finally asked.

"I thought you might... I just assumed that you would have..."

"Pick any one you like. There's no right way, Nasim."

Nasim smiled, closed her eyes, and pulled a book at random from the shelf. "*Canterbury Tales*!" she exclaimed. Then, turning to Peter, she said, "I can't tell you how wonderful this is."

THIRTY-FOUR

JANUARY 3, 2063

Scott took his oath the day before his committee - one that he really couldn't even claim membership in until the swearing-in ceremony - made the final additions to the Eden Project bill. They had sorted out everything from the building of new housing facilities - someone had had the poor taste to call them 'coops,' and the name had stuck informally for a while before the press had picked up on it - to the selection of handlers to the regulations that would govern artificial insemination and IVF and the number of children expected per woman and all manner of contingencies in the event problems arose. They had located a number of vacant buildings already owned by the government that could be converted to apartments while the coops were built. Purportedly, this was so that doctors could begin monitoring the women's fertility long in advance of the first inseminations, and, more implicitly, it prevented the uncooperative ones from disappearing while the framework was being established.

A few new Senators, hungry for their share of the attention that the Eden Project garnered, had been talking to Ruth. They had been the first to take her advice and call the women 'Eves' within earshot of the press corps, and, shortly after, the word matriculated into the lexicon of the general population.

Ruth had flown home the day before the swearing-in, in spite of Scott's standing offer of his guest bedroom for as long as she might like to stay. Even after Ellen had furnished the new place, Ruth had remained in the hotel, and now she was eager to get back home. Short of running for office herself, she had done everything she could for the Eden Project and was content to watch the outcome materialize from afar. And besides that contentedness, she was exhausted from the last nine months.

Alex had taken Scott up on the offer and had moved in for a few weeks - that had been before Ellen came, when Scott had just rented the townhouse and it was still empty. They had both slept on the floor until Ellen visited, and, appalled that they hadn't even bothered to buy themselves air mattresses and blankets, went shopping. Several weeks later, half the furniture from Wisconsin had arrived, and shortly thereafter, Ellen had come to stay permanently; but by then, Alex had found an apartment of his own and moved his air mattress and blankets into it.

The ceremony dragged on longer than Scott would have liked. The freshmen Representatives looked more numerous all lined up than they had as faces and numbers scattered across a map, and each one went in turn. Afterwards, though, he and Ellen and Alex went out to celebrate, a moment's pause to appreciate the long journey before trudging onwards the next day. It was odd not having Ruth there. Almost as odd as it was to spend an evening with Ellen, but Scott had saved for this occasion the news that they would almost certainly be at the top of the list to adopt one of the Eden children, and that had made even melancholy Ellen brighten up for a few hours.

The following week, when it came up for a vote, the bill passed the House with better margins than anyone had guessed. In the months since the election, public sentiment against the program had softened, and the perception that supporting the Eden Project was the 'right side,' the side with the moral backing, had become increasingly common. The stances of many of the more moderate House members had shifted accordingly, though the bill still barely eked by the Senate to a smattering of applause from the viewing gallery. When it went back to the House for the final vote after reconciliation, though, the last yeas could barely be heard over the cheering.

Several men whom he had only just met clapped Scott on the back when the tally was finalized, and outside a scrum of reporters waited for him - and for others, but mostly for him. The grin on Scott's face was irrepressible, and he thanked Ruth at some point in each of the tiny interviews he gave, hoping she would catch a snatch of one of those soundbites back in Wisconsin.

They celebrated again that night, Scott, Alex, and Ellen. With oysters and crabs and lobster they were told had flown in from Maine that morning and with champagne. And afterwards, when Scott and Ellen were lying in bed, he pulled her into his arms and asked her whether she wanted a boy or a girl and what she would name the child.

The real declaration of victory, though, he saved for the moment the President signed the bill. He had pressed Archer Soren for a spot at the signing with such persistence that Soren, who had no places to give, eventually surrendered his own. The moment was brief, an anticlimax to the months of campaigning and the thousands of hands shaken and tens of thousands of ballots cast and then the hundreds of hours of argument and compromise that had followed. A flick of a pen, a scribble of indecipherable letters at the end of a stack of printed pages, and it was done.

THIRTY-FIVE

"Delia!" Nasim didn't know what to do with her excitement, clapped her hands because it refused to be contained. "I've never... I've never even seen anything like it."

"I didn't think you would have," Delia replied, not sure whether she should be proud at the surprise or sorry that Nasim's life was so cloistered that she had never seen a moonstone. Nasim had been so excited by Peter's gift that Delia wondered how she had never thought to get her anything before.

Nasim picked up the little box and laid one finger on the pendant. It was cool to the touch.

"How does it...?"

Delia laughed, "How should I know?"

The moonstone was a sphere the size of a marble that shone with the bleached white of moonlight. Its surface was marred, though so subtly that her tracing finger couldn't feel it. But where those imperfections lay, the glow was reduced to a faint shadow. They came in all sorts now, but the original had been a replica of the moon, the worried face on one side and the other pocked with craters that no one living had ever seen. That was the sort that Nasim held now, a tiny moon suspended on the fine platinum chain.

"You like it?" Delia asked, while Nasim studied the dark side.

She clutched it in her palm, closing her fingers around the sphere. "It's the most beautiful thing I've ever seen. Will you put it on me?"

They walked into the woods in the early afternoon, past trees a few years bigger than when they had first started walking this path, past the fire ring that she and Peter had built, and to the pond. The water level was low, and the algae that used to choke out everything in late summer had arrived by the end of spring this year. A few dead fish already floated on the water, and flies buzzed around them, some venturing as far as where Delia and Nasim stood, their noses wrinkled in disgust.

"I don't suppose they'd clean this up, even for me?" Nasim asked.

Delia shook her head.

They retreated back into the woods, where a tree that had fallen in an ice storm that winter had made a natural bench.

"Maybe we can find another lake somewhere deeper in the woods," Nasim said.

But Delia shook her head again. "There isn't much more between our lake and the road, and after that it's all cornfields."

"Is it?"

"You didn't know?"

"Delia, there's so much I don't know. All these things. The moonstone and the woods and the cornfields. I suppose I could find out if I knew what to ask, but I wouldn't even know where to begin. I wish I knew what you know."

"But you *can* know those things. I can tell you those things. Ask anything. And if you can't think of the right question to follow it, I'll help you figure it out."

"What would it be like if I had a normal life?"

Delia sighed, "Nasim, asking what it's like isn't going to give you a normal life."

"I don't need a normal life! I could be happy just picturing myself in one, but even that myth is beyond me. I don't even know what to imagine."

"You know, you can do whatever you want after. They say you can stay because it's easy, because they think you won't want to leave your home and what's familiar. But you don't have to. You can do anything, and you'll just be a person, any person, with a normal life."

Nasim cut off Delia's thought, "Do you think that we could go somewhere before then? Do you think they might let me move to a different campus?"

"I don't know. Why, though?"

"Well, why not?"

"I just meant that you've never... never shown an interest in any other place. I'm just surprised, is all. But maybe they would. Do you know where you'd want to go?"

Nasim bit her lip. It wasn't the excitement she had hoped for, but of course Delia would be caught off–guard. But Enzo, surprised or not, he would be ecstatic, and that was what really mattered.

Delia didn't know what to make of the pause. "I know what they ask seems immeasurable, Nasim, and what they give you in return... but afterwards... Afterwards, you have everything. It's all taken care of, and the burden is gone. You want to move, there won't be a single person whose permission you need. You want to know what real life is like, normal life, you can do it to your heart's content. The only thing that they don't give you here, Nasim, is freedom. And you'll be able to see for yourself how little that's worth–"

"How *little*?" Nasim cut Delia off. "How can you say it's worth so little when you have it?"

"Nasim, you don't see the people outside the walls."

"Peter's going to take me! He got me a pass. I *will* see. In a few days, I will."

"But you haven't yet. You haven't seen the hunger and the poverty. What it was like when you were living out there... it's so much worse now. It was better for a little while, but that didn't last long. I haven't been out of the walls for almost two years because I can't bear to see it. I can't even imagine what it's like to live it." *And I don't know why Peter would take you there*, she thought.

Nasim traced the thick wrinkles in the bark beside her. "But they don't even tell us that," she whispered, ashamed for a moment that she hated the cage that kept her safe and the captors who kept her fed. Her voice quivered, "They don't even bother to tell us that we're better off here."

Delia scooted closer and put an arm around Nasim's shoulder. "You'll see it. You just have longer to wait, and then you can see whatever you want. You can live whatever life you imagined for yourself, and if you don't like that one, you can re–imagine it. And I can be there with you if you want, or Peter can, or Enzo. You can live outside the walls or come back to your coop, or you can live nowhere at all, just flying from one place to the next." When she felt the jolt of a sob in Nasim's shoulders, Delia squeezed her tighter. "I'm sorry I can't make this go away. I would do anything to share the burden with you. But there's an end, you know? Just focus on the end. It's only time that stands in the way."

They were late getting back to the coop. Enzo had already arrived for the evening. He watched them emerge from the tree line, his face so close to the pane of the glass door that the women saw his breath on it.

"I'm sorry, you know," Delia said as they approached the door, "about how I used to be about Enzo. You know that, don't you? That I'm sorry?" She had practiced saying it in front of a mirror, practiced it until it sounded sincere.

"You don't have to be," Nasim replied. "You've never done anything you have to be sorry for."

"But I am. I just… I would take it all back if I could. Everything I said about him. Because I hate to think that you think differently of me because of it."

Nasim stopped far enough from the door that Enzo hadn't yet slid it open in anticipation of their arrival. "You're my best friend, Delia. You're my best friend… and still, though, I never forget that the person who signs your paycheck is the same person who built this prison. It's never been any more complicated than that."

THIRTY-SIX

That it was a large black sports utility vehicle should have been no surprise. The men who had come to the door were both wearing suits, and one of them had one of the those things in his ear, but whether it was talking to him or he to it or whether it was involved at all in this process, she didn't know. She hadn't been the one to answer the door, but when she heard their voices, she hoped that Mina would say that she wasn't in. But Mina didn't; she called for Nasim, holding the door open for the men to enter.

They waited while she packed a bag. The rest, they said, they would send someone to collect for her, but there was no rest. Everything she owned was already packed. The drawers she took her clothes from were in a dresser someone else had had the graciousness to share with her. The mattress she slept on was one that someone had left next to the trash chute one day. The sheets she had borrowed from one of the other women, the only one who had two sets, and she used a sweatshirt as a pillow. Everything she had had had been sold by her uncle, the one who hadn't been willing to take them in. Her aunt had tried to stop him, but there had been other things - her own children - that had been more important. So everything she had salvaged still fit into that one suitcase, the suitcase she had crammed full and lugged away before her uncle could sell her, too.

They didn't tell her where she was going, and she didn't ask. She sat slumped in the back seat, her forehead pressed against the window, fog creeping across the glass with each breath and retreating in between. Her fingers picked at a flaw in the leather trim of the car. Half an hour later, they stopped, and one of the men, the one who had been driving, walked up a driveway and rang the bell. The woman who answered the door looked timidly at the waiting car, at the second man, at the tinted window that hid Nasim and then stepped aside to let him in. They emerged a while later, each carrying a suitcase. The way she dragged her feet, the way she kept looking down the street, it was as though she was expecting someone else to arrive, someone to rescue her or to wish her off or to do something that Nasim had no one to do for her.

Nasim pressed her forehead harder into the glass, smashing her nose onto the pane and refusing to look at the other woman, whom she could hear trying to breathe through the fear and the tears.

Three hours later, the car stopped again, this time in front of an L-shaped, seven-story building. From the expressway, she had seen Chicago pass by not long before, but this place was on the deserted campus of something else, she didn't know what. There were brick buildings and parking lots, all of it surrounded by a fence and by woods beyond. The men stepped out of the car and opened the doors for the two women, then grabbed their suitcases and walked in. The lobby looked like a hotel, a person standing behind the desk to check them in. Their names were on a list, their room numbers already assigned.

Nasim had never had a room to herself, never had her own bathroom. She had only stayed in a hotel once, she and her sister and mother sharing one bed and her father and brother sharing the other. But here there was only one bed and an armchair and a small desk. There were more drawers than she had clothes to put in them, and a television - one of the ones that was still a physical thing instead of a projection - stood on top of the dresser.

The man - her man, the passenger - had left without a word. For a while her eyes hung on the door. There was a lock on the inside. She hadn't seen one on the outside. She tried the handle. It opened. She walked into the hall, and no one stopped her. She got back on the elevator, took it to the ground floor. No one stopped her there, either. She smiled at the man behind the desk, her teeth clenched in fear, and walked past him towards the door beyond. When she was a few feet away, another man, again in a suit, stepped in front of it, his hands clasped in front of him. She tried to smile at him, too, but she bounced off his presence, skittered backwards, and hurried back towards the elevator, towards the room.

"Miss," the man behind the desk stopped her. "For you, miss." Her heart was pounding, and she wanted to run. He handed her thick envelope. "Save someone the trouble of bringing it up to you, miss."

She reread the contents of the envelope half a hundred times in the next days. It was the only thing she had to read, and it was the only thing that was important. An explanation of the legality of this detention, a federal law that mandated her service as an Eve, not so different, the letter noted, from conscription in times of war. An outline of the expectations, the obligations, the privileges of her position. A timeline in which completion of permanent facilities was expected. A slip that advised her of an upcoming appointment with a doctor. An invitation to request anything from the front desk and the promise that they would make every reasonable attempt to provide. The dining room schedule and a form to request meals compliant with a number of dietary restrictions.

She paged through, studied each sheet of paper front and back, trying to find the words that justified her imprisonment, that made them right and her wrong, but no matter how many times she read it, those words never materialized.

THIRTY-SEVEN

June 17, 2073

In the end, Nasim decided that an ordinary Tuesday with grey skies but no rain was the right day to use the pass. A car had come to collect them, a black SUV no different from the one that had deposited her in front of her coop in a distant memory that she tried very hard to suppress. It took ten minutes to get to the eight square blocks and three stoplights that constituted the downtown. A few people turned to watch the car as it drove by, but Nasim couldn't guess what reason they had. There were plenty of other cars, though perhaps not as new or as clean. Or maybe they always did that, eyed every car that they didn't recognize. Or maybe they knew that she wasn't supposed to be there.

The drab weather drained the color from the leaves, and a cold wind – more November than June – whipped the branches and rattled the street signs. The colors were bleak, dingy greys and once–white buildings, brick facades with paint peeling off to reveal the brown–red underneath. A third of the storefronts were boarded up, but the others were open, a handful of restaurants and sandwich shops were patronized by a handful of people each, a couple of places that looked like they sold everything overflowed with junk that a few customers picked through. In spite of the people, though, quiet pervaded. It felt more creepy than peaceful, maybe because the people wore the same washed–out colors that decked the buildings, giving the living the same air of decrepitude as the inanimate. Or else because it was like walking into a photograph of what was now a ghost–town, and these people were relics of a period before any of them suspected that this place was destined for abandonment.

When the car stopped in front of a boarded–up movie theater right in the midst of it all, Nasim sank down in her seat. The windows were tinted – no one could see her – and yet she felt so exposed that she wanted nothing more than to slink back into the cocoon she purported to hate.

Peter was watching her. She wished he would stop.

"It's okay, Nasim," he said, as she eyed a pedestrian a block away, certain that he had somehow seen her, known her, and resented her in the instant that his gaze had passed over the car. "We can sit here awhile if you want. Or we can have him drop us somewhere else." Without waiting for a reply, he instructed the driver to take them a block over, off Main Street, and when the car stopped there, there was no one in sight.

"I should have worn something different," Nasim said, her eyes on her red trenchcoat, her hands clutching at it as though they might manage to obscure the color.

Peter did eventually coax Nasim from the car, then linked arms with her, and together they walked back to Main Street. The sidewalks they traversed were cracked and grown through with weeds, and the road they crossed was lumpy with poorly patched potholes. On the other side, Peter held open the door of a small diner, "I thought we could start with some people–watching."

They were seated in a booth by the window, but the

scene inside drew Nasim's interest much more than what they had just left behind. In here, the air was warm and smelled of comfort foods, patrons chatted with each other or else with the waitress, and any silence that did threaten was interrupted by cutlery against ceramic, by the tinkle of the bell on the door, by the fry cook's shouting, "Food's up!" every few minutes.

Nasim watched with fascination as the waitresses, two heavy–set women with permanent smiles, bounced from table to table. One of them finally whirled to a stop at their table, plunking down two mugs and filling them with coffee while she asked, "Do you two know what you're having? Of course you don't, you don't even have menus yet. Love this, dear." It all came out in one thought, ending with her tugging at Nasim's red sleeve and winking. And then she was gone, stopping at three more tables to top off coffee before seizing a couple of menus for the two of them.

They had burgers with fries and split a sundae for dessert, and over the course of the meal, the trace of a smile that had appeared when the waitress had complimented her coat had gradually grown broader.

"Are you ready to brave the world again?" Peter asked when the waitress handed him the bill.

But Nasim's eyes were on the piece of paper in his hand, and the smile faded from her face, "Peter, I didn't bring any money."

"I've got it, Nasim."

"But did you bring money?"

He laughed, "Of course, I did."

"I... I didn't even think of it." Her eyes dropped to her lap as the false sense of comfort this place had instilled evaporated.

Peter spent the remainder of the afternoon trying to

recreate the magic of the diner, but the rest of Main Street looked even more glum now than it had before. They wandered through a few of the shops, where Nasim wondered whether she was allowed to touch the curios that lined the shelves; but the first time she tried, a woman asked if she could offer any assistance, and Nasim was afraid to try again. She was relieved when Peter noted that the shadows were growing long. She hadn't wanted to be the one to suggest that they go back, but she could think of nothing she wanted more than to sit in front of the fireplace, where the strangers around her were kept out by gates and no one wondered who she was.

"We could walk back," he suggested. "It's not far. Twenty minutes, maybe? We'd be back before dark."

But Nasim shook her head, and Peter summoned the car that was idling down the street.

When Peter arrived for his shift the next morning, Nasim was sitting on the couch, knees hugged to her chest. She greeted him with a silent nod and only after he had sat down next to her and asked her what was on her mind did she begin, "How can I have been so miserable here when other people suffer so much more? I feel like some primadonna to complain about my nice coop, my hot meals, my hours of leisure. There are people who would give anything to be here, aren't there?"

"Nasim," he put a hand on her shoulder, "we can only benchmark against our own lives. It's human that we suffer, not circumstantial. You wouldn't be any more miserable if it were worse. Maybe for a little while, but you would recalibrate."

"And if it were better?" her intonation fell. She wanted the question to go unanswered.

"You might be happier for a little while. And then you wouldn't."

"But what does that leave me with?"

"It leaves you with the fact that the only thing you can control is how you respond to the world around you. The winds, the waves, the tides, the currents, they do as they wish. You can set a course and fight them to stay on it, or you can see where they take you."

She carefully framed her response, "And if they leave you shipwrecked? Or sink you? Because you just went with it?

"I'm not saying take your hands off the wheel. That's it, that's where you have the choice. Sometimes you have to set a course and fight to stay on it or you'll wind up run aground somewhere, so you do it. Sometimes you have to tie yourself to the wheel to prevent being swept overboard, so you do it. And in that moment you decide whether you're going to do it happily or whether you're going to resent having to do it."

"And this relates to my misery."

Peter shrugged, "If you want it to. I think that people are remarkable in their ability to habituate to even the most profound despair. Will you let my metaphor go on a little? Something about stormy seas and the fact that gradually the fear of the storm wanes – even if it's just because you're too tired to feel it anymore. I also think that humans are remarkable in their ability to find suffering when there's little reason. Flat seas, steady breeze, but the sun is too bright, or the days are too short, or the hardtack is moldy. You adjust to your circumstances, you re–equilibrate."

Nasim thought about it for a few minutes, then said, "Peter?"

"Mm?"

"You're barred from using boat metaphors for at least a month."

THIRTY-EIGHT

After the first week, no one stopped them from leaving the building. There was a fence to keep them from wandering too far. But Nasim's desire to go outside was no greater than her desire to remain in her room, so inertia kept her in. On the computer they brought her in the third week, she followed the news about the Eden Project, which now rarely merited a full article. She found photographs of the coops as they were being built, foundation pits and construction equipment scarring the idyllic landscapes where she was supposed to produce the next generation.

She called Scott Davis one afternoon with a conversation she had spent a week rehearsing - a last appeal to any shred of humanity in him - but the person who answered the phone told her that he would be out of the office for the next four days on an agricultural survey of the Midwest to address issues that his constituents were invited to read about on his website. She called Eleanore, whom she hadn't seen since election night, but she couldn't think of a message to leave when Eleanore didn't pick up.

A few days later, Nasim heard Eleanore's voice behind her and turned around startled. She was being interviewed on the station Nasim had left the television on to break up the background silence that risked drowning her in its constancy. It was at a rally for something, some cause, someone else's cause. Nasim turned off the TV before anyone could tell her what it was.

She was more reluctant to call Sam, whom she hadn't seen since election night either and who had been so clear about the finality of the vote that she couldn't imagine what there was left to talk about. But Sam's number was the last one she had. She hung onto it for weeks out of hesitation to begin the conversation and equally out of hesitation to end it, the knowledge that once she hung up the phone, it would to a world in which there was no longer anyone to call.

In the days that she waited, she only sometimes moved from her bed to the chair, from which she could see a parking lot and woods beyond. The food that was served downstairs she could order from her room, and after she had done it a few times, they started sending her a menu of the day's meals so that someone didn't have to walk through the buffet each day with her on the phone and read off the cardboard placards.

She went out just once and walked the road back to the gate, though she didn't get close enough to the guardhouse to see the person she was sure was inside. She saw a dirt path leading off the road on her way back and took that as it meandered through the woods and spit her out somewhere on another stretch of pavement that she followed until she could see her concrete home again. The illusion of freedom, though, just deepened the solitude behind her own door.

She did finally call Sam, who answered right away.

"I didn't think you'd pick up."

"I wouldn't avoid you, Nasim."

"But you won't help me, either." She hadn't meant to

start with confrontation. She'd meant to win back an ally.

"I would do anything I could to help you. The question is what I'm *able* to do, not whether or not I'm willing."

"We could go on fighting."

Sam sighed into the phone, the crackle deafening for a moment before the silence swallowed it back up. "There isn't a fight anymore, Nasim. We had a cause that people cared about, people other than you, people who were never at risk of being thrown into a coop. But the attentions of those people... they're on other issues now. We had five minutes to convince them, Nasim. It's more than most causes get. Our minutes are up."

"But the people who cared then, surely they could be persuaded to care again?"

"The polling numbers are clear: the opposition to the Eden Project, it's melted into indifference. The proponents aren't much stronger than they were on Election Day. But our side... it's not a side anymore. What was moral certainty has disintegrated into... ambivalence, conditional approval."

"Sam?"

"Yes, Nasim?"

"Do you think this will fall apart in the next few years? Do you think it could? That maybe by the time I'm twenty, it won't exist?"

Sam was silent.

"Because it doesn't exist on is own. It has to be funded. And there's the budget every year. And maybe it'll get cut right out of existence? Or the presidential election, in two years, it might be an issue again. Maybe not *the* issue, but if it were to come up, and people were voting on other issues, a candidate opposed to the Project might win and repeal the whole thing."

"You can't put the toothpaste back in the tube, hon. It's not impossible, but-"

"I know! It's *not*, is it?" She said it too loudly, the hope in her voice jarring in the quiet around her.

"Nasim. The sooner you acknowledge that you've lost, the sooner you'll find the grace to accept your future."

Nasim hung up the phone not out of anger but out of fear of Sam's words. She didn't really believe it, what she was trying to sell Sam, but that hadn't stopped her hoping that Sam would validate the possibility, minuscule though it might be.

She called back right away, and Sam picked up.

"I didn't mean it. My hand just slipped."

"I know."

"Sam? Can I call you again? Even if there isn't more fighting to do?"

"Sure."

"Thanks."

"Do you need anything? Anything that I can send you?" Sam asked.

"No… There's everything here. I have my own room. And they gave me a catalog the other day to pick out things for my coop."

"That's good." Sam didn't know what else to say. "Call anytime you want."

"Thanks, Sam." She never called back, though.

THIRTY-NINE

OCTOBER 17, 2073

"What do you think, Peter?" Nasim asked. They were sitting on the couch, side by side, both of them reading paper copies of *The Divine Comedy*, Nasim's new, Peter's worn and dog–eared from when he had read it in college. An hour earlier, Nasim had mentioned that she might like to move to a different coop and then, without waiting for a reply, had gone back to her book.

"About moving?" He laid the book upside down on his lap, the old spine creasing deeply as the pages pressed open under their own weight. "Why, though? Have you seen a coop you like better than this one?"

"Not to another coop here. To one in a different facility." Nasim had forbidden Delia from discussing it with anyone and was pleased that she had kept her word.

Peter's subtle nod grew more obvious as he considered the possibility. "Did you have one in mind?" He hadn't expected such a rapid – or obvious – return on his endeavor to empower Nasim. Had it really been this simple all along?

Nasim laughed. "I don't even know where they are. But isn't there supposed to be one in almost every state? We could go just about anywhere."

"Have you picked a state, then?"

"Somewhere far from here," she said. "Somewhere with mountains or ocean or forests." *Especially the mountains that will relieve Enzo of his homesickness for a place that had never been home.*

Peter grinned. "Nasim, anything that would make you happy would make me happy. It would be nice to have different seasons or even a new view out the windows." And Nasim thought she heard in his response, too, that it would be nice to have something more interesting beyond the coop than a tired Midwestern town full of drab, resentful people with whom he had long since ceased to interact.

"I don't want you to talk to anyone about it." A surprise for Enzo, and Delia and Peter might as well think that each of them was the sole coconspirator. "Tell me about where you grew up," she said to mask her discomfort with what felt like a lie of omission.

"In Maryland."

"That's not new information, Peter. Tell me *about* it."

Peter moved the book to the table beside him, glancing at the page number before letting it fall closed. He leaned his head back onto the couch so that his gaze rested on the ceiling above him and smiled so deeply that it appeared in lines around his eyes. "Rolling hills and green fields and split rail fences. You'd never think to look at it here, but farmland can be so beautiful. The old, white farmhouses and the barns, half peeling red paint and half raw wood. The mountains there, they're low and ancient. They're not the mountains people put on calendars. They don't take your breath away."

"I've never lived somewhere that wasn't flat," Nasim said.

"There's beauty in flatness, too. You don't see the sky

the same way when hills block the view. Have you been west of here?"

"Not far," she replied.

"Far enough to see the Big Sky?"

"Is that a place?"

"Not a specific one." Peter said. "It's… when everything is utterly flat, the sky is so strikingly vast. Here you still have trees getting in the way of that, but further west, it feels like there's more sky than earth. I don't love it the way I love the hills, but it's beautiful all the same."

"And here?" Nasim sighed heavily. "I haven't seen the beauty here yet."

"Well, then that's as good a reason to move as any."

A smile crept across Nasim's face.

"Nasim," Peter said, his voice more serious. "There is beauty here, though, even if we don't always choose to look for it. Just remember that if they won't give you the transfer, or if the next place doesn't… doesn't live up to your hopes."

But Nasim's smile persisted. She put down the book she had been holding through the conversation and decided, "Let's have some popcorn and cider. And something caramel. Do you think they'd drizzle the caramel over the popcorn – real caramel, though, the sticky, gooey stuff? Or would that make a horrible mess?"

Peter posed the same question to the person in the kitchen who picked up the phone, and what arrived a few minutes later was an honest attempt but indeed a horrible mess. Together Nasim and Peter laughed and licked off their sticky fingers and watched as the light of late afternoon turned to dusk. They finished their popcorn and washed it down with tepid, spicy cider in glass mugs that stuck to their hands.

The two of them talked late into the night, something

Nasim couldn't recall having done with Peter since perhaps a few months after Enzo had arrived. They sat on the floor, their hands scrubbed clean, their faces illuminated by the flickering light of the fire that Nasim had lit. They went through the states one by one, starting with Florida and ending with Washington, telling each other everything they knew about each one. Everglades and bayou and the Mississippi, the Tetons and mesas and Yosemite and rainforest. She could feel herself blush when he said something nice about Washington, about his having been to Seattle and having wanted to stay longer, about the allure of the mountain looming in the distance. And they wondered where the facilities were and whether the coops were as big as hers and what they would see out of the sliding glass door that she was sure they would have there, too.

Only as midnight was closing in did Nasim's eyelids grow heavy, and she retreated to her bedroom with some reluctance. Lying in her bed she remembered and called out to Peter, "You can't tell anyone. You promise."

A few moments later his silhouette appeared in her door. "I promise, Nasim. I won't tell a soul. It's your dream to share." And then, as he turned to go, "I'm happy you shared it with me, however it turns out."

FORTY

The coops sprang up, their construction driven by the flood of money the Project had poured into an otherwise dry economy. Later people called it the Hope Time, this and the three or so years of optimism that separated the gloom of the Plague before from the years of economic depression that came after. The change in sentiment was lost on Nasim. Once she had made her three phone calls, she stopped following the news of the Project. What did it matter if she was in this room or another? She stopped listening to the other news, too, banished it even as background noise. It didn't drown out the silence, anyhow.

By the time men in black suits came knocking at her door, she no longer knew how long she had been in this place. She had closed the curtains and stopped counting the days, and it came as a surprise that there were buds on the trees when they led her outside with her same single suitcase, no heavier than it had been before.

There was a caravan of black SUVs in the parking lot and a stream of black-suited men and women, two flanking each Eve. Nasim recognized a handful of faces from the few times she had gone downstairs to eat, but she had never had a sense of how many women were there. Judging by the number of SUVs, by the line of them that stretched onto the road and back towards the gate, the building must have been close to capacity.

They drove for three hours, a black train snaking south. The car Nasim was in went faster than most, but even so, they never reached the front of the line; and when they turned off the expressway onto a two-lane highway, they had no choice but to slow to the pace of the car in front of them. They turned with all the other SUVs onto a smaller road and then a few miles later trickled past a gatehouse one car at a time.

The guards took Nasim's name and gave the men a number for it, and here the single line finally forked and then forked again, each Eve headed for a different coop. When they stopped, it was outside a long, low rectangle of a building, double doors propped open on either end and glass doors decorating the long sides of the rectangle at regular intervals. The lawn around the building was close-cropped, still winter-brown, though the buds on the scattered trees were swollen fatter than those she had seen earlier in the morning, and the woods beyond were showing the first glow of green. The two men walked her down the hall, windowless and fluorescent, the smell of fresh paint still stifling. The doors were numbered, but Nasim hadn't listened at the gatehouse; so the men knew - and she didn't - how close they were.

She had never chosen anything from the catalog they had given her. It was still lying next to the bed in her room - *her old room*, she corrected herself - and she wondered if they would give her another one now and ask her again or if she had missed her opportunity, if she would find an empty room behind one of these doors, if it would remain empty for the next decade and a half.

The space was furnished and far larger than the single room she had expected. The short industrial carpet of the hallway gave way to a patch of tile on the other side of the door in a sea of thick, cream-colored shag, and the walls were bright yellow. A deep, red couch faced the door, behind which was a round wooden table nestled into a bay window, and just to the right of that was a kitchenette with the glass door to the outside. There was a fireplace in the living room, too, and to the right was an archway that the man carrying her suitcase disappeared through. She followed him past a green-painted bedroom and to the hallway's end, a second bedroom, this one nearly as large as the apartment she had just a few months earlier shared with three other women. The bedroom walls were a Mediterranean blue, the ceiling bright white. A king-sized bed, sentried by tables on either side, dominated the center of the room, and a dresser on the left wall looked a dozen times too large for all the clothes she had ever owned. She peered through the doorway to her left, where a tile and glass bathroom adjoined the bedroom.

The man left her suitcase next to the dresser and then looked at her for a moment, not sure whether to say anything, to offer anything. In the end, though, he didn't; he departed in silence. By the time she followed him back into the living room, they were both gone.

Nasim felt a tickle of guilt at her pleasure with this space. The colors were vibrant, the carpet soft and luxurious on her now-bare feet, the furniture new and hers and nicer than anything she had ever had. There were lamps in every room, and the light they gave off was warm and comfortable; and the windows were enormous and turned opaque with the flick of a switch. The quilt on the bed and the pillows were real down, and the sheets were cool and smooth and silk. A bathrobe hung on a hook on the bathroom door, thick and white and softer than she imagined possible.

She stopped in the second bedroom. It was much smaller than hers, with a twin-sized bed and an armchair and no bathroom attached. She could think of no purpose for another room but the addition of a second Eve. She wouldn't even mind giving up the better room in exchange for the company.

Half an hour later, she had opened every door, every drawer and cabinet. There were dishes in the kitchen, linens in a closet in the hall; a second bathroom behind one of the doors off the living room and a coat closet full of cedar hangers behind the other. She sank into the deep couch and wondered what good a fireplace would do someone who didn't know how to build a fire.

FORTY-ONE

Nasim had worried that Peter's protectiveness would stall the project at hand if she showed any signs of faltering or, worse, that his recent pedagogical thrust would turn the plan into an exercise in which she had to come up with every answer. Delia, on the other hand, had grown excited about the idea of moving and seemed a more promising planning companion.

Sprawled across the couch, Nasim watched the fire roaring in protest against the chilly fall evening. Delia was seated on the floor rubbing Nasm's swollen, achy feet. "I really think Washington, or Oregon maybe," Nasim said.

They had rehashed the same details so many times that Delia had begun to suspect that it was just idle dreaming, and Nasim's insistence that it be kept secret had only strengthened that suspicion. "Have you talked to the others yet?"

Nasim was spared having to answer by the sixth breaking of her water.

The next time Delia drew the morning shift, they set immediately to work. Suddenly ready to take action, Nasim had imagined herself settled into her new coop – if she was destined to have one – within a month, two at most, but when they called on Monday, the assistant director of the facility pleaded ignorance about the possibility of a transfer; and he did so again when they, hoping to reach someone else, called on Tuesday. The man had further refused to forward their call to the director or to schedule a meeting or initially even to take a message; but he relented on the last point in the end. The director called back in the late afternoon, and Enzo picked up the phone, handing it to Nasim with the question, "It's for you?" The director, too, had no idea who might grant transfer requests but assured Nasim that that power resided in a different office. The best she was able to offer – and with hesitation – was the number to the national office, but the perceived bureaucratic stonewalling that was already infuriating Nasim was no more than some confusion and lack of authority on the part of the director.

When Nasim and Delia dialed the number on Wednesday morning, the phone rang in a low building on a sprawling federal annex deep in the Washington suburbs, where the Office of Personnel Management had relegated the Eden Project to two wings. The two of them imagined, though, that they were attempting to breach some concrete fortress in the heart of DC, and it might as well have been for as much success as they had. They persisted until, eight transfers in, they encountered a line that rang and rang, with neither person nor machine to answer. They had no idea who was supposed to have picked up, nor how that person related to the previous one, name also unknown, nor to the one before that.

On Thursday, they were prepared with a notebook to map their progress, and by the time Enzo arrived in the afternoon, the Deputy Director of Regional Affairs had surrendered the direct number of the Associate Director of Regional Assignment. By the end of the day Friday, they had instructions to file a Petition for Transfer, a mysterious document – heavy, dense, and unnecessarily complex – that didn't arrive for several weeks. Then, whether by the nature of the bureaucratic behemoth that they were pitted against or in order to discourage transfers without forbidding them, what might have been accomplished in a few weeks was convoluted into months of rubber–stamping and resubmission and, more than anything, waiting.

Nasim was surprised one day as she dialed the phone to realize that she never rehearsed the script beforehand anymore. The little jitter of nerves, the secret hope that no one would pick up on the other end to spare her having to complete the call - she couldn't recall when those had disappeared. She no longer feared that someone might, by saying no or by merely implying it, end their progress; instead she prodded and questioned and, if need be, argued. It was a fleeting moment of realization, interrupted by someone's answering the call.

Nasim's next insemination took place while they waited, and when the phone did finally ring, she thought it was the nurse confirming that an embryo had taken. Peter had just arrived for the afternoon shift, and with a quizzical expression he handed the phone to Nasim. "It's the facility director for you."

Nasim felt a pang of guilt for not saving the news for Delia, but her excitement bubbled over. After a moment of listening, she shouted, "Peter!" and without waiting for his reply, "we're moving to Washington!" She dropped the phone, indifferent to the sound of its breaking when it hit the floor. Grabbing Peter by the arms, she dragged him in circles as she skipped around him, alternately singing, "We're moving, we're moving" and shouting "Wash–ing–ton!" Peter would have happily joined in, but he was too winded from laughing. Later that evening, while Nasim called Delia to relay the good news, Peter tried to recall another instance when he had seen such exuberance in her, but that he could think of none was through no fault in his memory.

FORTY-TWO

There was a small desk tucked between the front door and the hallway that led to the bedrooms, and that was where Nasim sat every afternoon to write a letter. One each day. To the candidates who had been elected because of their opposition to the Eden Project and the swing votes that had just barely been swayed, to the people like Eleanore who had fought on her side. She wrote one or two to Sam, but she never sent those. When she had begun, they were difficult to write, well-reasoned arguments against her captivity here, letters that had gone through draft after draft before she had finally signed her name to them and walked them to the mailbox ten minutes away. Later, though, when she had run out of names, she had started writing to people in her own past, teachers whose addresses she had managed to dredge up and neighbors whose stance on the Project was impossible to guess. And then she had started through the list - the earlier one and its haphazard additions - a second time, and the measured rationale had begun to erode, replaced by pleaded appeals.

It was a cycle she had been through too many times already not to understand where it would lead: Hope, desperation, despair. Until she found some smaller grain of hope to hold onto, dug out from recesses of greater and greater improbability. She had once hoped for a normal life. Now her hopes peaked at what? Getting out after the first child or two? Escaping from this purgatory to a space with some degrees of freedom to compensate for her body's captivity?

The cycles sometimes took a week, sometimes an hour; so she might find herself writing a letter one morning and by afternoon collapsed into hopelessness, or she might spend four days without leaving her bed for anything but a shower after a week of unreturned letters and unanswered phone calls that left her wondering whether her phone line connected to the outside world, whether the mailbox was ever emptied.

She didn't know the word for the apathy that gnawed at her, for the feeling of flatness that settled on her, sapping her of the desire to write letters, the desire to escape, the desire to take the next breath. She had felt grief before and, in lesser doses, had felt sadness and fear. But this was something else, something she didn't know until those men had taken her to that first room and left her with the solitude and silence that lived there.

Mustering the will to escape the periods of darkness grew more and more difficult, the efforts to rally herself, more and more futile. She spent an entire day studying a flaw in the ceiling above her bed, a little speck of texture on the otherwise smooth white. And then a second day, too; and sometime during the second day, though she didn't know what time it was because she had never switched the window to transparent, she heard someone in the living room - the door closing, maybe a whisper, movement, though there were no creaks in the new floor to betray it.

Anywhere else, it would have been nothing, but here, it shattered the silence.

Nasim dashed to the bathroom door and threw her bathrobe over her, cinching it tight around her waist and then checking again that it covered her. She eyed her dresser, wondering how quickly she could get properly dressed, but she pulled the belt tighter still and then inched towards the sound.

"Hello?" she called.

"Hello?" someone echoed back. A woman. Just the one voice.

Nasim saw her first, standing in the living room, her eyes moving from the dining table into the kitchenette now, and in a moment she would follow that course to its end and see Nasim in the doorway to the hall.

"Hi," Nasim said, stepping into the living room. How could it be that the mere presence of another person made her feel like an interloper in a place that had been her home for more than two months?

"Hi. Cath." Cath extended a hand and Nasim unfolded her arms just long enough to shake it.

"Are you an Eve?"

"No, I'm a handler. Your handler. If you keep me, that is."

"A handler?"

"I… uh… I'm supposed to help you. With… with anything, really. They didn't explain? They didn't tell you I was coming?"

Nasim shook her head. "They don't really tell me anything."

"They thought you'd like me, that we'd be a good a match. Or the tests thought so, anyways. And they'll find a couple of others, too. Eventually. After all the Eves get their first handler. But for now, you've just got me."

"But what are you going to *do*?" Nasim asked.

"Everything. Anything. If you want a friend, I'm your friend. If you want a maid, I'm your maid. If you want a cook, well, I don't think you'd want me to cook for you, but I'd get you something. From the kitchen."

"For how long?"

"Until you're finished."

Nasim stood frozen a moment, sixteen and alone, and then she collapsed sobbing to the floor, and in an instant Cath was at her side. Nasim tried to explain about the darkness and the solitude and the silence and her fear that they were permanent, but her words were incomprehensible. She tried to tell Cath about the feeling that everything dear to her was water cupped in her hands, and no matter how tightly she sealed the gaps between her fingers, it all slipped out, one drop at a time. Her parents and Abbas and Maryam and her freedom and soon her free will and her will to live, too. But her sobs were too jarring to let the words pass by, and Cath didn't understand any of it.

FORTY-THREE

Once the final decision on the petition was reached, the rest followed swiftly. The approval had included not only the receiving facility – a place in the southwest of Washington, inland a ways from the Sound but still on the rainy side of the Cascades, their second choice – but also the number of the vacant coop that she was to occupy. The movers were scheduled for two weeks hence and would arrive a day early to pack. The facility director at this end had made Nasim a single gesture of kindness that represented the sum of the goodwill that the Eden Project had ever shown her: she had obtained for Nasim a floor-plan of the new coop. When Enzo arrived at midnight to relieve Peter, he found the two of them sitting at the round table, the paper spread between them.

"Enzo!" Nasim had almost blurted it out, but she instead looked at Peter, who understood and excused himself. For the whole twenty seconds it took for him to put on his shoes, she chewed on the words, and the moment the door closed behind him, she exclaimed, "We're moving to Washington!"

"What? Washington?" He was so perplexed that he

struggled to choose the next question. He settled for the most straightforward: "Which one? DC or the state?"

"State." Why did he look confused rather than excited?

The next easily answered question: "When?" She looked like she was expecting a different response. Her brow was set with confusion, but those lines were beginning to soften into an expression of disappointment.

"In two weeks." She could tell that he still had no inkling of how this was tied to him.

"Why...?" Realizing that one–word questions might be starting to sound antagonistic, he tried to think of more to add but was stopped short before he found the words.

Nasim's eyes had begun to glisten and she blew out a great sigh. Her voice a little louder, a little higher than usual, she said, "Enzo, you said it was like home to you! I can tell you're not happy here, and I thought that maybe if we went there, you know, with the forest and the volcanoes and what–not, that you would feel more... more comfortable. But you're looking at me like you hate the idea." She had managed to get through it all without her voice so much as cracking, but having finished, she burst into tears.

"No, no, no no no no." He wrapped his arms around her. "Nasim, I don't hate it. I just didn't expect it. I was confused. I don't know. I heard 'Washington' and I thought maybe DC, maybe you were moving there for some advocacy something? Or that the Project was moving you? Or that the fact that you could move meant you were suddenly free? I just didn't understand. That's all it was! It's a lovely surprise."

It was easy enough to convince her – she wanted to be convinced – although the reassurance required rehashing several times during the night. An hour later, sitting next to each other at the table, Nasim announced, "I want to get rid of everything. It's all got to go."

"Has it?" She didn't feel him cringe as he wondered whether he ought to have known the answer to that question, too.

"I want you to pick everything out with me. It'll be like it's ours instead of just mine."

"But didn't you already pick everything once? You don't have to change things for me," he offered.

"I didn't choose any of this. I just took what was already here."

The exercise gradually erased the discomfort of earlier. Together they thumbed through options on a tablet and filled the rooms of the new coop one by one with furniture, rugs, and art. "They've said that anything in the catalog is easy to get," she explained. "Other things are possible but not necessarily easy." Section by section, they marked off chairs and photograph frames and dressers and drew every item onto the floor plan. A leather couch and loveseat set in an 'L' around a low coffee table. A square table in the dining room. Two matching bedroom sets for Nasim's room and the handlers'.

At 3 AM, they were arguing over the merits of some bedside table that Enzo was pushing for.

"But it's hideous!" Nasim cried.

"That's the beauty of it, though!" Enzo retorted.

"Well, in that case…" And they laughed together and found they couldn't stop until Enzo was doubled over, clasping his sides, gasping for air. When he finally took a deep breath, he said, "I don't even know what was funny," and they laughed all over again.

They moved to the couch once they had finished the floor-plan. Nasim snuggled up next to Enzo. "I can't wait to see it. I know it's going to be beautiful, and you'll show me everything, won't you?"

"Everything."

"And what about after?"

This time he understood. "We can do anything after. We can stay there or go see the world or go see the world and then go back there. We'll have forever." He let go of her hand so he could touch her face. "Forever to do whatever you want."

"You promise?"

He laughed, "How many times do I need to promise before you believe me." Then he looked into her green eyes, his face suddenly serious. "Forever, Nasim. I promise."

She laid her head on his shoulder and thought awhile. Finally she said, "And you'll teach me to drive."

"You don't know how to drive?"

"Whose car would I have learned on, Enzo?"

"Okay. And I'll teach you to drive."

"And–"

"And that's enough promises for one day, isn't it?"

The sun had just broken the horizon behind them when Nasim sighed. "I just wish you were happy about it."

"I am happy about it," Enzo replied, his hand over his heart in sincerity.

"But not happy enough."

FORTY-FOUR

Cath had brought a suitcase with her, twice the size of the one Nasim had, full of clothes that she unpacked into the dresser in the second bedroom. The remainder of her belongings had been moved into her own apartment, a single, large room that she wouldn't see again until a second handler was assigned to Nasim. She went to the kitchen in the middle of the afternoon to see which baked thing was freshest and brought that back along with two meals - part lunch, part dinner - one of which she hoped Nasim would like.

Nasim had been quiet since her tears had dried up. She had broken away from Cath, retreated to her bedroom, stepped into the shower to wash away the staleness of the last two days and the mucous of the last hour. When she emerged, she found her towel hung in a different spot than usual, warmed by a heater, the function of which she hadn't bothered to guess, and her bathrobe picked up off the floor. She had left the bathroom door open and so hadn't noticed anyone come in, and the realization that someone had been there and, somehow worse, that she had failed to notice made her uneasy. In the bedroom, she found her bed made and clothes laid out on top of it, her nicest jeans - the ones without any wear showing - and a t-shirt not yet faded by washing. The socks she didn't recognize, but she put them on, soft, thick cotton, because, though she usually went barefoot, they looked as nice as slippers.

When Nasim opened her bedroom door, it was to an empty coop, and she choked on the fear that she might have imagined the whole thing, that she might have found herself so desperate for companionship that she had invented a comrade; and who then but she could have hung up her bathrobe and laid out her clothes?

Cath, though, returned a few minutes later with food. "I didn't know there was menu, so, of course, I didn't think to ask you what you wanted. Well, I thought to ask, but I didn't think we knew what was available, so I didn't. You see what I mean? But I got two things, and if you don't like either, I can go back for something else."

Nasim studied the paper sack, a full-sized grocery bag with the top rolled over on itself. "Whose socks are these?" Nasim asked, her eyes not moving from the bag.

"They're mine. I didn't, uh… I couldn't find any that weren't threadbare through the heels, so I thought… I thought tomorrow I could order you some new ones. If you'd like."

Nasim nodded.

"Nasim." Nasim looked suddenly at Cath, startled by the sound of her own name. "I think it's safe to say neither of us has any experience with this." She pointed at the space between them. "So I'm going to do what I think I should do, and I need you to tell me if you want something else or if I overstep or… or anything."

Nasim nodded again.

"We'll figure each other out soon enough, and then it

won't be so hard with the next ones because I can help you with them, with getting them whipped into shape." A smile broke on Cath's face. "And we can start figuring it out over dessert."

In spite of herself, a smile edged onto Nasim's lips, too. "How did you know I like dessert?"

"What kind of heathen wouldn't like dessert?"

They ate together, sharing the two meals that Cath had brought back and then the quarter pecan pie, and talked and laughed a little, though the sound of it startled Nasim to silence again. But Cath pried her with questions about her family and her favorite color and her path here and the books she liked to read.

When Cath stood to clear the dishes from the table, Nasim tried to help. "You have your job; this is mine. Go relax. I'll be done in a second."

"You're just worried I'll put you out of work," Nasim teased and then regretted it, fearing Cath might not hear the lightness in her voice. But Cath laughed, and Nasim relinquished herself to the couch and to the exhaustion of having done anything but lie in solitude in her own bed.

Seated side by side on the couch they watched a movie that night. It was projected onto the wall from a computer system that Nasim hadn't realized existed. "I thought they didn't want me to have any reminders of the outside world," she had said when Cath had asked where she had thought they had hidden away her media system. The movie was something stupid that had just come out, and Nasim's wandering attention drifted back into that flat space halfway through.

The next morning, she slept late, waking a few times an hour only to roll over and drift back into half-dreams. She felt Cath's presence in the coop, felt her hovering near the door but unwilling to come in. Towards early afternoon, though, Cath caught her in the moment when Nasim's eyes flicked open and then clamped shut again.

"I saw that."

"I hoped you wouldn't," Nasim replied, the gravel not yet cleared from her throat and her eyes pressed shut.

"Are you going to sleep all day?"

"Why? Did you have a better offer?"

"Coffee cake?"

Nasim opened her eyes, studying Cath's silhouette against the bright daylight that leaked into the hall from the other bedroom and from the living room beyond. "Will you flip the switch for me?" she asked, pointing to the opaque window beside her.

Nasim waited. She slept naked, and her bathrobe hung on the bathroom door. When Cath went into the bathroom to start the water unbidden, Nasim darted across the room to snatch the robe from its hook. She had hesitated a moment too long, though, and Cath caught her in her streak across the bedroom. She threw Nasim the bathrobe and laughing said, "There's nothing to be shy about. I don't mind as long as you don't."

FORTY-FIVE

Nasim almost succumbed to the urge to seize Enzo's hand when the plane landed. In the last thirty minutes, white–capped islands had poked through the sea of clouds: Rainier, Adams, St. Helen's, Hood to the south, Baker to the north. The smell of evergreen when the doors opened, faint and foreign, mixed into the staleness of the aircraft. A car was waiting for them on the tarmac, the driver there to pull them from the others, from the people flying for business or family or things about which Nasim had no knowledge. Most of their luggage had gone ahead with what little furniture had been moved and would be waiting for them with the new things that Nasim had picked with Enzo.

The drive took two hours, and Nasim savored the minutes, relishing them as though they were the flavor of real freedom: traffic jams and people in cars and miles of roads and woods and looming mountains. When they arrived, it was to a compound full of U–shaped, single–story buildings, wooden doors to each coop facing the inside of the U and glass doors looking out. There was no scarred, fluorescent hallway to traverse, and the smell of evergreen was overwhelming here, and of dampness and greenery; and a light rain tickled a shudder of excitement and chill from Nasim.

The four of them went in together, and again, Nasim fought the urge to grab for Enzo, to reassure herself by his presence that this new place was no dream. When they had all had a chance to peek into each of the rooms, Nasim said, "You must be dying to see your places, too. You shouldn't all have to wait. Enzo will stay with me while you two get settled, and then if we eat dinner together, you can draw straws after. You don't mind, do you, Enzo? It's only a few hours."

Enzo shook his head, and Delia and Peter left together in the car that was still idling outside. When the door closed behind them, Nasim threw her arms around Enzo. "Tell me, do you love it?"

"Of course I love it. It couldn't be better. I can't believe you managed to make this happen." His face was so serious, so earnest.

"Smile, though!" Nasim couldn't stop grinning.

They fell asleep together on the couch. Neither meant to, but they had departed so early that morning, and the excitement had drained so much from them that their conversation had trailed off into head nodding to which they eventually surrendered. The sound of Peter and Delia opening the door, bags of food from the kitchen in hand, startled them both awake.

When Enzo drew the night shift after dinner, Delia offered him her afternoons instead so that he could go see his quarters, but he declined. And as soon as it was settled, the others left again, exhausted and eager for their new beds.

"I'm not tired, though. Are you?" Nasim asked.

Enzo shrugged. "Not especially." He was looking more carefully now, running his hands over the things they had picked out together, touching each item as though verifying that it was real. "The only thing this place lacks is that horrible anachronism of a phone," he said.

"And a fireplace," Nasim added. She had known there wasn't one – she had studied the floor-plans, after all – but she hadn't *realized* it any more than she would have if there hadn't been any closets. It was an inconsequential disappointment today, though. "I'm sure there'll be a good place to make a fire pit somewhere," she concluded. "And we should see where we are, anyhow."

"Now?"

"What better time?"

They idled arm in arm through a mist so thick it might have been rain. Nasim had found an insulated raincoat, one she didn't know she owned and several sizes too big, that she was wearing now. She shivered into it, relishing the warm air it trapped against her body, a cloud of comfort against the damp chill beyond. Enzo, though, had nothing but the t–shirt he had worn to the airport, and his arms were freckled with goosebumps.

"Do you want to go back?" Nasim asked when she saw.

"I don't ever want to leave this moment," he replied. "Here with you in this... what is this? Rain? I don't even know. If we stay here all night, do you think the night will stay with us?"

Other than a cat that they saw dart across the road in front of them, the scene was devoid of any movement. All the creatures were snuggled away somewhere warm and dry. The desolation made them feel as though the night belonged solely to the two of them, as though everything else had relinquished its claim.

It was hours later when they found her coop again; they hadn't gotten lost so much as willed themselves to forget the way back. When they saw her door, though, they were both shivering and soaked through, and Enzo ordered hot chocolate for them while Nasim stood in the shower, waiting for the hot water to wash away the chill in her bones. It wasn't until Enzo padded in wearing a dry pair of her sweatpants and a baggy sweatshirt and carrying the hot chocolate some fifteen minutes later that she had finally stopped shivering.

FORTY-SIX

Although she still suffered the same bouts of apathy, their duration, if not their frequency, was tempered by Cath's presence. After the first morning, she insisted that Nasim get up before noon, which effectively ended her multi-day stints in bed. Some mornings she even half desired to get up and pushed the bell at the side of her bed, a summons for Cath to come prod her. And with someone pressing her to do something, even if only to watch a movie or go for a walk, she found herself divorced for hours at a time from her meditations on her plight and on the impossibility of escape from it.

After a week's interlude, Nasim sat back down at her desk to write a letter. Cath was showering and when she, towel-clad, made her way across the living room to her bedroom, she paused over Nasim's shoulder.

"Whatcha doing?"

I'm wishing you were out of a job, Nasim thought. "Why are you here?"

"I don't know. Something about me matched something about you. Said the tests, anyways."

"No, I mean, why did you even apply?"

Cath shrugged. "It was the most important thing I could do? The biggest contribution I could make to my country? To more than my country, really. I wanted to join the foreign service when I started school, but by the time I was finished I wasn't so sure that was for me. All the schmoozing, you know? But this appeared at just the right time. Just the right thing.

"And anyways, unemployment for recent graduates is something like fifty percent, and suddenly the government announces that they're hiring three million people. No qualifications necessary, well-paid, housing and food provided, and full retirement benefits after fifteen to twenty years. All you have to do to start the process is take a personality test. I don't know anyone who didn't apply." In reply to Nasim's skeptical expression, she added, "Literally."

She was standing in the doorway to the hall, her towel clutched in a hand above her breasts, and when she turned to go dress, Nasim shoved the letter she was writing into the drawer of the desk.

"So what were you writing?" Cath asked, reappearing with the towel wrapped around her hair now, her jeans tight around her thighs and a t-shirt hugging her chest.

"A letter."

Cath laughed. "You don't have to tell me if you don't want."

"To my sixth grade Spanish teacher, but that wasn't necessarily representative."

"Representative of…?"

Nasim shrugged. "Never mind. You know what would really be great?" Nasim forced a smile across her face, wondered how unnatural it looked.

Cath thought about it for a moment. "A chocolate cream

pie?"

"How do you always know?"

"Because the moment you get that look, all I have to do is suggest something delicious, and that's always *the* thing that you want."

"What look?"

"That smile. Yeah, *that* one. You know, it's a miracle that you're as freakishly thin as you are given what I see you eat everyday."

"It's all about the volume. Skip your salad, and you can fit in an extra piece of pie." Nasim wrinkled her nose, her tongue playfully thrust between her teeth, the tension of the moments before fading.

"That's the most ludicrous thing I've ever…" Cath had picked up the phone and begun dialing. "I'd like to order a pie for B112. Chocolate cream, please… Yes, the whole thing… Nothing else… Pick up, please… Thank you."

"The whole thing?" Nasim burst out laughing.

"You're walking over there with me to pick it up, so I figured you could fit in an extra half pie."

"How long's it going to take?"

"Six hours. Has to chill before we can eat it."

"Six hours!?"

"I'm kidding," Cath laughed. "They made them this morning. I saw them when I picked up breakfast. We can go over now and get one."

It was the first time Nasim had seen the kitchen, the first time that she had been anywhere on the campus other than to the mailbox, and the sun on her skin felt just hot enough that it might thaw away some of the apathy still frozen inside her. Cath grabbed her arm and began to skip, dragging Nasim behind.

"C'mon! Let's earn you some more pie!" But Nasim

was laughing too hard to do anything but double over.

They really did eat the whole thing, half of it during the two movies they watched - much better ones lately since Cath had assembled a list to choose from - and the other half just sitting on the couch cross-legged facing each other, each with a plate on her lap. They could sit like that for hours and talk, and they did until the sky was turning grey with morning. Between yawns, Cath said, "You don't mind if I go to bed, do you?"

"Not until we finish this." Nasim, her eyes barely open, pointed to the last little sliver of pie.

"Can't that be breakfast?"

"Not much of a breakfast."

"Breakfast supplement, then?"

"Oh, all right. I'm exhausted, too, I guess." But the last piece was no more than three bites, and she was so tired she didn't want to stand up, so she finished it rather than move. "Oh, God, I can't believe we finished that," Nasim said as she fell backwards into the couch. "I'm sleeping here tonight."

"You're not. You're sleeping in your own bed." Cath half-pulled, half-coaxed Nasim into her bedroom, undressed her, and saw her into bed before stumbling back to her own room.

FORTY-SEVEN

Delia was on duty and paying no attention to the time, but Nasim had been watching the projection on the wall, counting down the moments until Enzo would show up. The last of the new furniture had been delivered – a cherry coffee table that he had insisted was, now that he had seen it, the only coffee table he could ever imagine wanting – and her excitement for him to witness this place in its final state kept threatening to bubble over. When he was five minutes late, Nasim pointed out the time to Delia, who went to the door to put on her shoes and jacket. But instead of Enzo, there was the slip of paper, folded in half, that Delia picked up. Nasim snatched it from her hands before she could read it.

Nasim,

There aren't words that will make this easier to convey. No words, either, that will make it easier to hear or understand, so I'll use the only ones I have. The more I know you – the more I love you – the more sickening this system becomes. I have no choice: I can't stay here.

I can't be complicit in the horror of your imprisonment.

I'm going.

This tears at me. In losing you, I'm losing the most important relationship of my life, one so profound that it feels like you have become part of my soul now. I hope one day you'll find it in you to forgive me for the part I've played in the Project. I know I'll never forgive myself.

I'm so sorry.

—E

Nasim's knees buckled, and she gasped for air. The paper was clenched in her hand, her cold sweat mingling with the ink, and the room spun around her. Delia tried to help her to her feet, tried to ease the paper out of her hands, but Nasim fell forward, biting back the nausea washing over her while her four limbs gripped the ground. When the room stopped spinning around her, when the roiling paused, Nasim sat down on the floor. She was certain that she had misread the note, misinterpreted the message, but she couldn't look at it again, not with Delia at her side, not without divulging the contents; so she clutched it tighter. Delia, though, refused to leave Nasim, who finally begged, "Will you get me a nurse?"

"I'll call one."

"Please, go!" And the urgency in her voice was just enough to override Delia's certainty that calling would be faster than going.

The ink was running when Nasim uncrumpled the note, but there was no ambiguity in the words. Nasim rolled onto her side, curling herself into a ball as sobs wracked her body with such force that when the nurse entered he mistook them for convulsions.

The nurse lifted Nasim and carried her into her bedroom, but there, too, she responded neither to his

C. E. Rowland

questions nor to Delia's panicked echo of them. Instead, her eyes traced the words she could still picture written in the air in front of her, and the ink of those words continued to bleed. It seeped into the near future, poisoning tomorrow: without him. It smeared into the recent past, tainting her last memories of him when he must have known he was leaving but gave no sign. It ran in both directions, blurring all the sharp lines, blotting out future and past, a tide of ink that blackened everything it touched.

The nurse counted her pulse, tried to hold her still and coach her breathing, but she couldn't hear him over the sound of grief rushing in her ears. Delia, too, tried to touch her, tried to speak to her, but the pain was too deep to reach through.

Nasim grasped about for anything to hold on to, anything to buoy her. A week from now, he will be gone. A week ago, who was it who was here? A month from now, I'll be in this place – his place – surrounded by him, without him. A month ago, I thought we had forever; he told me we had forever, and what he said meant nothing. A year from now? A year ago. A decade from now. All of it washed into black. Everything I see is swallowed into nothing. A decade ago, before Enzo, I had something then. I had... darkness and loneliness and hatred and...

And she felt herself sucked her to inky depths, her limbs too heavy to fight, her head too light to resist.

The nurse had called for help – he had come without any sedatives – and it arrived just then, but her breathing was already stabilizing, and she was beginning to come to.

Delia, meanwhile, having failed to reach Enzo in his room, called security and asked them to fetch him. She was too eager to get back to Nasim to look at the crumpled note that she picked up from the floor. She stuffed it into her pocket and hurried down the hall.

When Enzo arrived with another man, it didn't occur to Delia that he was being escorted rather than accompanied. That Enzo should ignore her, fixating instead on the door at the end of the hall behind which he would find Nasim, seemed only right. That his feet slowed as he approached Nasim's room, she didn't notice.

The nurses had gone; Nasim was alone.

"They came to get me. I didn't have a choice but to come. But I won't come back again." His tone had gone flat and cold.

"But what...?" Nasim's voice stuck in her throat. "What's...?"

"It's all in the note, Nasim." His body was rigid, his face betrayed no emotion at all. "It's not more complicated than that. You don't deserve to be here. I can't be party to that injustice."

"You're the part that makes the injustice just a little less," she whispered, her eyes brimming with tears.

"You know that isn't true. You know my being here makes me just as culpable as they are."

But I forgive you your part in it.

FORTY-EIGHT

SEPTEMBER 25, 2063

"Have you always been so…"

"So what?" Nasim asked. She was seated at her desk penning a letter that she had said was to her aunt. Cath was lying on the floor beside her, propped up on her elbows, a book open in front of her.

"I don't know. Melancholy?" she tried. "Yeah, that fits."

"Am I melancholy?"

"Aren't you?"

Nasim thought about it awhile. "I don't know."

"Nasim, you're depressed."

"Am I?"

"Aren't you?" And then, when Nasim failed to reply, Cath answered, "Of course you are. You barely get out of bed in the morning. You don't eat anything unless I put food in front of you, and then you don't touch it unless it's sweet. You have no desire to do anything. No desire for anything at all, as far as I can tell."

"To be somewhere else."

"We could go for a walk. That would be somewhere else."

"That's not what I mean," Nasim said.

"That's my point."

"I don't feel sad, really, though."

"Do you feel anything?"

In the silence, Nasim rolled her pen through her fingers. "No," she finally said.

"You need purpose," Cath said. "You need to fight for something."

"I do…" Nasim trailed off.

Cath had moved closer to Nasim and was kneeling beside her now, trying to entice Nasim to look at her, but Nasim was still focused on the pen, on the sensation of a seam in the plastic as it touched each finger in turn. Cath's eyes were skimming the letter, the contents of which she had guessed long before but never had the chance to verify.

What was it, exactly, that made the seam feel so different from the rest of the pen? Three hundred fifty-nine degrees of rotation elicited barely a sensation. It all came in the last degree, a feature all but invisible but the only aspect of the pen that stimulated a response in her fingers. Thumb, index, middle; thumb, index, middle.

"Here, hand me some paper. I'll write one, too," Cath said.

"You don't have to help me. I'm not asking you to."

"I've never seen someone as unhappy as you are, Nasim."

"But it's you I'm trying to put out of a job."

Cath shrugged. "They picked me because we'd like each other. How can I see you suffer and not do anything about it?"

Nasim still hadn't looked up from her pen.

Cath took a sheet of paper from the drawer, wrote a few unpracticed lines to the senator she had voted for, stuffed the words into an envelope. Nasim was still entranced by the pattern - thumb, index, middle - by the time Cath had looked up an address.

"C'mon, Nasim. Let's go to the mailbox. Write that one tomorrow." She eased the pen from Nasim's hand and waited for Nasim to realize its absence. When she did finally look up, Cath was trying to smile at her. "Some fresh air, maybe? And something delicious? Or a movie? Or we can talk, if there's anything you want to talk about. Anything at all, doesn't have to be serious. We can talk about your favorite kind of cloud, if you want, or your favorite vowel."

They trudged to the mailbox together, Cath the whole while trying to coax something from Nasim - a smile or a laugh or just a nod. She succeeded but not until she had dragged Nasim on to the kitchen, where they made off with a dozen cookies that had to be spatulaed off the hot cookie sheet for them. Somewhere on the way back, Nasim reached her hand into the bag for one of the cookies and burnt her tongue on the still-molten chocolate chips, and Cath's laughter - at Nasim's impatience and her predictability and her swearing - finally elicited a smile.

The first smile was the hardest to earn when Nasim was like this, but the others didn't come easily, either. They watched a movie that afternoon, one that Cath had remembered as being much more uplifting than it turned out to be, and afterwards Nasim tried to go to bed.

"But it's only seven o'clock."

"I'm tired, though."

"Tomorrow will be better."

"..."

"Why don't you take a shower? That'll wake you up a bit, and then we can do something."

"Do what?" Nasim sighed.

"I'll think of something while you're in the shower. Something irresistible."

Nasim said nothing but obediently stripped down in her bedroom, pausing on the cold tile in the bathroom before stepping into the running water. She tried to imagine washing away the weight on her shoulders, tried to imagine the warmth radiating through her skin to the deeper spaces where she couldn't feel anything.

"Are you alive in there?" Cath asked.

"Is this what being alive feels like?"

"How about we build a fire in the fireplace and roast marshmallows, and I'll tell you about all the embarrassing things that happened to me growing up. You don't have to say anything. You don't have to laugh. You can just watch the flames, if you want."

The fire was already going, and the marshmallows had appeared from somewhere with skewers to roast them on when Nasim emerged from her bedroom dressed in the old t-shirt and sweatpants and thick socks that Cath had laid out for her. The latter had recently appeared in her dresser, though she hadn't asked where they had come from. Cath had already started on her first marshmallow and handed a skewer to Nasim with her free hand.

"Okay, so embarrassing story number one," Cath began.

"It's okay, you don't have to."

"I don't mind."

"Just sit with me. It's enough." Nasim sat so close to Cath that their legs were touching and after a while leaned her head on Cath's shoulder, her eyes fixed on the flames.

FORTY-NINE

I'm trying to be strong enough to keep myself intact and to still find love and sympathy in me for you. To be strong enough to forgive you each time I remember how much I'm suffering, to be ready to forgive you if you come back.

What if you came back and the wound was already healing? You wouldn't be able to replace the piece of my heart you took.

There is one detail in every moment that eviscerates me. In this one, it's the warmth of your hand that should be closing over mine as I wake up. In the last, it was the sound of different birds outside, chattering about a place that I would never have come to but for you. When I open my eyes, it will be the ugly bedside table that I see first, one you chose, one I never would have picked. Every instant a reminder of the moments that have ceased to be. And you? You're trapped in no such prison.

There is no trace of my Enzo in you, this person who left. This isn't some manifestation of a part of him that's now become the whole; this is something that was never there, displacing everything that was him. But Enzo will find his way back. There's no other ending to the story.

When people say that life isn't fair, what they mean – what I thought they meant – was that Fate isn't fair. That my parents died, and then Abbas and Maryam, that I survived without having been vaccinated and that the price of that extraordinary luck was the sentence that I'm serving now in this horrible place. Fate deals Her cards without regard to the recipient. They aren't supposed to be fair, the things She does to you. But the things that other people do to you... weren't those supposed to be the things you earned? They say that, don't they, that you reap what you sow?

It's no more than a mistake. One that he would fix if this – all this, these walls and these rules and these people and this – weren't in the way. Because Eden hadn't taken enough from me already. A dozen years of my life and the ownership of my body, they weren't enough. So it gave me a good thing, the only good thing I've ever had, and then took it away again. To what end? Just to see me suffer a little more?

I will get him back.
I will get him back.
I will get him back.
I will get him back.

...

Nasim lay on her side, her eyes fixed on the wall opposite her. She was naked, and though she had just showered, the water wouldn't wash away the odor of grief that clung to her; she could smell it again already, the sweat that came with the sobbing. And in the respite between, in the moments when the tears dried briefly and the snot cleared from her blocked nose, she shivered under the comforter. Delia sat on the bed beside her holding Nasim's hand in her own.

Enzo had slipped out without Delia's noticing. He had stayed only long enough to speak his bit. At the moment he left, Delia was on the phone with Peter, relating what had happened – or what little she understood of what had happened – warning him to be prepared for his shift. She had assumed that Enzo was still in the bedroom and had thought to leave, but when she peaked in, it had been just Nasim, her body shaking again.

Nasim had fallen asleep with Delia sitting beside her, and when she had awoken, disoriented and eyes swollen, Delia, who could think of nothing to help but perhaps a shower, had pulled her towards the bathroom. Nasim had offered no resistance. Her feet had stumbled one after the other in the direction that Delia led her, and she had allowed Delia to undress her. Delia had eased her into the shower and disappeared to find some comfortable clean clothes. When she had returned, Nasim had sunk to the floor of the shower, her head between her knees, the water running in a curtain over her face.

Delia had been drenched in the moments it took to reassure herself that nothing had happened to Nasim, whose shoulders shuddered and jerked with sobs again. The water's washing away her tears had done nothing to disguise the redness in her eyes. Delia had turned off the water and tried to lift Nasim to her feet but wound up drying her off as best she could where she sat.

She had finally coaxed Nasim up and led her back into

the bedroom, where Nasim had collapsed onto the bed. The drops of water left from the shower were already indistinguishable from the beads of sweat popping from her skin. Delia, mystified and impotent, had changed her own soaked clothes for those that she had laid out for Nasim, and that's how she found herself sitting before Nasim's blank gaze, their hands clasped.

The silence stretched for hours, perforated by intermittent crying, quiet sometimes but loud more often. Delia shifted closer to Nasim at some point, but otherwise the scene was frozen. A slow snow of crumpled tissues found its way to the floor around the bed. Once Delia asked again. Asked what was wrong, what had happened, but the question only elicited in reply another fit of tears and such violent gasps that she feared Nasim might lose consciousness again.

Barely aware of the space beyond her, Nasim failed to notice the man who appeared to tell Delia in a hushed voice that Enzo had resigned and to relay that Peter would soon arrive to assume what would be a twelve–hour shift.

FIFTY

MARCH 21, 2064

"Do you think they've already met each other if they're arriving together? Maybe they were on the same flight or something," Nasim said.

They were writing their letters. Cath had had her own names to add to the list, her own set of elected officials, her own history's-worth of neighbors, teachers, professors. She had called her relatives to urge them to support the cause and to get still more names from them. They did it every day, the phone calls and the letters their morning ritual, the reason to get out of bed.

"Or maybe they had some kind of training," Cath offered.

"Like what?"

"I don't know. It's odd that we found out they were coming two months ago and they're only just now arriving."

"Well, how long did it take you to get here once they'd picked you?" Nasim asked.

"A week."

"Are you serious?"

"I didn't have a choice," Cath explained. "It was either be here in a week or decline the offer. They were pretty clear about that. And then there was a half-day orientation where they took me around the campus and gave me the phone number to the kitchen and told me that I'd better make sure you made all your appointments. That was it."

"Maybe it's because you were perfect for the job already." Nasim made a face, nose scrunched and head shaking, that Cath mirrored back at her.

"Are you excited?" Cath asked.

Unwilling to voice her answer, Nasim replied with her own question: "They're really coming tomorrow?"

"I think they've already arrived, but they're probably getting the orientation now. They're not supposed to show up here until tomorrow morning. Come to think of it, I guess I'd better have my stuff packed."

Nasim's face darkened. She hadn't even thought about it, that Cath would be moving into her own apartment, the one that she had only seen briefly the day she had arrived.

"Oh, don't look like that." Cath said. "It'll be exactly the same, just in finite doses."

"It won't be the same, though."

"Nasim, I'm not going anywhere. I'm here until you're thirty-five at least. That's as far away from today as the day you were born."

"I don't want…" Tears welled up in Nasim's eyes in spite of her efforts to fight them back.

"You *do* want other handlers, Nasim. Twenty-four hours a day for the next two decades? Eventually, I would drive you crazy. It might take a year or two, but it would happen. This just gives you two more people to lean on. And they're going to be as well matched to you as I am. You'll love them. They'll love you," Cath promised.

"I know." Nasim kicked at the pillow that she had thrown off the couch when they sat down. "It's just…"

"I know. Perpetual change. Perpetual discomfort. But it's a good change. It's a change that will make you richer. And I don't really foresee any other changes. The whole point of the campus and the coops and the handlers is to build a secure environment for you. So really, this should be it. Last change."

"I guess," Nasim said with the beginnings of a smile, "I could always fire both of them if I can't stand being without you."

"You're such a piece of work, they'll probably quit before you have a chance," Cath teased.

"You should be so lucky! Then you'll have me all to yourself again."

"Are you okay?" Cath asked, serious again. She knew Nasim well enough to know that laughter more often disguised than displaced the pain.

"No."

"But you will be." There was no doubt in the statement.

"You promise?"

"Of course," Cath said.

"And… and we'll keep writing letters, won't we? You'll still help me?"

"Nothing could make me give that up. If you stopped writing, I'd still do it." Though she knew the impulse was irrational, Cath couldn't shake the feeling that the letters that she penned might count towards giving Nasim a sense of purpose.

"You'll stay while they're here, right? Tomorrow morning?"

"What, you think I'm gonna grab my suitcase and duck out of here the first chance I get? C'mon, Nasim. Who would tell them they need to order desserts with every meal if I didn't hang around?"

"I'd starve if no one told them," Nasim replied.

"That's exactly what I thought. By the way, do you know how you want our shifts to work?"

"Can't you just decide?"

Cath almost said, "No," but then saw the plea on Nasim's face. "Why don't you just have us work eight hours? We can rotate the shifts or draw straws or something to see who gets what each week."

"And you'll stay tomorrow morning," Nasim instructed.

"I promise."

Fifty-One

What am I supposed to do with all of this pain?

What do I do with the love? Am I supposed to leave it mired somewhere in the past's mud. But it's in me; it's stuck in me. It won't let go without some doing. Do I turn it into hatred, into indifference? Do I spit it up, leaving it in a puddle on my floor, purging it with my breakfast?

What do I do with the pity, the certainty that you were driven to something you will regret by – what? possession? insanity? Do I turn it into contempt for your blindness, your weakness, your foolishness? Do I feed it to my anger and take pleasure when the pity that I feel becomes deserved, when you are indeed a pitiable person?

And what of my anger? I try to soothe it with my certainty that it was not you – not the real you – who made this choice, but still it festers in the moments of doubt that are becoming more and more frequent. And even if it wasn't you! People who have had far less, people who have suffered far more – truly suffered! – have had the courage to find happiness. The entitlement, the arrogance to run in cowardice from something distasteful, the anger that bubbles in me when you say that you had no choice, that froths at the pain that you could have spared me if you had just a shred of empathy, it's putrid and toxic, thick-black-tar anger. How do I scrape that off my soul?

I thought once that the depth of my love for you was unknowable, and it's to those immeasurable depths that you've cast me so that, lost in grief, I can't imagine a surface above me. The darkness is too deep even to feel through.

I have to remind myself that you're hurting yourself, too. I dig into the deepest recesses of myself to remember the certainty that you love me – because that's fading so quickly, that certainty – and then, with great effort, I can muster the conviction that you're suffering, too (albeit at your own hand). That I know you well enough to know that this is not the right thing for you. That your turning tail is not a sign that you don't love me, that you don't have the desire to fight for me; it's a symptom of self–harm that stems from some origin that is not me. And then I forgive you again. And I love you again. And all I want is to help you through this time to the other side, when you will decide what is right for you. And I am so confident that being here, being with me is right.

Lucky you. You're where? Wherever: somewhere that you've never seen me, surrounded by people who have never met me, by things I've never touched. We've never shared the sights that you see. And here – what of here? The place that I am because *I moved here for you.* I can't take a step without touching a floor that I tread because of you. I can't take a breath without breathing the air that I breathe because of you. I'm ensnared in a tangle of reminders of you, suffocated by your panorama enclosing my life.

Everyone here thinks of you every time they see me, and I can't help but see it in their eyes.

Lucky you, free of me and my shackles and my burdens, free of the bothered conscience that kept you up at night. Free to live out whatever reality feels better than this one, and free of me to live it.

...

The weather had changed on the day Enzo left, a warmth unusual for the season replacing the cold spell that they had arrived to. For almost a week, the sun beat against the closed shutters of Nasim's room, spilling in through the skylight over her bed and bathing the rest of the coop in yellow warmth. When the weather turned sour again, the sky clouding over and the seasonal grey mist returning, Delia pulled on an extra layer against the nighttime chill before leaving her apartment for her shift. She turned the collar up and thrust her hands into the pockets, where one of them encountered a crumpled piece of paper, the origin of which she didn't recall until she unfolded it.

Nasim was as likely to be awake as she was asleep, no matter that it was the middle of the night. But regardless, she would be in bed and indifferent to the world. It wouldn't be difficult to talk to Peter.

He was sitting in the chair in Nasim's room when Delia arrived and beckoned him from the hall. She pressed the note into his hand and followed him into the kitchen, where they sat on opposite sides of the square table that had replaced the round one of the old coop. He read the note carefully, then folded it along its crease and smoothed out the wrinkles.

"It's a finer line we walk than I think anyone would

care to admit."

Delia was taken aback, "Is that a defense of him? Or a condemnation of us? I don't even know whether you're talking about his moral high ground or the fact that it sounds like they were fucking."

Peter shrugged, "All of it?"

"You think they were fucking?"

He shrugged again, "I don't think it matters. Her heart's broken, the same as if they were. It seems like he loved her, the same as if they were."

"Did you know?"

"Think how the intimacy that we share with her would look to anyone outside this circle. No one would be surprised if any of us were fucking her. She loves us all. We all love her. We're all in love with her. So no, I didn't know *this*. I didn't know what bound them. I didn't know why he left. But aren't we all guilty of... of whatever he's guilty of?"

"You're no help at all, Peter."

"What do you want? I don't think there's any clarity for us here, Delia."

FIFTY-TWO

Peter and Delia arrived together while Nasim and Cath were eating breakfast. Until the knock at the door, Nasim had hoped that they might not show up, that something would delay them at least another day. And though she hated that she had even had the thought, it wasn't lost on her that a simple car accident could prevent any upheaval whatsoever in her own life. But they arrived right on time, unharmed.

She had been given their names in advance but knew nothing else about them. They were both as young as Cath, probably just out of college. Possibly here, she tried to reassure herself, not because of any special love for the Project but enticed instead by the benefits and job security. Cath was the one who opened the door to let them in while Nasim surveyed them from the table. The two of them looked from Cath to Nasim and back, not sure who was who. They stood there in silence, each waiting for the other to speak first. If they had spent the past two months in training, it hadn't been in niceties.

Cath finally said, "I'm Cath, Nasim's third handler." She said it without intending any hierarchy, but it jarred Nasim, and she almost corrected - "first handler" - before realizing what that distinction would imply and stopping herself.

They shook hands with her, offering their names, their attentions really turned towards the person at the table. Nasim's long black hair was pulled back from her face in a loose ponytail, and her pallor was exacerbated by the trepidation welling up in her. There were dark circles around the green eyes that surveyed them.

"So you're Nasim," Peter said, taking a few steps towards her. Cath stepped in front of him, though, just enough to arrest his progress.

"Nasim prefers that we not wear shoes in the coop."

Peter hesitated a moment, weighing the intention of the gesture and the authority of the speaker, and then his face relaxed, and he pulled his shoes off, retreating to the door to set them down. "Of course," he said, with a smile that seemed genuine enough. "I should have thought to ask."

Delia, who had hung back, took her shoes off, too, and followed Peter around the couch to the table.

"Peter," he offered his hand.

"Delia," she offered hers.

Nasim took each in turn, wishing they had just appeared like Cath had, without ceremony, knowing instinctively to take her shoes off at the door. But there had been some expression her brother had used sometimes, *If beggars were horses... something something something.*

Cath rescued them from Nasim's silent stare. "I brought enough breakfast for everyone in case you haven't eaten," she said, pointing to a paper bag on the counter. "Croissants and a couple of bagels. Butter and jelly and such in the fridge." Cath was sitting in her seat again, her back to the kitchenette. "And plates in the cabinet above the sink, and flatware in the drawer to the right," she finished.

"What would I do without you?" Nasim mouthed to Cath while the other two rattled around the kitchen.

Cath smiled back and shrugged.

When they were all seated, the focus drifted back towards Nasim, who could think of nothing to say but, "I think eight hour shifts would be the best."

Cath covered her mouth to hide a smile that she couldn't suppress by force of will. That Nasim was looking at her and couldn't help but see it, only made it worse. She coughed to disguise a laugh she couldn't stifle, while Nasim, her glare giving way to an eye-roll, turned to Delia and said, "I'm sorry. I'm not good at this. This," she repeated capturing the four of them in the circling of her index finger. "I don't really know what to say."

Why had they sent her a man?

"I'm not any good at it either," Delia confided, and at least the discomfort was something they shared.

Peter looked from one to the other, and after chewing on the thought finally said, "It's no surprise, really. It's not as though any of us has ever been in this situation, and the Project hasn't given us any sort of script. So what that leaves is... if you want to tell us what our shifts are, by all means. We won't be put off. We'll have ample time to do all the rest when you're ready."

Nasim nodded, her jaw clenched. They weren't bad, these two people. They were nice and... and they weren't Cath. She forced herself to think, *I'm not losing Cath; I'll still have Cath*, and repeated it two more times, trying with each iteration to really believe it, to *know* it.

"Eight hour shifts. Midnight to eight, eight to four, four to midnight. Once a week you'll, uh, you'll draw straws to decide who gets which shift for the week. We can start it... What day is it?"

"Sunday," Peter answered.

"We can start tonight. At dinner. And until then… Until then…"

Cath broke in when the silence dragged on too long. "Maybe until then, Peter and Delia can each spend half the day with you and me, and I can show them some things?"

Nasim nodded and looked at Delia.

Cath started, "Peter if you-"

But he had already pushed back his chair to go. "Shall I come back around two, then?" He asked Nasim, reaching out to touch her shoulder, but the answer came from Cath, and his hand stopped short.

"Two is fine."

FIFTY-THREE

MAY 31, 2075

I'm scared. I'm scared for the present. I don't know what I'm doing. I'm adrift in this moment, can't find my feet, can't find anything.

I'm scared for the future. I don't even know what I want without you. I can't imagine what life without you means, can't even begin to comprehend it; and I don't want to. I don't want to live it, that life without you. I want to return to the seed of happiness I had finally planted, my tiny family intact – you are my family: you and the ersatz home I tried to make with you; you are my home. That seed, that little bit of happiness that I deserved, that was love. The happiness I had always wanted, it was love. The days were finally bearable, and that was love. And what if I get it back, the love and the happiness and you? Will I spend every day fearful that you'll change your mind again? That on a whim you might leave again?

But what wouldn't I give to get it back?

How many times did you lie to me, Enzo? How many times did we talk about the future – about the possibilities of it – after you'd already made up your mind to go? Every day that passes now the seeds of doubt sink their roots deeper into my past. How many times did you lie about dreams and futures and forevers?

Even in retrospect, even with hindsight, I can't see the signs. When the person I trusted most deeply deceives me, how can I trust anyone? How can I trust even myself if I'm so blind?

I could learn to trust you again if you came back.

Why is it not enough that you destroy my waking life? Not enough that you cut my present and future out from under me. Not enough, even, that you sour my past. You appear in my dreams, too, to leave me all over again. Or worse, to make me think that you've never gone, so that I wake thinking that I've dreamt the nightmare that is my real life. Your actions make you for the person you are, such a monster that you even haunt my sleep.

But if I can't have you back, then I'll take the fragments of fiction over reality.

...

"How long do you think she'll go without speaking?"

The exhaustion of grief had so overwhelmed Nasim that she spent most of the day asleep and then would lie in bed awake for half the night, drifting in and out of half–dreams. Peter and Delia had been returning to their own apartments less and less, first only to sleep on alternating shifts and shower quickly, and eventually only to retrieve a change of clothes. Instead they traded off sleeping in the second bedroom, each spending the other half of the night drowsing on the armchair next to Nasim's bed. During the day, they read or sat in silence or spoke in hushed whispers out of earshot of her bedroom, but having so little to do for her and knowing no one in this new place, even silent company was better than passing the hours alone.

Delia looked up from the book she was reading. "I'm more worried about how much longer she'll go without eating."

"They won't let her for much longer."

Delia put her book down and studied Peter's face. "I haven't reported that she hasn't been eating."

The implicit accusation hung for a while before Peter replied, "You know I wouldn't say anything."

"What do you think Enzo is doing?"

"Who knows."

"Jesus, Peter. You're the world's worst gossip. What do you and Nasim talk about all day?"

"Books, mostly. Ideas... We spend a lot of time not talking, too. Funny that I've never really wondered what you do, either."

FIFTY-FOUR

"They told us yesterday that most handlers have the food delivered," Delia said, walking across the campus with Cath.

"But if you have it delivered, you can't have a look at what they've got baking. And, more importantly, you can't smell it. They might tell you they've got fresh cookies when what they mean is that they've got cookies from yesterday they're trying to get rid of because they're already baking the afternoon pies; and what you really want is to get a piece of the pie action."

They were halfway across the campus, and Nasim was curled up on the couch holding a pillow and repeating the mantra, *I'm not losing Cath. I still have Cath.* Any desire to understand the origin of her fear was lost somewhere between the mantra and the tears she was fighting back. *I'm not losing Cath.* She hugged the pillow to her chest. *I still have Cath.*

"It'll just take a while. She's had a rough time. When I started, I don't think she had really had anyone to talk to in ages, and it all just came spilling out. I don't know how it'll be with two more people, exactly, but I'm sure it won't take too long for her to warm up to you."

"She really likes you?"

"It's a two-way street."

"Were you nervous? When you started? That she might not?"

Cath laughed. "How could I not have been? Not only is that the job, but if after they chose me from all those applicants, chose *my* tests from the pool, I failed at the one thing that I was practically guaranteed to succeed at, what would that say about me? It'd be like being told you're a math prodigy and then have trouble learning your times tables."

"But for me and Peter... we don't come in on the same terms that you did." Cath thought she was going to say something about the past two months, but if that's what she had meant, she changed her mind. "You had the luxury of setting the expectations. We have to meet them, and we don't even know what they are."

"Yet. You'll learn them. That's why I'm helping you through the day. And you can ask me anything. Delia," Cath stopped at the door to the kitchens, "She needs so badly to just be loved. I want you to promise me something. I know we don't know each other at all, but promise me anyways." She didn't wait for a reply before continuing, "If you don't love her, leave. She's suffered enough loss that she can take another, but she hasn't had nearly the love that she deserves; and we're the only ones here to give it to her."

Delia nodded, then said, "I believe in this, you know. The whole of it. Eden and Nasim, and anything I can do. I... uh... I would be doing it myself if I could. The children, I mean. But since I can't... It's an honor just to be here, to help in whatever way I can. There's nowhere I would rather be."

Cath pushed the door to the kitchen open, and the smell of baking pies flooded out. "Nasim doesn't want to be here," she told Delia. "Don't tell her that you do. She might misunderstand. She might think you want *her* to be here."

Nasim pulled her knees to her chest and hugged them there, the pillow wedged between. *I'm not losing Cath.* She pushed her head into the pillow. *I still have Cath.*

When Cath and Delia returned, Nasim had surrendered to the tears. Delia stood uncomfortably at the door while Cath wiped them away.

They ate lunch not long later, though Nasim had retreated so far within herself that she was inaccessible even to Cath. The couple of hours after lunch they passed by watching a movie to mask Nasim's withdrawal. When Peter arrived thirty minutes into the next movie, Delia left with relief, and at dinnertime Cath repeated the trek to the kitchen, this time with Peter in tow.

They drew straws at eight, though in the absence of straws, they had to make do with the flatware, the handles of which were indistinguishable. Spoon for the night shift, dinner fork for the morning, dessert fork for the afternoon. To Nasim's relief, Cath drew the spoon and so stayed while the other two disappeared.

"I can't do it, Cath." She had retreated to her bedroom. Since the men in suits had dropped her off, no one but she and Cath had been in her apartment. The whole thing had felt like her own private space, a cloister of solitude that she and Cath inhabited, but now the living room had been desecrated by the presence of other people.

"Of course you can do it. They're both going to love you as much as I do, Nasim. It'll be like having three of me instead of just one."

"Will you stay with me tonight?"

"I am."

"With me, though. Here."

"In your room?" Cath asked.

"Please."

"If that's what you want."

"My sister and I used to share a bed. Until she got sick, we did. Even though there were all those other empty beds in the house."

"I promise they'll love you as much as I do, Nasim. No one could know you and not love you."

The weeks that followed were uncomfortable, but Peter and Delia were kind and patient, even when Nasim wasn't. She sometimes attempted to fight the feeling of resentment that they stole hours from her time with Cath, tried to conceal it, at least, but she rarely cared enough to succeed. And when Peter and Delia failed to do the things that Cath had done, when they didn't hang her towel on the heater or didn't know to bring dessert even when she hadn't asked for one, she only sometimes bothered to hide her impatience. But Delia managed to pry a good mood from her sometimes the way Cath could, and Peter made her feel the safety that her brother had, a feeling she didn't even remember existed until she recognized it suddenly one afternoon. And both of them adapted to Nasim's frustrations and then rose to her expectations, and they both contributed gestures of their own love to the framework of habits that lured Nasim out of bed each morning.

FIFTY-FIVE

June 6, 2075

I barely feel anymore. The repetition of the pain or the exhaustion or some combination have sapped all the feeling from me, left me mostly numb. In little snatches I can reflect a glimmer of the anger that you must think consumes me. Not for the reasons you think, though. Not because you've eviscerated the future we'd imagined together, not because you did so without even a hint of warning, either. Not because you waited to do it until I had stuck myself in this place that you wanted, in the shadow of the mountain you wanted. The thing that really roils in me is that when you'd had enough, you just shrugged your shoulders and said, "Sorry," and that was the end of it. Is that all I've ever been worth to you?

But this is an old story, isn't it? I'm not living something exceptional, am I? People love, people leave, hearts break. And that's better isn't it? To suffer average suffering instead of... instead of exceptional suffering. There's some consolation in that, isn't there?"

...

When Nasim woke, it was to Delia shaking her shoulder, rousing her in whispered fear. "Nasim. Nasim, wake up."

Nasim's hands, pressed between her thighs while she slept, felt sticky.

"You were shouting," Delia said, her voice more relaxed now that Nasim's eyes were open and her cries abandoned somewhere on the other side of the curtain of sleep.

Nasim pulled the blanket back and the sheets, a red handprint left on them in evidence. Her thighs were stained with blood, and beneath her the white sheet was spotted with concentric circles of bright red and brown and black.

Delia's eyes widened. She grabbed for Nasim, as though she might be slipping away, but then went instead for the phone.

Nasim's face was expressionless. She tried to absorb the feeling of another loss as she sat naked on her bed, but a voice whispered in her ear that she had already lost everything, so how could there be anything more to lose?

Delia tried wrap to Nasim's bathrobe around her shoulders, tried to wipe the blood from her, tried to move her out of the bed, but Nasim was frozen. The nurse arrived not long after, trailed by a second with a wheelchair. They lifted her out of the bed, dropping her limp arms into the bathrobe and pulling it snug around her body before wheeling her out of the coop. Delia followed them, called Peter – who had gone home to sleep in his own bed this once – on the way out the door and then left the phone in the hall as she ran after the wheelchair.

It was unusual that an Eve make it so long without a miscarriage, the doctor reassured them. Nasim sat on the examination table, and Peter and Delia stood nervously in the tiny space beside her. As much as they tried to control it, the doctor told them, the body was an instrument of Nature, and in Nature, some things thrive, and others whither. She should take some time to recuperate, and they would simply try again. It was still early enough in the pregnancy that he prescribed only three months before the next insemination.

Nasim was wheeled back to her coop, laid back into her bed, the sheets of which were white and clean again. The bathrobe had disappeared, replaced in the doctor's office by a set of her own clothes, and now a fresh robe hung on the wrong hook on the outside of the bathroom door. Delia, too weary to stay, retreated to the handlers' bedroom, and Peter assumed a spot on the bed beside Nasim where they cried together.

FIFTY-SIX

"I was thinking maybe popcorn and a fireside book this morning." Peter handed Nasim her towel as she emerged from the shower.

"What's it like out?" The windows had still been opaque when she had gotten into the shower, though even the lazy winter sun had been up for a few hours already.

"Miserable. Ten below, and I couldn't see five feet in front of me on the walk over. I couldn't tell if it was actually snowing or if it was just wind blowing what's already there."

Nasim shuddered at the thought. Winter, harder to bear than the rest of the seasons.

"We'd better turn up the thermostat and switch on every light in the coop." Nasim had finally learned how to ask for things, though her requests still sounded like group activities.

"Already done."

"Did you set it at seventy-three?"

"I thought that's what you might like."

Nasim smiled, "Maybe seventy-four today."

"What kind of popcorn do you want?"

"What do you mean, 'what kind'?"

"Buttered or caramel corn or kettle corn or cheese?"

Nasim's towel was wrapped around her hips, her eyes meeting Peter's in the reflection in the mirror. "All of them."

He couldn't help but laugh. "All of them?"

"That's what I said." She smeared a cream on her face that Delia had given her when the crisp autumn air and her frequent showers had dried out her skin. "Why, what kind would you have picked?"

"Oh, I don't know, I always liked the cheese and caramel mix. So I guess I would have settled for just two of them."

"What a bore you are, Peter," Nasim said, her green eyes flashing back to his reflection. "Tell them that if they make me a caramel apple, they can just send two kinds, but otherwise, I want five. At least."

"What's the fifth?"

"Tell them to be creative." Peter turned to go place the order, but Nasim stopped him. "Oh, and Peter?"

"Mm?"

"Don't pick it up. Not in this weather. Make one of them bring it."

"But how will I know what cookies to bring back if I can't tell which are freshest?"

"Don't be ridiculous." He turned to go again before she finished, "Just ask them which are freshest, and tell them to bring a dozen."

By the time Nasim had dressed - all her ragged clothes had been replaced in the months when Cath had been her only handler - the fireplace was lit, and Peter was sitting on the floor in front of it, his back against the side of the couch and his book open on his lap.

"They didn't have anything but Red Delicious on hand, so I told them to skip the apple."

"What kind of cookies?"

"Oh! I forgot the cookies."

"You didn't."

Delia or Cath would have kept the farce up awhile longer, but she had the sense that Peter teased her not because he enjoyed it but because he saw that she liked it. "I didn't. Spice cookies came out this morning."

"Peter?" Nasim began, sinking onto crossed legs before the fire.

"Mm?"

"How many Eves are there?"

"About a one and a half million," Peter replied.

"In the world?"

"They're all here."

"Here?!"

"Not on this campus," he clarified, "but, as far as I know, no other country has an Eden Project yet. I saw something a while back about the UK, but I don't know that that's gone anywhere."

"What about here? On this campus? How many?"

"I have no idea," he admitted.

"Will you find out for me?"

"Of course, I will."

"About this campus and about the other ones. I don't even know where the other ones are. And about other countries. You'll find out and tell me. Isn't it strange that I don't know?"

"No stranger than that I don't know, I suppose."

"You'll find out, though?"

"Of course, I will," he reassured her.

"What are you reading?"

"Dostoevsky."

"Any good?" she asked.

"I think so."

"I finished my last book. Maybe I should read that one, too."

Peter hesitated a moment, weighing his reluctance to feed the melancholy inside her against his obligation to fulfill her request. "How about this? I'm halfway through already, so why don't I start something new. We can read it at the same time. Book club for two. Let's read *Dune*. I read it so long ago I don't remember anything except that it was excellent."

"Display next to the fireplace," Nasim commanded the computer, and the text appeared on the wall in front of her. "Do you think if I hadn't been an Eve, you still would have been picked as a handler?" she asked, ignoring the words that were gently scrolling up the wall. "Like, do you think it's just what you were meant to do? Or…?"

"I don't know."

"Of course, you don't *know*. What do you *think*, though?"

"I've never really thought about it."

"No, I guess most people don't spend as much time exploring the alternatives."

The silence that followed while Peter waited to see if Nasim would continue was interrupted by a knock at the door. A snow-covered man in a thick parka, his hood still cinched around his face, was stomping his boots in the hall outside. He thrust a paper bag at Peter and left wordlessly.

"Don't they usually use golf carts to deliver?" Nasim asked.

"Indeed, they do."

They both laughed at the image it conjured, the parka-clad man climbing back into a golf cart and maneuvering it through the blizzard that was howling outside. Peter tore open the stapled bag in the kitchenette, and the coop smelled instantly of cookies, not just the spice cookies he had mentioned, but there were sugar cookies and chocolate chip, too. And piping hot apple cider and three dozen tea bags and just the two kinds of popcorn - cheese and caramel - because he knew she wouldn't want the others, anyhow. Nasim had been drawn from her comfortable spot on the floor by the aroma and hovered behind Peter, waiting impatiently for him to plate the food.

"We can't just eat the popcorn out of the bags?"

"Have to mix it up. It's better that way."

"Three kinds of cookies."

"Don't sound too disappointed," he teased.

"Peter?"

"Mm?"

"You'll find out about the other Eves for me?"

"I will."

FIFTY-SEVEN

Something was pulling her into frigid depths, the water black around her and only far above could she see light. It had her ankles or her legs – a cinder block tied to her feet or a tentacle or gravity – tugged her down, the water around her so cold that she had become aware of the nerves in the back of her eyes, of the bones in the depths of her ears, suddenly perceptible because they had turned to ice. Her lungs, just full, were being squeezed smaller and smaller, and the reflex to breath was itching somewhere in her mind. *Don't.* Her hands wanted to reach for the light above her, already fading, but she forced them down, feeling for what was sinking her. There was something – was it something? – but her fingers were too numb to feel.

Her lungs convulsed – once, twice – but she had kept her throat closed. The reflex, though, the unfulfilled promise of air made her even hungrier for it.

The light was further. Maybe too far already. Even if she were free at this moment.

Her lungs convulsed again – twice, thrice. *Don't.*

Her hands had forgotten their task. They were stretched towards a surface that was barely perceptible anymore.

Her lungs convulsed again, and this time she couldn't stop it. Her airway opened, the water poured in; she suddenly became aware of every alveolus as it burned with the cold of the water that filled it.

And then she could see herself. In spite of the blackness, she could see her legs pointed down, pulled by nothing, her arms raised over her head, pointed at life. Her hair waved softly overhead, trailing her continued descent into unknown depths.

From outside herself, she saw a hand that she couldn't feel grab her wrist and yank her back. Pull her up and up into the light she couldn't see. And they emerged together from the cold she couldn't feel into air that might have been warm.

She could see herself prone beside the water. It was Cath who was kneeling over her, water dripping off the end of her nose, her mouth forming words Nasim couldn't hear. But she knew what they were, she knew that they were shouted: "Get up! Get up!"

And Cath raised a fist over her head and brought it down like a hammer onto Nasim's chest.

...

Nasim awoke with a gasp that filled her lungs from empty. Her back arched, her whole body rising up with the force of the breath she took, with the force of the life coming back into her. There were rivulets running down her skin – water, not sweat, because she could still feel the penetrating cold of the drowning in her. Her senses were slowly awakening: the darkness of the room on which she had not yet opened her eyes, the spring of the bed beneath her body, the sensation of the goosebumps popping up on her wet skin.

She opened her eyes.

Cath was on the bed, straddling her on all fours, desperation etched into her face. "Get up, Nasim!" She grabbed Nasim's shoulders and shook them, "Get up!"

...

Nasim opened her eyes to a dark room. She was naked on top of her bed, but she was warm and dry. Her hand was over her breast, and she could feel the steady companionship of her heartbeat pulsing under her palm and the rise and fall of her chest as she breathed the fresh ponderosa air. From beside her she could hear Cath saying, "Nasim, get up."

...

Nasim awoke snuggled deep into her warm bed. The room was brightly lit by the sun. Cath was standing next to her. "Nasim, it's time to get up."

FIFTY-EIGHT

JUNE 29, 2065

"Just because I don't mind having them around doesn't mean that I don't miss the days when it was just us."

"I know, Nasim. But if you could go back to 'just us,' you'd miss them being around."

"Possibly." Nasim signed the letter she was writing and stuffed in into an envelope. Cath had just sealed hers.

"Do you want to take them now, or do you want me to mail them on my way back to my apartment?" Cath asked.

"You take them later."

"You sure?" Last year, hot summer afternoons had enticed Nasim out of her coop with some regularity, but now she almost never left it.

"Yeah, I don't want to go."

"I was talking to Delia about-" Cath started.

"I don't want to know."

"Why?"

"It's something you're both worried about. I can tell. From... from knowing you. I'm sick of hearing what you're worried about. Just... just let me be miserable."

"Nasim, listen to yourself."

"What I'd give to not have to."

"Nasim-"

"No! I'm not going to be reasonable! Why do I always have to be reasonable?" Nasim pounded a fist onto the desk. Then she stood, drew her hand back and turned it to smash her knuckles into the wood. Cath grabbed her arms, dragging her away from the desk. Nasim tried to wrench free, but Cath had a firm grip; and Nasim's desire to fight fizzled. They collapsed together onto the couch, both breathing heavily.

"I don't want to be reasonable anymore," Nasim whispered when she had caught her breath.

Peter and Delia had only seen flashes of the darkness that punctured the monotony of depression. It was Cath who bore the brunt of the anger bubbling through the apathy. It was Cath, too, who had the hardest time touching Nasim through the darkness because it was only with Cath that Nasim felt comfortable enough to sink ever deeper.

"I don't know what to tell you, Nasim. Do you have a choice? What would you be if not reasonable?"

Nasim sulked in silence.

"What we can do is write letters and make phone calls. And that's what we do. We fight all we can. What else is left?"

"Nothing's left."

"Well, so then, what? We can do that - we can keep fighting - or we can give up. What's the third choice? What else is there?" Cath asked.

"There's nothing."

"So pick one, Nasim. Keep fighting or accept it."

"We *are* fighting," Nasim's voice grew louder.

"Then act like it's going to make a difference!"

"It isn't going to make a difference."

"Maybe that's why you're so miserable all the time.

Maybe if you believed even a little bit, maybe if you had even a little hope-"

"Stop!" Nasim jumped to her feet. "Stop talking about it like it's your cause. Stop talking about it as though... as though it can hurt you. It hurts *me*. It steals *my* life. What does it matter to you?"

Cath swallowed the hurt she felt, dismissed the words that the pain evoked in her, tried to recover her patience again. "*You* matter to me, Nasim. The fight matters to me because you matter to me. Because it hurts *you*. Because it steals *your* life."

"It isn't fair!" Nasim cried.

"It isn't fair."

Nasim threw her hands into the air, her fists clenched, her lungs bursting with the breath that fed her anger, and then she deflated, falling slowly to her knees, her hands catching the weight of her torso and her chin sinking to her empty chest. "We're not going to win."

Out of words, Cath knelt next to Nasim and held her, and when Delia appeared at the door an hour later, Cath waved her off.

"Nasim?" she finally whispered, not sure if one or both of them had fallen asleep there while the sun set and the room turned black.

Nasim didn't move, but Cath heard her grunted reply.

"C'mon. Get up."

Nasim shook her head but let herself be dragged to her feet. When Cath tried to move her towards the couch, though, she pulled away and trudged instead into her bedroom, where she collapsed onto her bed. Cath followed her.

"You haven't eaten anything since breakfast, and you barely touched that."

Nasim's face was buried in her comforter.

"Maybe if you showered? You could eat and then..." But that's not how it worked when Nasim was tangled in anger and hopelessness and apathy, when she had sunk to the depths that she could reach only in the safety of Cath's presence. So instead Cath went out to the living room to call Peter and tell him that he, too, need not come for his shift. Then she returned to Nasim's room and undressed her, coaxed the comforter out from under her and tucked it in around her.

Cath sat next to Nasim that night, as she had the night after Delia and Peter had arrived. Nasim's hand clutched hers, the only sign that Nasim even knew she was there. Eventually the headboard felt too hard on her back, and she lay down and fell asleep not much after.

Cath awoke the next morning before Nasim did and eased her hand free so that she could switch the window to opaque before the pre-dawn grey brightened to day.

"What am I going to do about you?" she asked the back of Nasim's sleeping head. "If my being here mires you deeper in that tar, should I go? Or is it that you need someone who loves you to go there with you? Nasim, what are *you* going to do about you? What are you going to do with all that pain?"

FIFTY-NINE

When Nasim opened her eyes, the cloud-filtered light of mid-morning illuminated her bedroom. She felt a warm hand gently squeezing hers. Delia's, she realized as she opened her eyes. Cath stood at the foot of her bed. She looked the same as she had the day she had left. The same wisp of hair – too short for her ponytail – bothering her eye, the same red nail polish, too. Nothing was different: not the cut of her clothing, not the line of her waist. Her face, her smile, the creases across her forehead, they were unchanged, too. And she still sank her weight progressively more into her right hip as she stood. "Get up," Cath said.

Don't want to, Nasim thought.

Cath shrugged, "Your life." She had probably meant to leave it at that, but couldn't resist adding, "Just saying that the act of getting up today will make doing it again tomorrow that much easier."

Nasim squeezed Delia's hand then let it go. "I should get up today."

Delia tried to mask her surprise. It was the first that Nasim had spoken. "Do you want to shower? Or eat? What should we–"

Cath was looking out the window now, talking through Delia. "Croissants, maybe. And you stink of grief. You should shower."

"You can order breakfast while I shower," Nasim said to Delia. *And you can shove it,* she thought to Cath. She had been standing under the hot water, her face raised to it in wonder at how this could be so different from the water that had drowned her the night before, when she thought to add, "Croissants!"

By the time breakfast had arrived, Nasim's desire for food had waned, and she found herself tearing chunks of pastry off either end to make it look eaten.

"At least don't go back to bed," Cath prodded.

Fine, Nasim thought, and she trudged across the living room. *Can sleep here just as well.* She slumped into the couch, Delia watching her with silent curiosity.

Peter – now back on a regular rotation with Delia after the upheaval of the past month – three days later found himself walking a few paces behind Nasim, who had been goaded into a walk by the ghost of Cath.

"The fresh air will do you good," Cath called after them.

Just doing it to get away from you, Nasim thought as she watched her own feet step one in front of the other.

When Peter and Delia crossed paths during their shift change, Peter motioned for Delia to step into the damp night air. Even outside, he kept his voice low. "She's doing much better than I thought she would be."

"How can all this have happened this way, Peter? I'm still not satisfied with any of the answers."

Peter shrugged, "Are there answers that *would* satisfy you?" And ignoring Delia's look of annoyance, he continued, "The point is that Nasim is doing better than I expected. Interspersed in that deep darkness, I catch an occasional glimmer of her doing something perfectly normal. She went for a walk today. Unprompted by me. She's mostly ignored me, actually. I don't know that she ever noticed my following along. But... you know, when he first left it occurred to me to wonder if a person could die of grief. Or maybe that's not quite the right sentiment. Maybe what I wondered was whether a person could die of the cumulative weight of life's injustices."

"And then the child," Delia added.

"And then the child," Peter agreed.

"But she seems... okay?"

"So you think so, too?" he asked.

"It's not a high bar," Delia replied.

"No, but it's something."

Sixty

"C'mon. We're going outside. You and I - both, together - are going outside." Delia was pulling Nasim to her feet from the cozy depths of the couch, where they had been sitting since breakfast.

"Go outside if you want, but I'm not coming."

"Nasim, when was the last time you left your coop?"

"I had a doctor's appointment last week." She felt a tide of panic rise up in her as she remembered the one piercing scream that had come from the exam room next to hers. It had rung in her ears all day and kept her up most of the night, too.

"That doesn't count."

"It should." Nasim folded her arms across her chest.

"The leaves are so beautiful, though. In four weeks, they'll all have fallen, and everything will look bleak and dead until spring, but right now...! And it's warm. And the sun is shining. And the colors, Nasim."

"I can see the colors from here." She glanced over the back of the couch at the bay window and the wooded landscape that lay beyond the green lawn.

"Ten minutes. Give me ten minutes outside, and if

you're not enjoying it, we'll come right back, and you can glue yourself back to the couch and wallow in your self-pity."

A trace of anger crossed Nasim's face. "Self-pity?"

"I'm not judging," Delia shrugged. "I'm just... it shouldn't prevent you from feeling the sun on your skin every once in a while."

"That has nothing to do with why I don't want to go. I'm just not interested. Go yourself."

"You know I can't."

"I give you permission. Go."

"That's not that point, anyways," Delia argued.

"If the point is that I should go, then the answer is that I don't want to. I don't see what else there is to discuss."

"Nasim, *please*."

Delia was nothing if not persistent. Once she dug in her heels, a disagreement could easily go on longer than a walk would. "Fine. Ten minutes," Nasim conceded.

They left through the glass doors, sat side by side on the edge of the tile to put on their shoes. Delia had handed her a windbreaker as they left. Like most of the clothes she wore, she had no idea where it had come from and whether it belonged to her or whether it was lent.

No more than a minute into the walk, Nasim was already regretting that she never wore a watch. Her legs were leaden, and though the sun was warm, the breeze wasn't. Her hands were cold, but she could feel her armpits already growing sticky with sweat under a sweater and the windbreaker, both zipped to her neck. She could barely see the ground in front of her feet through her eyes squinted against the brightness.

Delia's pace was easy, but she stayed a half step ahead of Nasim and, in doing so, set the direction towards the woods. When they reached the tree line, Nasim looked back, wondering how long they had been gone, but the coop looked too close to have been more than a couple of minutes' walk.

"How long's it been?" she asked.

"I didn't look to see what time we left."

"Well, what time is it now?"

"Twelve thirty."

Delia led the way down a narrow dirt track that, but for a few logs that lay across it and that they clambered over, seemed well-kept.

"What time is it now?"

"Twelve thirty-two."

They walked down two more twists in the path, and a small patch of prairie opened up in front of them. The path cut across it, but Delia walked a few steps to the right instead, where she sat on a downed log. It was no more than fifty feet to the other side of the field. The line of trees across from them was decorated in green and orange and yellow, and the grass was shoulder-high and sandy-hued; and the wind whipped it in swirls and bent it in waves. The meadow was lower than the woods around it, and from the edge where the log was, they had a view of the whole thing.

Seated side by side, they watched the wind playing in the grass and tearing leaves from the trees. A gust showered them in orange and yellow and crackling, dry brown. The sun was angled on their backs, lighting up the trees across from them and replacing the warmth that the wind stole. Somewhere in the space between the sun and the wind, Nasim forgot her pain for a handful of moments.

By the time they returned to the coop, Peter was waiting to begin his shift. Delia disappeared when she saw him, so when Nasim turned to say something to her about the walk, she was already gone.

"I haven't had lunch yet," she said instead to Peter while she sat at the glass door and took off her shoes. "I'm thinking something warm. And cheesy."

"Have you ever had tomato bisque with cheddar in it?" Peter asked.

"Like dipped a grilled cheese in it?"

"No, the cheese is just in the soup." Before she could answer, he said, "You're going to love it. I'll be back in twenty minutes."

Nasim, windbreaker still on, sat down on the couch. The sense of losing herself in something else was fading, the draw of her turmoil within growing, but she could still feel the warmth from the sun; and when she closed her eyes, she tried to recapture the play of the wind.

The bisque was decadent, the last few bites more molten cheese than soup, and Peter had brought a mille-feuille, too.

"Nothing for you?"

"I already ate," Peter said.

"It's better to eat with company, though."

"Even if company already ate?"

Nasim nodded.

"I'll remember that," Peter replied.

"I have no doubt."

"Books this afternoon?"

"Movie, I think. Can you find me something about... I don't know. Fall? Something about fall," she confirmed.

"And popcorn?"

"Always popcorn."

"What kind?"

"The usual."

Peter called in an order for cheese and caramel popcorn and picked the right movie and ate with her, though he wasn't hungry.

SIXTY-ONE

Nasim was sitting in her old living room cross–legged in front of a nascent fire that Cath was nursing. Her dream self had tried to start it, but her fingers had felt impossibly stiff, her arms unwieldy, and Cath had pushed her aside

When one of the big logs caught, Cath turned her back to the flames and faced Nasim and said, "You're going through the motions, Nasim. There's no fight in you, but the seed of it is still there."

"I'm not going to fight."

"When you're strong enough to fight, the fighting will heal you. It will give you purpose. You don't have to win the first battle, but at least take a step towards the battlefield."

"It's not what I want," Nasim replied.

"Write a letter like we used to. It's a sign of life."

"Cath, I hated writing letters. I did it out of hopelessness. And later I only did it for you."

"*We* only did it for *you*, Nasim. If you aren't your own advocate, who will be? People like Peter and Delia? People like Enzo? Are those the voices you want representing you?"

"How were you any better than they are?"

"That's the point: Anyone you lean on will eventually let you fall. All you have is yourself; you have nothing else. Peter, Delia, Enzo, me – you can't count on any of us."

Nasim drew a sharp breath, but she held her retort in her lungs for a count, then sighed it out.

Cath shrugged, "See? You know I'm right."

In response, Nasim willed herself awake.

It was the first time she had woken up alone since Enzo had left. Delia was talking to someone at the door, mumbled words Nasim couldn't make out. She waited through a moment of indecision, hoping the conversation would conclude in that time. Then she slowly climbed out of bed, pausing at the edge and again wishing that Delia would return. Nasim gradually made her way to the shower, listening at each step for the door to close; but it didn't, and she turned on the water herself and stepped in.

Nasim was unaware of how long she had been standing in the water, her forehead resting against the shower door, when Delia spoke, "You're up!? It's early. If I had known, I would have–"

"It doesn't matter," Nasim cut her off. Then less tersely added, "It's fine."

Delia waited until Nasim had turned off the water to say, "There's breakfast if you want any."

She ate more than Delia expected her to and then pulled a book from the shelf and settled into the couch. Delia watched it all in silence, worried that this progress – this sudden chain of normal events – was fragile enough that acknowledgement might shatter it.

"You can read your own book instead of staring at me," Nasim eventually suggested.

When in the early afternoon Delia finally asked her what she was reading, Nasim closed the book over her finger to look at the cover. "*Siddhartha.*"

"Do you want lunch?"

"It's the right time for it."

But lunch arrived, and Nasim poked at the potatoes and prodded the fish and did very little in the way of eating. Then, still staring at the mess of food on her plate, she announced that she was going to take a nap. She stood up from the table and, eyes fixed on her feet, trudged back to her bedroom as Delia shoveled the last couple of bites of food into her mouth before hurrying after Nasim.

"Pathetic," Nasim heard Cath call after them.

She was still in bed when Peter arrived. He and Delia convened briefly in the kitchen so that she could relay the day's development. "Those few hours could have just as well have happened three months ago. It's not that she was her normal, happy self, but she seemed like her normal, melancholy self. You know what I mean? Run-of-the-mill depression instead of this grief she's been mired in. And then it came back. But still."

SIXTY-TWO

The passage of the next year was marked by the increasing frequency of the doctor's appointments that Nasim had endured since her delivery by suit-clad men to the room outside of Chicago. By early spring, a nurse had been assigned to visit her coop every morning to take her temperature and collect a urine sample.

"It'll be a reason to get up in the morning." Cath was standing in the bathroom doorway waiting for Nasim to tire of her shower. "And a reason to get out of the shower," she added, glancing at her watch and weighing the difficulty of rushing Nasim against the likely impatience of the nurse who would arrive in the next few minutes.

"It's a shitty reason."

"I didn't say it wasn't," Cath replied.

"What do you think they'd do if I didn't get out of the shower?"

"Nothing you'd like."

The water turned off, and Nasim stepped out from behind the fogged glass.

"But what do you think?" Nasim asked again.

"Nasim, if I could think like they do… I'd probably kill

myself."

"Do you think if I asked they'd give me a mirror that doesn't fog up?" Nasim wondered.

"I think they'd line your coop with mirrors that don't fog up if you asked."

"But how would we test that? That they were really the kind that didn't fog up?"

A third voice called from the living room, "Hello?"

"Shit!" Nasim started. That she sulked and dragged her feet didn't make her any less nervous about being late, about being in trouble. "Stall him, would you?"

"What's he going to do with me?" Cath laughed.

"I don't know. Stall him anyways." Nasim had rushed into the bedroom to dress, her towel held like a cape between her naked body and the door of the bedroom in case the nurse appeared there.

Cath disappeared down the hall. "She'll be out in a minute," Nasim heard as she hopped on one foot into her socks.

It was only a few seconds before she appeared breathless in the living room, her unbrushed hair dripping onto her t-shirt. The nurse was a man - why were all the people here men? - tall, with a shaved head and a smile Nasim would have preferred he keep to himself. He was standing in front of the couch and seemed willing neither to sit nor to allow access to it.

"Cups for the urine samples." He handed a bag with seven sealed containers to Cath. "And this." He handed Nasim what appeared to be a pill, but it was too dense, too solid. "You swallow it. It'll transmit your internal temperature to a computer a few times a day."

Cath leaned in close to look for herself. "And when it...comes out?" she asked.

"I'll be by every morning to pick up the urine sample, and when the computer alerts us that a temperature reading fails, I'll bring you a new probe." He looked at Cath, "Don't worry. They're disposable."

Nasim rolled the capsule between her fingers.

"If you don't mind," the nurse said, watching her.

"Oh, of course." She placed it in her mouth.

"It's easier with water." But she had already swallowed it.

The nurse took a small device from his back pocket and touched the screen a few times. "It's working," he said. "If you've no questions…"

"No," Nasim said, and Cath shook her head.

"Have a nice day, ladies."

When the door closed behind him, Nasim turned to Cath. "So, not *really* a reason to get out of bed. I can pee in the cup the night before."

"Well, it was a reason to get up today. We'll deal with tomorrow when we get there."

"Think us up something to do, would you?"

"Breakfast might be a start," Cath suggested.

"But for the rest of the morning."

"We could…" She stopped before mentioning writing letters. She knew Nasim would dismiss the idea, didn't think she could bear to hear the defeat in Nasim's voice again. "I don't know. We'll think about it over breakfast?"

"Cinnamon rolls?" Nasim wondered.

"I'll call it in."

Over breakfast - cinnamon rolls and Earl Grey - Cath suggested, "We could go down to the gym."

"Nah."

"I've been. It's really nice. Has a pool and everything."

"Nah."

"There's that theater on sire that opened a couple of months ago."

"We can get anything they'd play in the theater here and sit on our own couch. Why would we go there?"

"I used to love baking cookies when I was growing up."

"Yeah, but when you have someone who'll bake them for you, why do it yourself?"

"So if that's all no good, what is good? What do you actually want to do?" Cath wished she were better at concealing the impatience.

"I don't know."

"You only know what you don't want?"

"I guess I've never really… had anything I liked to do," Nasim said.

"What about growing up, though?"

Nasim shrugged. "I played 'cops and robbers' with my… my brother and sister." She always stumbled over any mention of them.

"And?"

"And nothing. I did my chores. I helped my mom cook. I read, but I do enough of that now. More than enough."

"What kinds of things did you *like*, though?"

Nasim shrugged again.

"Nasim, how are we going to come up with something to do if you don't like doing anything?"

"I don't know."

"Board games? Cards?"

"I don't know. I've never played," Nasim said.

"Never? Okay, there's a thing we can rectify. I have a deck of cards in my apartment. I'll go get it."

"I've never been to your apartment."

"You want to come?" Cath was surprised at the implied request.

"Why do you sound so skeptical? You've spent the last three years basically living here, and I've never even seen where you live."

Cath's apartment was a single room. Though the space was large, it was furnished as though it were tiny. A twin-sized bed stood opposite a small couch, a coffee table set in front of it doubling as her dining room. One wall held the same style kitchenette that Nasim's coop did - all appliances and no counter space.

Cath could see Nasim's eyes hesitate on the empty spaces. "It was the furniture I had in my dorm. I'd buy more, but, I don't know. This seems like enough. Here, I've got them." She held up a deck of cards. "It would be more fun to play with four than with two."

"There's the Eve next door... I've sometimes seen her and thought we could maybe be friends, but then... Well we could've asked her, but she's on bedrest."

"Who told you that?" Cath asked.

"Peter did."

Neither of them said anything more about it, and they passed the rest of the morning playing two-handed euchre.

SIXTY-THREE

Nasim's nose was deep in a book when Cath cleared her throat and, when that failed to elicit a response, said, "All you do all day is sit there."

And what should I be doing all day? Nasim thought.

"You consume. You listen, you watch, you read. Why don't you produce? Why don't you speak and act?"

I'm doing what I want to do.

"Easy things aren't fulfilling. You're just distracting yourself from the reality, but there's so much more to life than distraction, Nasim. Seize it! Drive your destiny."

Drive my destiny? It's insulting to suggest that the reason I'm here is some failure of mine.

"If you do nothing to resist, who else could be to blame?"

Why are you here? You left. You couldn't stand to be here any longer. You thought you were suffering watching me suffer, so you left; and you should have stayed gone.

Cath stood up from the chair where she had been sitting, took the three steps to the glass door, and gazed out. "You're changing the subject."

But what did you really feel? Nothing! What you felt

was nothing *to what I felt. Some poor distorted reflection, some shadow of the real thing, maybe. At least Peter, at least Delia, they never pretended to feel it. Because what did that accomplish? Other than to amplify the misery of my... my shit lot. More pain to go around!* Nasim wished that Cath would turn around.

No one else has ever had the arrogance to think they feel what I feel. No one else has ever thought that their making themselves suffer might somehow heal me. No one else has ever been so stupid. She wanted to see Cath's face.

Countless people have told me that the only way to live with this is to accept it. They've spent twelve years whispering it in my ear: That fighting the pain makes it worse. That gouging the scar never lets it heal. That I could be happy – or whatever it is that I'm capable of being – if I just stopped digging my claws into the wound.

But not you. "Cut yourself again to remind yourself of the injustice," you told me. "Let me scratch myself to feel it with you," you begged. So I did. Again and again, I scraped off the scabs, dug at the raw flesh, until I'd torn all the way through my body, until the nerves didn't exist anymore, until the pain I felt was soul-deep.

And then you left.

Because your cuts hurt.

And you left me with festering wounds.

And the only thing I'd ever learned to do was to claw them open as soon as they stopped oozing.

There was so much pain in me that I didn't even feel you leave, a blister on my heel when my arms were peeling off.

Cath still had not turned around, but Nasim didn't care anymore.

After you'd gone I wished... for so long I wished that

you could feel the pain I felt. You deserved to know what I really suffered. For teaching me to hurt, you deserved to have to bear it. For choosing to be weaker than I have ever been allowed to be, you deserved it. You think what you fled was pain enough to break you? Feel mine, too!

Nasim's eyes dropped to her white knuckles clutching the book she had been reading. She tried to quiet the sound of blood rushing in her ears, willed her heart to slow. And then she opened the book again and resumed reading.

When the sun set a few hours later, Nasim turned to Peter, who, when he was ahead in his reading, had taken to doing crossword puzzles in the hours of silence. "I miss my fireplace," she said.

The air was damp and the evening, cool. She flirted with the idea of trying the heat, though she was sure the furnace had been shut off for the summer. A fire would indeed be perfect, but Peter was nevertheless surprised to hear her say it. "I'm willing to bet that we could find a place on the grounds for an illicit fire pit," he offered.

He couldn't see her expression well with the already–dim light now fading into dusk, and so he strained to hear whatever he could in her voice. But her answer required no interpretation: "Let's go find the spot."

"Now?" He stifled the surprise in his voice and added, "Or maybe tomorrow when it's light out."

"Now," she said and stood up from the couch, stretching her stiff legs. She was at the door by the time he caught up to her, and then she regained some of her lead as he seized two coats from the closet before hurrying after her into the mist.

She had only walked the grounds a couple of times and so chose the direction at random. After a few minutes, she slowed the frenzied pace she had set. "Do you have any thoughts on where?" she asked Peter.

He couldn't help but laugh. "What are we doing out here, Nasim? You've been cloistered away in your coop for the past two months. You've barely spoken a word. And now we're going nowhere in particular, but we're going there like bats out of hell. What's going on here?"

The way Nasim looked at him with uncharacteristic big, doe eyes unsettled him. It felt like she was seeing everything for the first time, like she was drinking in so much at once that she barely saw him at all. "We're looking for a place to put a fire pit so that we can have fires. Do you have a suggestion, or no?"

In her hurry, she had started walking again before he said, "Yes, I do. This way," and she turned to follow him back the way they had come.

Cath's ghost – silent since Nasim's reprimand – trailed sullenly behind them

SIXTY-FOUR

When Peter arrived in the morning, Delia was with him, and Cath joined them in the living room.

"She's still asleep," Cath said. "And I can't imagine she'll be up much before the nurse comes for the urine sample, but you'd know better this week than I would."

"That's about right," Peter said. "So that gives us two hours. Won't take more than forty minutes, I wouldn't think."

It took even less time than that to hang the decorations they had brought, ribbons and garlands, half autumn-colored and the other half decorated with balloons and *Happy Birthday*'s. As they were finishing, Delia went to the kitchen to retrieve a cake they had ordered, one with Nasim's name written across the top in frosting.

So many of Nasim's birthdays had passed without anyone's noticing that she herself rarely noticed anymore. Once her sister had died, there had been no one left to care. The first birthday that she had had with Cath, she hadn't mentioned. Cath only found out weeks later when she had said something about Nasim's being sixteen and Nasim had corrected her. Her eighteenth birthday had been lost in other things, and her nineteenth had occurred in one of the week-long periods in which she had refused to emerge from her bedroom. There had been no question among the handlers that there ought to be a party this year; that it be a surprise had been Delia's idea.

Nasim was woken up by Peter, Delia, and Cath singing to her and carrying a cake lit with twenty candles. She flushed an embarrassed red at so much attention suddenly focused on her, and by the end of the song she was crying.

"Nasim, what's wrong?" Delia asked, angry with herself for having pushed for the surprise.

"Nothing," Nasim tried to smile through her tears. "Nothing's wrong. It just reminded me. Of... of friends I used to have." She hadn't told Peter and Delia about her brother and sister, though she had never thought to wonder why she was unwilling. Delia had once pressed her about how she had managed after her parents had died, and Nasim had implied that her aunt and uncle had taken her in. This scene, though, brought back her birthday a decade earlier, when her parents and two siblings had woken her singing, candles planted in an enormous stack of pancakes that they slathered in syrup and ate as a family. It was the only time her mother had ever made pancakes and one of the rare occasions on which they had eaten American food at home. The memory had been buried, a reminder of the happiness that had existed on the other side of the wall of pain she never looked through any more.

She wiped the tears away, succeeded this time with the smile, and blew out the candles.

"Okay, now shoo," Cath said to Peter and Delia. "I'll take care of the shower. You two can manage breakfast, I trust." Cath laid Nasim's bathrobe across the bed as Peter and Delia left and went to turn the water on.

"I was surprised," Nasim said when she was safely boxed in by the glass walls of the shower.

"That was the idea."

"I didn't think you'd remember."

"Twenty's no insignificant thing."

"It's also…" She couldn't finish the sentence, wouldn't have known what words to use even if she could. *The beginning. The end.* In the next couple of months, one of the appointments would be for the first insemination. No letter she could write, no phone call she could make would stop that now.

"I know," Cath said.

"I-"

"You shouldn't worry about it today. Today's only one day closer than yesterday was, and you weren't worried about it yesterday."

"But today it can happen, and yesterday it couldn't."

"Nothing's going to happen today. You don't have your next appointment until next week, and nothing's going to happen then, either. They'd have told you. You can worry about it tomorrow. Today, we're celebrating."

"But you don't-"

"We're celebrating *you*, Nasim," Cath insisted. "Three people who love you are celebrating the fact that you exist for us to love. Bask in it for a while."

Nasim wiped the steam off the glass of the shower door so she could peer through to where Cath was standing on the other side.

"Okay."

"I'm going to go pick you out something nice to wear. You can't come to your own surprise party looking like a slob."

Peter and Delia had retrieved a stack of pancakes from

the kitchen. Eggs and sausage and bacon, too, but it was the pancakes that Nasim wanted, thick and fluffy with real maple syrup.

She returned again to her tenth birthday. It had been the only time they had had maple syrup in the house, and she had poured herself only a little, imagining how her father must have balked at the price, imagining that her mother must have been the one who had insisted that they not buy the imitation stuff. But her father had smothered his pancakes in it. "My eldest daughter will only turn ten once," he had said and then plunked the bottle back down in front of her. She had been too shy to take more, but on her second helping of pancakes, she had been more liberal.

Now, though, she had no hesitation. She took what she liked. She left what she didn't. She had things her parents would never have imagined. A heated towel rack, windows that turned opaque with the flick of a switch. But they had had things that she could scarcely imagine. Purpose, fulfillment, maybe even happiness.

"Are you going to pass that along, or are you keeping all of it?" Delia asked, pointing to the bottle of syrup in Nasim's hands.

SIXTY-FIVE

Once again Nasim found herself sitting in front of the fireplace of her old coop. Cath was fumbling through a pile of kindling beside her.

"I'll do it," Nasim said.

"You never do it." Cath replied.

Nasim laughed. "You haven't been here in a long time." Cath reluctantly gave up her position in front of the hearth, and Nasim's experienced hands readied the tinder and kindling. When the first log caught, she sat back on her heels and enjoyed the radiant warmth kissing her face. Then she said, "Are we here to rehash the same conversation?"

Cath shrugged. "You're the one who doesn't want to live – really live. You're the one sulking, tail between your legs, waiting for your life to make itself more palatable. So, yes. I expect we'll keep having it until you decide to do something."

The first log was burning brightly, and the second one had just caught. It was hot now, sitting as close as Nasim was, but she didn't retreat. Looking into the dancing flames, she said quietly, "I have a choice: I can find happiness within the boundaries, or I can break myself against the wall. Acceptance isn't the story anyone wants to hear, is it? But we all have our walls; we're all born into limitations of happenstance – time and place and poverty and humanity – but you, Cath, you only see mine. If every hungry man were precluded happiness until sated, if every exploited woman were precluded happiness until liberated, if every sick child were precluded happiness until well, what world would this be?"

Cath objected, "Those are not the same, Nasim. There is a difference between what you suffer at the hands of God and what you suffer at the hands of men. One is the fate you're dealt, the other is the one you submit to."

"I hate the cage I'm living in, but perhaps it's not so small that I can't find the space for peace inside it. The injustice hurts so deeply, but maybe I can know the pain without also suffering from it. I am *not* submitting, Cath. I won't ever submit. But neither am I willing to suffer any more at their hands, neither will I fight only to be beaten – not defeated, but simply beaten. What you never understood, Cath, is that I have a side, yes, but I'm not a conscript. To assume that I lack the free will to choose the battles I will fight, that assigns me as little value as they do."

"You're speaking the words your oppressors want to hear you say," Cath retorted. "Just think how much trouble you could have saved them if only you'd come around earlier. When Eleanore came knocking at your door, you could have told her to shove it, and we all would have been spared a lot of contention." The logs shifted suddenly, falling in on themselves, and in a moment the fire was smoldering and smoky.

Nasim pulled a poker from beside the fireplace and pushed the logs back upright, stoked the flames, and waited for the smoke to dissipate. "You and Eleanore and Sam, you all told me that if I poked and prodded the world just so, I could see realized the outcome that I wanted. But I never had that power. I never had control over any of it. None of us does, Cath. None of us controls this web. We act as though we do, our expectations reflect that illusion. We think that if we do it right, we'll get what we want; that if we don't get what we want, it's because we've done it wrong. But all we can do is poke; we have no control over how the world responds."

"And so why bother trying, right?" The frustration in Cath's voice crescendoed. As she spoke, the fire cooled, some of the flames died out, and grey smoke began to collect in the corners of the fireplace.

Nasim fanned the embers until they burst back into flame before she replied, "We bother trying because that's what it is to be alive. To poke at the world and prod it and shake it and sometimes even break it. Without the knowledge of what our actions will elicit. Without the expectation that we can foresee the results."

"Ah! You've found it! The key to happiness!" The contempt in Cath's voice stung. "Set your expectations sufficiently low, and you'll never be disappointed!"

Nasim shook her head gently. "Choose never to expect that you control what is beyond your control, and you have also chosen never to be disappointed. I have finally learned, Cath: Pain will find me wherever I am. But I am the master of my response to it. I choose not to suffer anymore."

Nasim's face was flushed with the heat of the fire, which popped and crackled as it burned. Her eyes hadn't left the flames since she had first lit them, but now she turned to face Cath's silence; and all she saw behind her was an empty room.

In that instant, Nasim felt the gravity of reality pulling

her from the dream, and when she opened her eyes it was to the feeling of being rent so completely from the dreamworld that, though separated from it only by a single moment in time, all of it was lost to her: an arm's-reach away but untouchable, a second before but unknowable.

The first rays of the rising sun illuminated a bird that had perched on her skylight, and as though it sensed her gaze, it took flight as soon as her eyes landed on it and left behind only a square of unbroken blue sky above Nasim's bed. Nasim closed her eyes once more, attempting to retrieve any memory from the dream, but she could feel even the sensations of it that she had carried with her across the threshold of sleep fading away. It wasn't until sat up to stretch a half hour later that she noticed that Cath's ghost had disappeared from her room.

SIXTY-SIX

FEBRUARY 12, 2066

On her twentieth birthday, Nasim stopped writing letters and began waiting for the call that would eventually come, the one that would schedule the first insemination. Her relief at the end of each day that it hadn't yet happened did little but compound her certainty that the next day it would.

A call did come a week after her birthday to remind her of an appointment the following Tuesday, and she spent the intermittent days in an inconsolable ball sunk into the couch. Peter walked her to the appointment, and she had been happy he had taken her by the arm: she was certain she wouldn't have made it there but for his weight pulling them forward. The appointment was been no different from the usual ones, though, and when the doctor told her she could dress, she nearly cried in relief.

When the real call came in February, they told her what would happen, told her that if she wanted to bring one handler in particular she should arrange it. She took Peter again, but only by chance, clutched his hand when the doctor came in with a box and showed her a needle-less syringe. She pushed her heels hard into the stirrups. The thin cotton robe she was wearing blocked her view of the doctor, and she clenched her jaw waiting for the pain of the needle that she had been too frightened to ask about; but it never came. She felt nothing but the cold lubricant, and then the doctor left. A nurse waited in the cramped room for fifteen minutes to ensure that Nasim didn't sit up in that time, and then he, too, disappeared.

"It didn't hurt," she whispered to Peter when they were alone.

"I should hope not."

"I thought it might."

"Honestly, Nasim, the speculum is a lot bigger than that syringe."

"The needle, though."

Peter couldn't help but laugh. "There's no needle, Nasim. What good would it do?"

Nasim shrugged.

A phone call a week later informed Nasim that the insemination had failed. She breathed a sigh of relief - another month of freedom. The month felt short-lived, though, from the exam room at the other end of it. Cath was with her this time, and it was Cath who clutched Nasim's hand and Cath whose face betrayed a grimace of disgust when the doctor pulled out the box with the syringe and a vial of sperm.

"Doesn't she have a right to know who the donor is?"

"Of course," the doctor replied and then turning to Nasim said, "You declined last time, but you can change your mind at any point."

Nasim shook her head, though, and wished the process would move faster.

When the call came to inform Nasim that the second

insemination had failed, she received the news with fear creeping into her belly. She remembered having read something about *in vitro* fertilization or having heard about it in the news. Something controversial about the way the law was being written, something debated before the men in suits had picked her up. But the fact that the debate had fallen silent, that she had heard nothing about it since was little reassurance.

Delia insisted that they couldn't attempt something like IVF without giving her ample warning. "It's not something they can just sneak into a regular appointment. And why would they? It's not as though they weren't open about what was going to happen last month or the month before, right? If they didn't hide that, why would they hide this? We can just ask them if you're worried about it."

"I can't."

"I'll call if you want me to," Delia offered.

"I don't know if I want to know."

"Wouldn't knowing make it-"

Nasim interrupted Delia with a quick shake of her head.

She had never, not since her earliest memories, known a woman to give birth. It wasn't anything her parents had told her about, not something she had learned about in school, either, since it had stopped being relevant. She had only a vague understanding of how the process proceeded naturally and none whatsoever of how artificial insemination played into it. She doubted very much that IVF - whatever that might entail - could be as benign as insemination had turned out to be. And as to what came after, what would happen once the pregnancy took, she knew even less about those nine months.

"How many times do you think they try insemination before they switch to IVF?"

"Nasim, I have no idea. Why don't we just call and ask?"

But Nasim shook her head again and surrendered herself to the fear that gnawed at her and to the hope, however perverse, that this time insemination would succeed.

They called again a week after the third appointment, which had been no different from the last two. Cath answered. Nasim had already crouched in the corner of the couch, occupying as little space as she could, bracing for a recurrence of the fear from which she had had a week's respite. But when Cath hung up the phone, she announced, "It took."

They studied each other in silence, neither knowing what to feel.

"At least it's done," Nasim finally said. "I wanted it to be done, and now it is." Her voice was flat, and her face had relaxed until there was no expression discernible on it.

SIXTY-SEVEN

July 22, 2075

"Nasim?" She was standing by the window when Delia walked into the room. The sun hadn't yet cleared the low buildings of the compound, and the birds were still the only sign of life.

"I'm going to get a cat," Nasim said.

"It's...?" Delia looked at her watch. "Very early."

"Cat wouldn't mind," Nasim replied. "I saw one a while ago who looked awfully pregnant. Find her, find her kittens. If they're weaned, I'll take one."

"How could you tell it was pregnant?"

"She," Nasim corrected.

"What?" Delia had only gotten up to use the restroom; she had thought she was coming back to several more hours of sleep.

"You said 'it.' If she was pregnant, she's obviously a 'she.'"

"But–" Delia's brow was deeply furrowed.

"Because I know a pregnancy when I see one, Delia. Frankly, I'm surprised you don't."

Delia wracked her mind for a response and finally said, "Should we have some coffee first?"

"If you want."

They had drunk their coffee, picked at their breakfast, and set out in search of the cat well before the morning's dew had dried. They found her, a little calico with swollen nipples and vacated belly, crunching on the fragments of chicken bone that last night's raccoons hadn't bothered with. She eyed Delia with suspicion but approached Nasim, rubbed up against her leg, allowed her head to be scratched.

"I don't think her kittens will be far, but I doubt we'll find them without mama's consent," Delia said.

The cat had rolled onto her back, and Nasim tickled her white chest. "She lost them," Nasim said.

"What do you mean?"

"She never nursed. Look," she pointed to the nipples, soft, uncalloused, and dry. Nasim picked up the cat and said, "If I'm wrong, she'll come back for them. But I'm not wrong."

"And that's how she now has a cat," Delia had run into Peter when she had gone to retrieve lunch at the kitchen.

"You're serious?" he asked.

"I don't know why I wouldn't be."

"Does it have a name?"

Delia shook her head, "Really, Peter? That's what you're going to ask?"

The kittens had either been lost or abandoned; the cat never so much as glanced out the door once she had been carried inside. Instead she relished Nasim's attention, following her from room to room, curling up on her lap while she read and next to her pillow while she slept. To Delia's horror and Peter's amusement, Nasim let the cat sit on the table while they ate.

Nasim could feel it building in silent moments between her and Delia, and then finally one day: "Really, Nasim, I don't see why she can't just wait the twenty minutes it will take us to eat. She could even sit on your lap."

"My lap's not comfortable for her when I'm sitting in a chair. I'd have to cross my legs, and..." Nasim stuck out her chin and continued, "And no, she's fine where she is."

"Well then maybe we ought to give her a plate so she can eat with us."

"Don't be sore about it," Nasim scolded.

"Well, she's having a bath. On the table. While we eat. It's weird."

Nasim shrugged, and a flicker of a smile crossed her face.

"It's not funny!" Delia insisted. And they both burst out laughing. The cat, who had been cleaning her face, paused her washing to watch as their laughter tapered off and then, unprovoked, started up again. Nasim was rubbing tears out of her eyes, and that became funny in itself.

Peter and Delia both noticed the change in her – not just her recovery from Enzo's departure but some profound calm that she had never possessed – long before either put it into words. The question of whether it would last remained unspoken between them until, after some months, they both dared hope – though still dared not voice their hope – that some existential change might have wrought itself in her.

During one morning shift change in the early spring, Delia found Peter sitting alone in the dining room.

"Where is she?" Delia asked.

"She told me that she wanted to go for a walk, and when I started to put on my shoes, she told me she was going alone. Just said it. 'I'm going alone.' And walked out the door." Peter's expression, as much as his tone, betrayed the bewilderment was still resonating.

"And you…?" The accusation – *And you let her?* – was left unfinished.

Peter's loss for words following Nasim's announcement had been so complete that he found himself struggling even now to find some. "What choice did I have?"

Delia plopped into a chair, her face shifting from serious to amused. "Where did this person come from?" she laughed. "How has she grown all this confidence and self-assuredness and… and chill? And what did she do with our sweet, anxious Nasim?"

"Delia, if you had heard her just now…"

They waited together for Nasim to return, and when she did, she said nothing of her trip – nor of the irregularity of it. Instead she sat down at the table, too, and said, "If we're all here, shouldn't we eat together?"

SIXTY-EIGHT

June 12, 2067

She hadn't known to expect the morning sickness, though somehow Peter had. He explained it while holding her hair out of her face and told her a second time when she was no longer distracted by her own vomiting.

"People used to do this voluntarily?"

"I think more with the aim of having children to raise than from the joy of growing them in their bellies."

They were seated across from each other at the table now.

"Shall I order breakfast?" Peter asked.

"Something… innocuous, please."

"Eggs?"

"Eggs are the opposite of innocuous."

"Toast?" he suggested.

"Mmm. Cinnamon raisin toast. Buttered while it's hot. And it had better still be hot when it gets here. It would be so much simpler if they hadn't taken my stupid toaster. But Peter?"

He had already walked over to the phone to call in the order. "Hm?"

"Have them deliver it."

The toast was cold by the time it arrived, as Nasim had known it would be when she asked for it. Even had it been hot, though, it was unlikely she would have picked at it with any greater enthusiasm than she did at the cold slices, the butter congealing on top of them.

"I hate this, Peter."

"I'd be happy to order you something else."

"That's not what I meant."

Peter nodded. "But if that *had* been the problem, there'd have been such an elegant solution that I thought it was worth a try."

Delia arrived before Peter could offer any other solutions.

"You're far into your morning," Delia said, half to herself. She took Peter's seat as he slipped past Nasim and squeezed her shoulder.

Nasim shifted her gaze from the bread in front of her to Delia, her eyes wide and sad.

"Already not a good day?" Delia asked.

Nasim shook her head.

"You know, I'll always be here to listen, Nasim. But you could also see someone if you wanted. A professional, I mean. To talk about the fact that… that a lot of days aren't good."

"What's there to talk about? I don't want to be here. They don't want me to leave. It doesn't seem like there's much else to say." Now Delia, too. Nasim wanted empathy, not answers.

"Not about that. About the way you feel. About dealing with the way you feel. About learning to live with… this."

Nasim shrugged.

"There are other things, too. Other than talking. They could give you something," Delia offered.

"Drug me into happiness?"

"I don't think that's quite how it-"

"I'm already just a body to them," Nasim interrupted. "I'm not going to feel good about it, too."

"Nasim, please don't get angry. I know you wouldn't be here if you had a choice, but what was the alternative?"

"That I not be here."

"But what would that have meant?" Delia asked.

"That Scott Davis not have started his little campaign. That Ruth Clayborn had kept her matronly urges to herself. That a few more voters had thought about what it means to use a woman's body as an incubator." Her eyes flashed dangerously at Delia, daring her to press any further.

Delia shrank in her seat, looked at the walls around her hoping they might offer up an argument for their own existence. "But those are things you had no control over. Those are factors beyond you, Nasim. Where would *you* be if you weren't here?"

She offered no reply, so Delia answered her own question: "Dead, probably." *Isn't here better than dead?*

"Or vaccinated," Nasim retorted.

"But you *weren't* vaccinated. You had infinitely more control over that than you did over Scott Davis's running for office or the way two hundred million people cast their ballots. But still, you weren't vaccinated."

"I'd rather be dead than here," she finally said, pushing back her chair. Her uneaten toast had been reduced to a pile of crumbs. She picked up the plate, looked at Delia to see if she would protest, and then threw it at the wall, careful to miss the plate glass of her sliding door. Then she slunk into her bedroom, closing the door behind her, and lay down on her bed.

The room looked different with the door closed. Was it

the first time she had seen it that way?

Why hadn't she asked them when she had had the chance? They hadn't been well off, but Nasim had never thought of her family as poor. Surely they couldn't have been unable to afford it. And if they had been, if they had really been destitute and somehow she hadn't known, even then there must have been a way. They could have scraped up enough money from somewhere or found a clinic or something.

Maybe they hadn't understood the danger. Her parents were immigrants. They spoke English, but they rarely spoke to Americans. They lived in an immigrant community. They worked with immigrants. They shopped in stores run by immigrants. Maybe the message had never penetrated far enough into her neighborhood for them to hear it.

There were other reasons for some people. Ruth hadn't wanted to give up having children. But if her parents had felt that way - and how could they have without her knowing it? - then surely they would have vaccinated Abbas. And themselves.

Some people objected on religious grounds. At the beginning, especially, some fundamentalist religious groups had claimed that the Plague was God-sent and that the worthy would be immune. But those voices had fallen silent, either because they found themselves no more immune than anyone else or because they had eventually slipped into a doctor's office and quietly taken the prick in the arm. And if her parents had been adherents of any such group, again, wouldn't she have known? They would have made for poor fanatics if they had kept their beliefs concealed even from their own children.

"Nasim." It was Cath at the door. Was it really that late already? "Can I come in?"

Nasim didn't reply, but the door cracked open anyways, and Cath peered through to the other side. When she saw that Nasim's open eyes, she went in.

"Can I get you anything?"

Nasim shook her head.

"Late lunch?"

Nasim nodded.

"Anything in particular?"

"No." Then Nasim added, "Why does it seem like all I ever do is eat?"

"Because you never actually eat, so we're always trying to force some calories into you. It's a conspiracy."

Nasim laughed in spite of herself.

SIXTY-NINE

Peter had delivered the news first thing in the morning. No one had bothered about it while it was being debated, but it was on TV now, having already been settled, and he had rushed to her coop, afraid that she would catch wind from some other source. He had burst in on Delia and Nasim eating breakfast.

Nasim, Delia, and the cat – sitting on the table – had stared at him quizzically as his breathing had slowed and a feeling of sheepishness had welled up in him at his perceived urgency. Finally he had said, "I thought you would want to know that they're going to require the daughters of the Eves to join the Eden Project, too."

"You thought I would be dying to know that?" Part incredulity, part reprimand.

"Well, not exactly." Silence from her as she had waited for more. "I thought…" *And once it would have been true.* "I thought you would be better off hearing it from me than from someone else. That's what sent me over here in a rush, and now I don't think it anymore. I just feel a little foolish." He had felt a sudden burst of pride at this role reversal – her calm against his concern – and whatever part he had had to play in it.

Now, a day later, Nasim was studying Peter from across the living room. She knew that he would look up from his book within a few seconds, and she made up her mind just as he met her eyes. "There's something I need to do," she said to him. "Alone."

"What is it?"

"Alone," she reiterated. "Entirely alone."

He channeled his growing curiosity into a question she would have to answer. "And when do you need to do this thing?"

"It'll take some time. I'll start today. I need you to give me a few hours' of privacy."

"It's not a problem for me to take my reading to the handlers' bedroom for a while, Nasim."

She shook her head. "I need real privacy."

Peter shifted in the armchair and his gaze traveled the room in search of an escape as his curiosity gave way to discomfort. "You know I'm not allowed to just leave you here. You cowed me into letting you take that walk by yourself, but that doesn't mean we can make a habit of this sort of thing."

Nasim rolled her eyes. "You leave all the time to pick up food."

"That's different. That takes twenty minutes."

"So make it take longer." Delia would never have agreed, but Nasim knew that Peter wanted to say yes. That desire did little to diminish his fear of violating explicit rules of the Project, however, particularly in light of the increased scrutiny that Enzo's unusual departure had likely catalyzed. She pushed harder, "This is a journey I need to take, Peter. Give me two hours. No one will know."

"Not even Delia?" he asked.

"Not even Delia."

He was slow to put on his shoes; he dallied at the door. When Nasim heard the latch click behind him, she heaved a sigh of relief. A voice nagged her not to waste a minute, but she shrugged it off. *This will take whatever time it takes.*

She had been reflecting on the beginnings of the Eden Project in the past few weeks, but Peter's announcement about its extension to another generation had been what spurred her to this action. She wanted to talk to Scott Davis, a man who had existed in her mind as a monodimensional villain for so long that her memories of him – and even of herself in the scenes that they shared – had taken on a fictional quality.

He was the age I am now, she thought. *He had a wife, a career, the desire for children,* she recalled. *He fought for his cause because he knew it to be in the public interest, to be righteous.* It still disgusted her that there were people who valued her life less than they did her eggs and her womb, but he had believed he was right as steadfastly as she had known that she was. *We have that in common,* she thought, *that certainty.*

For the two hours that Peter was gone, Nasim contemplated Scott's choice, humanized him as best she could, and exercised her ability to accept that humanity. And when that had exhausted her, when her empathy had run dry, she picked the book up off her lap and resumed reading. It was enough for now; it would take whatever time it took.

Peter knocked before he entered the coop, something he hadn't done since the day he had met Nasim, but he didn't await Nasim's reply before opening the door. "Have you finished?" he called from the foyer, and Nasim laughed:

What Peter must think she was doing.

"Quite."

"Completely?" Peter asked, surprised, as he walked into the living room.

"No, of course not. I'm finished for the day."

"And you're not going to tell me what it's about?"

"And you're not going to ask," Nasim replied.

Peter quieted the impulse to push further and instead turned the subject to something that had been on his mind as she had asked him to leave. "You've met a few prospective handlers to fill the vacancy that Enzo left."

Nasim nodded.

"You haven't said anything about them. Any good matches?"

"No."

Someone in administration had asked him to do some digging. It was the first such request he had accepted, and he had done so only because he felt it was in Nasim's best interest to have her requirements for a new handler known. "What are you looking for that they've lacked?"

"I'm not looking for a new handler," she informed him coolly.

SEVENTY

The first labor lasted an eternity. A nurse - another man, Nasim noted, in the sea of men - had been coming to the coop once a week to coach Nasim and the handlers on what to expect, but the pain was well beyond anything that he could have described.

Cath was with her when it began. She was the one who called the nurses, who helped them put the extra sheets on the bed, and who, between those tasks, was at Nasim's side to soothe her when she cried out in pain. She gritted her teeth when Nasim crushed her hand and told Nasim to breathe as she herself tried to breathe through the nails digging into her skin. Cath said all the things they had told her to say, and Nasim failed to hear them over the pain and the anguish that alternated in a rhythm that her body dictated.

Cath tried to stay when the shift change came, but Peter was coming on duty, and the thought of him there brought immense comfort, where Cath provided so little. So Nasim shook her head. Cath offered to stay even with Peter there, but Nasim shook her head again, gritting her teeth this time not in pain but in fear that Cath might force her to confess that she wasn't wanted. But Cath didn't offer again, simply left when Peter took Nasim's hand in her stead.

Peter was there in the hours when Nasim wished she could die. After every wave of pain, she choked out a few curses at the Project that had put this thing inside her and the people who had enacted it. When it began, it was inaudible sentiments loosed through the curling of her fingers into fists, and as the pain grew in frequency and intensity, the thoughts eked out of her in mumbled words and much later in cursing screams. And then she would remember that this was the first of a dozen. And at every iteration, that thought came more quickly - a deeper rut in the track in her mind - and lingered longer. Eleven more times after this. If she could but will the rise and fall of her lungs to stop. If she could but find a knife to plunge into her belly. If she could but claw her heart from her chest. Then she could be free. Then this could be the only one. Then she would be her own master.

There was an end, though, to this time. A baby, a girl. Wiped clean and plunked into Nasim's arms. But a second later, "That's not supposed to…" and wrenched away again, one nurse disappearing with the girl while the midwife and the other nurse waited for the afterbirth.

Nasim cried through the rest of it, cried while they took the bloodied sheets from her bed and gave her a warm water bottle to hug, cried when Peter helped her into the shower to wash away the sweat of the last fifteen hours. The Project she could hate. Scott Davis and Ruth Clayborn and every person who had voted to put her here she could hate. The people who didn't answer her letters, the people who never called her back, she could hate them. And if she tried hard enough, she could hate Peter and Delia and maybe even Cath for their complicity, and the people who cooked her food and the people who took away and brought back her laundry and the people who cut the grass and changed the plantings in the flower beds. But of those, the only one she had really, truly hated had been the thing growing inside her. And in the instant the girl was cradled in her arms, that hatred had been rent from her, and then a moment later, the girl had gone, too; and the love that had bubbled up in that second fizzled and sputtered and turned to something else.

SEVENTY-ONE

Nasim had instructed Peter to leave for the afternoon. It was the fourth such time, and he had offered no objection. Now she sat on the couch, her eyes scanning three dozen images of a late-middle-aged man projected onto the wall across from her. It hadn't been difficult to find Scott Davis. He had only lasted two terms in the House before he lost a primary to someone with a more popular take on the next big issue, some job creation campaign that Nasim had never had reason to hear of. In those two terms, the Eden Project was the only noteworthy thing he had done, though even in that he was just a cosponsor preceded on the bill by two other dozen names.

Nasim was unsurprised to see that he had been one of the first people to adopt an Eden child. He and his wife had been among the first to get a second one, too – to ample criticism from the public – and some people had speculated that that was the sort of misuse of power that would cost a man a primary.

A few years' silence was broken by a perspective piece he had written about family life in an era when families were rare. He had gone back to practicing law, and he wrote about the challenge of keeping pace with his colleagues – or even wanting to – when the thing that truly gave him purpose was being a father to his children.

Nasim pointed to the next of the projected images, and a column of text scrolled down the wall in response. She absent-mindedly scratched the cat's ears as she read.

He had run for city council the following year, an uncontested race. The position afforded him occasional press coverage, spawning a few articles about his throwing the opening pitch at a minor league baseball game, manning a hotdog stand at the county fair to raise funds for local schools, which had seen dramatic funding cuts as student populations had plummeted. There were a few things about his children, too. The younger boy had won a spelling bee, the older one, some wrestling match.

There had been less in the last few years. After three terms, he had decided not to seek reelection (to the dismay of an editorial writer for the local paper, who had proclaimed that it was the incumbent's duty to run if the position would otherwise go vacant), but he was still a 'prominent citizen;' and occasionally someone wanted to solicit an opinion from someone like him. From, Nasim thought, a washed–up politician, mediocre former lawyer, ex–city councilman. From, the newspapers said, a local civic leader and family man.

A way to contact Davis proved more difficult to find, but a couple of weeks later, she coaxed someone into giving her Alex's number. She dialed it impulsively, then wondered as it rang what she would say if he picked up.

"Hello?" She was surprised that she recognized his voice this many years later.

"My name's Nasim. You tried to recruit me once to be your… your face for the Eden Project the first time Scott

Davis ran for the House."

Silence on the other end, and then, "Yes, I remember you now. Hard to forget the only person, as far as I know, who's ever thrown a salad at Scott." He chuckled at the memory and preempted her objection. "I can't say I wouldn't have wanted to do the same in your place, but I certainly wouldn't have had the balls."

"I want to get in touch with him. Do you have his number?"

"Straight to the point, eh?" Alex's face appeared on the wall in front of her as he activated his video feed. His hair, which had been streaked with grey years before, was all silver, its original color forgotten. His face was more weathered, lines where there had been none before, but he smiled more easily. "You're not going to track him down and kill him, are you?"

Nasim switched on her own video feed and studied the enormous face projected on the wall. It had sounded like a joke, but he could just as well have a serious interest in her response.

"No." She waited to see if that would be enough of an answer. She wondered how much of her he could see – she had never bothered to check the settings. Could he tell that she was pregnant?

"You promise?" he asked when she said nothing further.

"I just want to talk to him. I… there are some things I want to say."

"I'll ask him if he minds."

"Alex," the urgency in her response startled them both. Then more softly, "Don't you think I have a right to speak to him?"

"Probably," he conceded, and while she waited for the remainder of the response she thought was coming, he punched in a number that flashed below his face.

"Thank you."

"I… Just don't–"

"I don't blame you. Anymore. I used to, but I don't now."

Though it wasn't what he had started to say, Alex nodded in reply; and the call ended with that silence.

SEVENTY-TWO

"You can't lie there all day."

"I can."

"Not every day, though," Cath insisted.

"I can."

"Nasim, you need to eat."

"I won't. They can't force me to."

"Nasim, please." Cath had been hovering on the verge of tears since she and Delia, huddled on the couch together, had heard the screams and cries that marked the end of Nasim's latest trial. The pain had been so complete, so destructive that Cath had felt it tear her apart by mere association. "Please get up," she begged.

The quiver in Cath's voice frightened Nasim, and she rolled out of bed to quell it. Her legs caught her and then nearly buckled in surprise, the first time they had felt her weight in almost a week, their muscles sapped by the many meals she had refused.

Nasim sank to the floor in the shower, the glass and tile cold until her body and the hot water warmed it. Cath knelt on the other side of the fogged glass and pressed her forehead up against it.

"Will you write a letter today?"

"No."

"I think we need to. Both of us. We should write. Or make a few calls."

"What's the point?" Nasim asked.

"That you can't stop fighting."

"I haven't stopped fighting!" Nasim hammered her fist onto the glass above her, landing it where Cath's face had been. "I wish I could! I wish I could... wish myself into oblivion. I wish my body would just let me go!"

"Then do something with the fact that it won't."

"Fine." *I'll write your stupid letters. I'll make your stupid phone calls.*

When Nasim finally dragged herself to her feet, Cath had laid out her clothes on the bed, laid out paper on the table - not at the desk where she had written before, but on the table where they ate - two sheets across from each other.

For twenty minutes, Nasim stared at the blank page in front of her. She had had the words memorized, the ones she had struggled to come up with at the beginning, but now she couldn't remember how they began, and without the beginning, she couldn't find any of them. She thought about the mailbox. Was its belly full of her letters, never picked up, a time capsule of her misery that no one would ever read? She thought about the phone calls she had made. Could it have been a person at the other end, one person with a thousand different voices, one person who was sometimes there and sometimes parroted a recorded message and sometimes just beeped at her?

She rolled the pen through her fingers, feeling the seam that ran up the length of plastic.

Nasim could feel Cath's eyes on the blank sheet of paper in front of her, could feel the disappointment and the tears held back by nothing more than a pair of paper-thin eyelids. She began to transcribe the only thing she could remember, the list of names. The first fifty came easily, and then the next twenty or so, written one per line on the front of a page and the back. The names that came after had been added later, names Cath had brought with her or names that she had dredged up from the most remote recesses of memory. The manager of the grocery store her mother had always gone to. The name of the woman who lived next door to her aunt and uncle. Those she hadn't repeated enough to remember them now, so when she reached that part of the list, she signed the paper and stuffed it into the envelope before Cath could see what she had done.

She stood up from the table, stripped off her clothes right there, and left them in a pile on the floor while she took herself back to the comfort of her bed. Cath hurriedly finished her own letter, but before she could follow Nasim, Peter arrived to relieve her.

Most of Nasim's hours slipped by in numb darkness, but she occasionally pulled back far enough from that enveloping fog to see the thoughts that were marching through her mind. Why hadn't her parents vaccinated her? For hours at a time, it seemed as though the answer to that question could resolve everything. If they had been unable, then the blame for her being here lay wholly at the feet of a society that refused to protect its weakest. That a child should suffer a lifetime of this burden, that two other children should die because their parents lacked the resources to procure a vaccine that couldn't have cost more than a few hundred dollars, for that she could blame Scott and Alex and Eleanore and Sam. But if they had been unwilling, then the blame rested on them alone. Then all that she had suffered, all the loss she had felt, her imprisonment here, it was all their fault.

If she could but know the answer. If she could but have five minutes with them, with one of them, to ask the question.

And why had she never pressed the matter? She had been old enough to understand what the Plague meant, to know that there was a vaccine, but the fact that she hadn't received it had never been a point she had thought to question. And if not she, then why hadn't Abbas asked? He was four years older; he had been sixteen when their parents had died. Surely he would have thought about it before then. Undoubtedly he could have convinced them.

And once they had died, once it was just the three of them left, why hadn't Abbas done something then? Why hadn't he taken them begging at a clinic? Why hadn't he thought to scratch at the door of someone like Eleanore? Why hadn't he protected her when her parents had failed?

SEVENTY-THREE

May 4, 2076

She should have dialed Scott's number as soon as she had hung up with Alex. She had told herself at the time that the conversation she wanted to have with him merited some preparation, that it would be imprudent – or at least hasty – not to give it some thought beforehand. But now the waiting had given it importance, and that importance had made her nervous; and the nervousness caused her to wait longer still. Each time she reminded herself that it would take as long as it took, another voice replied, *But we're only waiting on you here.* Every time she repeated that she could bear the discomfort of the situation without suffering from it, too, the anxiety in her stomach clenched tighter and insisted, *No.* She was sixteen again, powerless again, alone and terrified again, no matter what words she whispered to herself in protest.

Twice she had asked Peter for an afternoon alone and had stared at the phone number for so long before she had screwed up the courage to make the call that, with relief, she had had to concede that she might not be able to finish it before he came back and so was absolved of the responsibility for another day. Then she had had to wait through a week of Delia's daytime shifts. The first morning that Peter was back, she steeled herself, asked him to leave until lunchtime, and began as soon as the door closed behind him. "Turn on the video feed," she said to the computer as it dialed. She wanted to do it face to face.

At the first ring, she kicked herself for failing again to check the video settings. She hadn't been able to decide whether she minded his knowing that she was pregnant, hadn't been able to decide whether that would feel like an accusation or whether it wasn't his business anyways. And having failed to decide, she had now failed even to find out whether he would see the wringing of her hands, whether he would note how she unconsciously touched her swollen belly.

She considered hanging up just to check quickly, promised herself that she wouldn't use it as an excuse to delay again. But the phone rang a second and third time before she made up her mind, and then Scott picked up.

"Hello." Whatever uncertainty and hesitation Nasim remembered from her single conversation with the inexperienced candidate of years earlier was gone; in a single word, he sounded important. It's no wonder people still sought him out for soundbites.

Nasim tried – but failed – to convince the butterflies in her stomach that they lacked authority over her. Remembering that Scott could see her, she thrust her hands behind her back lest she do something with them that betrayed her nerves. "Do you know who I am?"

"You look familiar," he said. He sounded sincere, but it had been his business to remember people – or to pretend to remember – for long enough that it might just be his habit now.

"Nasim," she reminded him. Just as it had been with

Ruth, she was only ever a first name. A first name and a face.

"Of course." He activated his video feed. He was smiling – the same smile that she used to hate so much, the one that she had always thought had made people choose him instead of her. "That's a name that brings back memories."

Nasim struggled to reconcile his nostalgia with the stale self–righteousness that she had braced herself for.

"You grew up," he added.

And you grew old, she thought. His face was much more haggard than in even the most recent photos she had seen, but the years had softened the edge, too. He didn't look hungry anymore; he looked happy, like that smile might be permanent.

She realized he was waiting for her to say something. "Alex gave me your number."

"I know," he said. "He told me. I should have recognized you with the warning, but I didn't." He laughed. "Two pre–teens at home, you know. Everything with them is urgent. They seem to take up all my working memory." He was tapping the side of his head.

She noticed that her hands had migrated to her belly, and she shoved them behind her back again, wished again that she knew what of her he could see. The words that she had picked out so carefully deserted her, and she could think of nothing else to say, nothing to preface it: "I forgive you."

He was slow to respond, chewing his thoughts for a full minute before he replied, "I'm not sorry, though." The smile wasn't permanent, after all. "I'm sorry that you were…" he searched for a word before settling on "compelled. Against your will. I'm sorry that anyone was. But I can't apologize for the way it turned out. It was the only way; I stand by that."

She wondered if he wanted her to agree, if he wanted her to confess that it had indeed been the only way and that it continued to be. "It doesn't matter anymore. Whether you were sorry or not, I would be here. Reality unchanged. I still forgive you." Her hands had drifted back to her belly.

"I did everything I could to make it... humane. But I only had so much sway, you know. I never... I always cared about the people. I never thought of you as anything but a person."

Nasim tried to smile at him. She hadn't expected that his words might mean something. "I didn't know," she admitted.

"Ruth cared, too, you know. She could have just sorted things for herself – she could have had it any way she wanted it – but that wasn't how she did things. Maybe that doesn't mean anything to you because she wanted... this," his eyes dropped, he must see her belly, "and you didn't."

Nasim shrugged. She had thought much less of Ruth than she had of the others, of Scott and Eleanore and Sam, because Ruth was like her. Because when she thought of Ruth, she couldn't help but try to understand how Ruth could have wanted this, and she didn't want to understand.

"I'm glad you called," Scott finally said. "It's been a while since Alex warned me. I thought you might have changed your mind. But I'm happy you didn't."

Nasim nodded. She didn't have anything else to say, didn't even know how to say that. Finally, "I'm glad I called, too," and she held up her hand in a parting wave before hanging up.

SEVENTY-FOUR

JANUARY 15, 2068

Nasim wrote a real letter the next day and the one after that. She still couldn't remember the words, but she found some new ones. They weren't as carefully chosen as the old ones, but what did it matter? Cath wouldn't know.

If she had thought about it, Nasim might have been surprised at the relief she felt when Cath drew the night shift, but instead, she trudged back to her bedroom, annoyed that she had bothered to get up to witness the drawing and making note not to do so again in the future. Peter, who was still on duty from that afternoon, followed her.

"You know, Nasim…" he waited, hoping for an acknowledgement that she was listening before continuing. Though none came, he went on, "There are reasons - hormonal reasons - that you might be finding yourself more depressed than, uh, than usual. It's not uncommon after childbirth-"

"Get out of my room."

Peter fell silent. Nasim crawled into her bed and rolled over, turning her back to him. She listened for his footfalls leaving the room, but perhaps she had missed them in her own movement. The silence outside her was perfect.

Peter broke it, "It's not for me to tell you how you feel, Nasim. Or how you ought to feel. But it is my place to suggest a solution if I see one. The doctor prescribed these for you." He placed a blue pill on her bedside table, his feet crunching into the carpet with each step. "To take the edge off. They won't change the way you feel, but they might make the pain a little more tolerable."

She heard his footsteps leaving this time, strained to hear any other threat of disruption to her silence, and then settled back into its comfortable embrace. The auditory mirror to the void that had opened up inside her, to the black hole into which everything she had ever felt - pain and joy and loss and hope - disappeared.

Delia came the next morning, tried to coax Nasim out of bed, tried to tempt her to eat. When she failed, she settled in beside Nasim and spent her shift offering kindness, words, distraction, touch. The whole time, Nasim wished that she would leave, wished that she would let the silence mend itself, but she didn't wish it enough to speak, so Delia stayed.

Peter appeared for only a moment in his shift to place a glass of water beside the untouched pill on the bedside table, as though the memory of its presence might spur her to consume it.

Cath's presence she felt more than heard. Someone entering her bedroom, someone choosing the floor over the armchair that had been dragged in sometime in the blurred hours since the child. Someone who stayed all night in that spot, whose breath never faded to sleeping, who stirred just enough to be noticed.

Nasim couldn't tell if she was awake for all of it or asleep. The one ran into the other so seamlessly that she wondered whether she could be both at once. Her thoughts were only half her own, mixed in with characters she didn't control. And those thoughts were half replaced by nothing, by void that might last hours. But throughout, she remained aware of the silence around her, bothered by every interruption of it.

Delia came again and Peter and Cath and Delia and Peter and Cath until the sequence lost a starting point and became instead a cycle of the ebb and flow of silence. And the cycle broke and re-formed at a point that must have marked the beginning of the following week, but what difference was the order?

The space within Nasim lured her deeper and deeper. Between her toes she felt the squish of the black tar that trapped her. She heard, for the first time, the companionship that her own voice offered, one that spoke every word she wanted to hear and never one too many. She summoned shadows of people she had known, the dream characters - her brother and sister and her parents, Sam and Eleanore - and turned their shades into color likenesses. She gave them life, made them speak - first in her voice, and later she gave them their own voices. A parallel world for her mind to inhabit while she willed her body to wither.

Peter, Delia, Cath, Peter, did it matter? She gave them their own likenesses, too, though she policed their voices more closely. And as the voices in her mind grew louder and more numerous, the preservation of silence outside mattered less and less.

It was Abbas who one day said, "Sister, how can you lie

here like this? How can you be mired in apathy so profound that you can no longer feel the pain?"

To which she replied, "How can I bear to feel the pain anymore?"

"But to lie here and pretend that the pain is not real does not mean that it isn't."

"How can something that exists only inside me be real when I can't feel it? If I don't feel the pain, it's not real."

"Sister, you can't be you unless you can feel. What are you now? A shell that contains a void within? Where is Nasim in that? Is she the shell or the void?"

"I'm here."

"If you were, you would feel the pain. You're not here. You don't exist anymore."

"I *do* exist," she whispered. "You're the one who doesn't exist anymore, Abbas." But there was little enough conviction behind the words that she barely believed them herself.

SEVENTY-FIVE

May 23, 2076

Peter was greatly relieved to learn that he would no longer need to leave Nasim to her mysterious plan. He never asked what had transpired, and Nasim never offered an explanation. Instead they returned to a normal rhythm of reading. What had once been amicable conversations about plot points and characters had gradually metamorphosed into heated debates about human nature and philosophy and literary merits. Nasim had started pestering Peter to request passes, too, and at least once every few months they would travel to the nearest town beyond the fence of the campus to eat a meal and watch the people. They would imagine the lives that passers-by must live, would spin elaborate narratives and delight in the incorporation of tidbits they picked up by eavesdropping. They retreated together into the woods, where they had made a fire ring, and built fires that they tended all night. Sometimes they would fall asleep in the radiant warmth and not wake until morning, when there was nothing left but hot cinders and dew.

With Delia, too, Nasim went into the woods. They had soon wandered all the paths and then struck off on their own, through the sparse undergrowth under the old evergreens and through the blackberry bushes and occasionally into a marsh that they always thought they would manage to navigate without getting too wet - and never did. They picked blackberries and mulberries and ate them until their fingers were stained blue. When they found a huckleberry tree, too sour to enjoy, they set their minds to baking a huckleberry pie. Once they dragged Peter with them because he had promised them that he would show them how to fish, but when his jury-rigged fishing pole pulled a fish from the water, they begged him to throw the thrashing thing back.

Nasim still sometimes fell quiet. There were days when she pushed at her food, days when the cat on her lap was the only thing that gave her pleasure, days when even that was not enough. On one such afternoon, Delia asked her to think about putting it into words. "I know you have before. You've told me about the darkness and the void and the numbness. You've told me the *what*, but *why*, Nasim? Why are you there? I don't think you'll find a way out until you know the answer to that question."

Nasim's response came quickly, "It doesn't matter that I'm stuck in the darkness. Eventually it will pass. And in the interim it hurts - or maybe it doesn't because I don't feel anything - but the pain or the emptiness, whichever it is, it doesn't matter."

It wasn't until weeks later, as they sat side by side on a log overlooking the marsh that they had - this once - decided not to venture into, that Nasim added to her first reply. "It's funny: I realized once before that my pain had nothing to do with happiness or freedom - or the lack of either - that pain was just a part of life. And that suffering was a choice, or - maybe better said- that not suffering could be a choice. But in accepting that, I forgot to ask myself where so much of that pain was coming from."

A rustling sound in the rushes not far from where they were sitting caused Nasim to pause. They watched together, hopeful that they might catch a glimpse of something interesting. The rustle ceased, though, and their curiosity went unsated.

Eventually Nasim continued, "I heard Ruth once in an interview say she was born to have children. I envy her that sense of purpose, the clarity that she had in it. Sometimes I envy people who believe in God, too. To go through the motions of life, finding joy only in a moment here or there... I wonder how different an experience that would be if you felt that you were carrying out some greater Will, that you were an instrument in some larger Plan. That you were here for a Reason.

"I have many moments of contentment, and occasionally I steal a second or two of unabated joy. But there's never been any fulfillment for me. That's why I keep tripping and falling into that void, Delia. Because I have no purpose here. Because I'm prevented from doing whatever it is that I was meant to be doing."

"I hadn't ever looked at it from quite that angle," Delia admitted.

Nasim smiled at her, "That's because your purpose is here. Because your fulfillment comes in taking care of me and, through me, in taking care of the whole next generation."

Delia looked away, not wanting Nasim to see that she was right.

"There's nothing wrong with it," Nasim reassured her. "It's not much different for Peter. I know that either of you would do anything for me, and you would do it because you love me. And you love me for who I am, but a part of you also loves me for what I am, for the fact that I'm an Eve. Cath and Enzo didn't have that. Or if they did, they forgot it. They lost the higher purpose, and once that was gone, all that was left was a person they loved in pain. *Complicit.* They both used that word. That's what happens when you lose the purpose in it. The captive's pain becomes senseless, the keeper becomes complicit."

The rustling began again, and again they looked in silence. This time they were rewarded with the appearance of a river otter that popped its head out of the water to contemplate them. After a few minutes spent regarding each other, it retreated back into the rushes.

"So what is it, then? What's your purpose?" Delia asked. When Nasim failed to reply she added, "What would bring you fulfillment?"

Nasim was silent for so long that Delia no longer expected a reply, but finally it came: "I wish I knew."

SEVENTY-SIX

APRIL 19, 2069

She hated this one more than the last one, the parasite growing inside her, sucking its life from her own. If she could have strangled off the blood that fed it, she would have happily done so. Each time it stirred, she imagined her body closing up, crushing the limb that touched her and hoped that by sheer force of will she might spur her muscles to act. But she was no more able to manage that than she had been able to stop her heart from beating the many times she had wished that, too.

"At least you've been through it this time," Cath said to Nasim. They were seated side by side on the couch in silence. Cath had attempted to select a movie to pass a few hours, but Nasim had declined each one. "You know, so you know what to expect. I can't imagine how horrible it must have been, all that going on without having a sense... of what was happening."

"What kind of people do you think they were?" Nasim asked.

"Who?"

"My parents," she said.

Puzzled, Cath replied, "You knew your parents."

"I don't think I knew them after all."

"What do you mean?" Nasim shrugged, but Cath persisted, "No, really. What do you mean? You think they weren't your real parents, or what?"

Nasim waited so long to reply that Cath had been sucked back into the daydreams that kept her occupied in the long hours of Nasim's silence. "I don't even know why they didn't vaccinate me. How could I know them and not know that simple thing?"

"Is it a simple thing?"

"It seems like the only simple thing. You have a choice. Get your child pricked in the arm to save her life. Don't get your child pricked in the arm, and ensure her a future of - what? - either death or this."

"But if it's simple, if that's all there is to it, then what don't you know?"

"Who were they!? Who were they that they made the choice they did? Who were they that I'm here now? If they'd died a little sooner, if... I hadn't been old enough to take care of myself, I'd have wound up in some foster home. You know what they would have done to me there?" Nasim's nostrils flared wide, her eyes bored into Cath. "They would have pricked me in the arm! Some government home where no one knew my name, some orphanage where unwanted children accumulated so they could be forgotten, that would have been a better home to me than the one my parents gave me! *That* would have saved me from this future!"

"I don't-"

"If I could just know why," Nasim interrupted. Her right hand was clutching at her left arm, its nails digging into her skin. "Why they did it. Why they didn't."

Cath waited this time, thinking Nasim might finish the

thought. "Then what?" she finally asked.

"Then I could know why I hate them."

"But you don't..." Nasim's knuckles were white, her arm now showing the first trickle of blood where her nails had broken the skin. Cath saw it, and it silenced her.

"I would know whether they were ignorant or short-sighted or selfish. I would know whether this was the future they envisioned for me, or whether it was death. I would know whether they thought we'd survive by some other miracle of God or man, some miracle other than a vaccine that could have saved all of us. Or whether we were really so poor that they couldn't afford to buy our lives. I would know who they were."

"Nasim, you're hurting yourself." Cath pointed to the four trickles of blood interrupting the pallor of Nasim's arm.

"Myself? This body is just the shell that keeps me here. It's as hateful to me as the Project, as my parents, as Scott and Eleanore, as you. All links in the chain, all the people who have tied me down here, and this body, the shackle."

"But that's-"

"It's the worst betrayal of all, that my own body should work against me. Worse than the people I never knew who put me here. Worse than the people I trusted to protect me who failed to. Even within *myself*, Cath," the disgust showed plainly on Nasim's face, "even *within* me, I'm not safe from betrayal. If I had instruments to do worse to this, I would happily use them."

Nasim raked her nails down her arm, tearing the skin in four tracks smeared first with the blood that had already collected on her nails and then dotted with what welled up from underneath.

"Nasim!" Cath grabbed for her hand to stop her, but Nasim had already dropped it into her lap.

Cath's eyes met Nasim's blank expression, and Nasim shrugged.

"It doesn't matter, Cath. All this hatred, all this bile, and I've nowhere to spit it. So I'll just keep choking it down."

In a whisper that she was sure Nasim didn't hear, Cath replied, "That's the fuel you burn in the fight."

That evening, when Nasim was lying in bed, her room black and silent, she tried once again to will the thing out of her body, to crush it in her belly, to smother the life from it. But it still moved and kicked and lived.

SEVENTY-SEVEN

Nasim handed Peter the books from the shelf one by one. She did it slowly, running her finger along the worn crease in the spine, smoothing down the bent corners of the covers, tracing the titles. A few of them she fanned through just so that she could smell the paper and glue.

"That one goes," she said as she finally relinquished the book she was holding.

Peter placed it in the third pile on the floor in front of him. In the first pile were the books that she would take with her when she left; in the second, those that would go into storage until she decided on a place to settle. The third pile contained those that she was willing to part with permanently.

When they had cleared the first shelf, Nasim turned around to survey the results. "Shit," she said and started laughing. The first pile dwarfed the other two. "That's going to make for a heavy suitcase."

Peter looked at the two books that had made it into the third pile, which the cat was now sitting atop. "You really hated these, huh?"

Nasim laughed again. "We're starting over. Two piles

this time. One for storage, the other to go with me."

They sorted through the first shelf again, and then the second, before Nasim gave up. "They're all going into storage," she said as she started reshelving the books haphazardly. "Except one. I can take one with me. And I can't choose right now. I've already had to make too many decisions today, even if none of them stuck."

When the two of them sat down for lunch (and the cat assumed her usual spot on the table) twenty minutes later, Peter said, "It's one of those times of reflection, isn't it? The end of something. It makes you think about the journey."

Nasim shook her head. "Just say it, Peter. Whatever it is, it doesn't need an introduction."

Peter put down his sandwich. "I was going to use the introduction as an opportunity to eat, but we can do it your way. It's been on my mind the last few days that when Enzo left, you withdrew so far that I thought you might never come back to us. I thought there was a chance you would decide that too many people had hurt you, that it wasn't worth risking your heart anymore. Or maybe something even more basic than that. I was afraid you wouldn't be willing to lean on anyone anymore. That you would retreat to self-sufficiency. But you didn't."

"Maybe that's just how naïve I am."

"You know that's not what I meant," Peter sighed.

"It's *my* contribution to the conversation, not yours."

"Well, regardless, I think about it, about how thankful I am that you came back."

"You can eat your sandwich now, if you want," Nasim replied. Peter's thoughts might be mired in the past somewhere, but hers were all on the future. "I know where I'm going," she told him, and when he looked puzzled, she continued, "After this."

C. E. Rowland

"I thought you were going to wander aimlessly. You very specifically said that not having a destination was the point."

"Well, yes. But I know where I'm going after *that*."

"And?" he asked.

"Peter, I'll have grandchildren one day. Granddaughters. I couldn't do anything for myself, and I didn't even try to do anything for my daughters, but I can do something for my granddaughters. I'll do what Scott Davis did when he believed in a cause. I'll shake the right hands, and I'll smile at the right people; and I'll go to Washington, and I'll change things."

"It might not be that simple," Peter replied.

"It doesn't matter whether it's simple. It doesn't matter whether I fail the first time or the tenth. It's the thing above all others that's worth doing. It's the only thing that's worth doing."

"Haven't you done this before, though? Didn't it just make you miserable?"

Nasim shook her head and smiled. "You can't see the difference? I was fighting a battle that had already been lost, and I was only fighting it for myself. That was desperation. This is a world apart, Peter: This is a fight that hasn't even begun yet, and I'll be fighting for the millions who can't. How could I shirk that responsibility?"

Only half of Peter's ambivalence - part pride, part concern - came through in his words, "It's going to be a long fight, Nasim, and a hard one to win."

She only shook her head again, and her smile deepened, "It's why I'm here. Because it's going to be long and hard, and no one but me would ever do it."

"But first you'll wander awhile?"

Nasim laughed and confirmed, "There's plenty of time.

First I'll wander awhile."

SEVENTY-EIGHT

JUNE 8, 2069

The second child was a boy, though Nasim never learned that. This time the nurse didn't hand it to her. She didn't even see the thing, just heard its cry as it was swept out of the room.

The labor had been much easier, much shorter. It had bridged Delia's shift and Peter's, and again she had been relieved when Peter arrived.

When the afterbirth had come and the midwife and remaining nurse had packed up the bloody sheets and left her with the hot water bottle, Peter sat down beside her. He took the hand that was hanging over the edge of the bed, held it in his own, but before he could say the words he had wanted, she said, "You can go now, Peter."

He almost said the words anyhow, but instead he took the glass on Nasim's bedside table into the bathroom, refilled it, and replaced it.

When Peter left, Nasim rolled onto her side, her knees drawn up to her chest, her whole body in a protective embrace around the water bottle at her center. Her eyes fell on the blue pill beside the glass of water. It had remained there, undisturbed, since Peter had placed it there more than a year before. She had never really looked at it, never noticed that its color was two shades lighter than the blue of the walls. It was a long oval, half the size of the temperature probes of which she had swallowed so many.

Could there really be relief in something so innocuous?

With everyone gone, the silence washed back over her, familiar and welcome, and in it she retreated to the safety of the space she had carved out in her own mind. Abbas was there, reaching out to her. He kissed her on both cheeks. She couldn't tell whether he had grown into a man here or whether she had shrunk into a child, but it seemed to her that they were well-matched, though neither of them had a form.

Here, there was no child inside her, and there never would be. There was no pain to feel, just emptiness, the safety of void. And occasionally the company of Abbas. All the other characters had disappeared as she had grown to hate them one by one. The hatred had fizzled out now, swallowed back up into the chasm like all the other feelings she had had, like even the memories of feelings she had had, but the characters had never returned. Sometimes Maryam came, instead, but usually it was Abbas.

The focus of her eyes had drifted, but the pill snapped back into clarity. A little, blue thing. Would it make her want to breathe again?

When Cath came by later, Nasim was still meditating on the pill.

"Do you think if I took it, I could accept all this?" Her mind encompassed the campus around her, but her eyes never left the pill.

"Accept it?"

"You know, resign myself to it. People have been

telling me for years that this is reality." Her hand moved unconsciously to her belly. "That once I know that, I'll... find some peace."

"It's been a long day, Nasim. Tomorrow or next week or next month, you'll-"

"What? Want to fight it some more? Miss the pain of resisting?"

"You'll-"

Nasim interrupted again, "I don't have any fight left in me, Cath. I'm too tired. I didn't know this point existed. I didn't know you could be too tired for even apathy. But I'm here." She waited awhile. "So what do you think about it?"

"About giving up?"

"No, about the pill.

"I never thought it was a bad idea."

"So you think I should take it?"

A flicker of a smile crossed Cath's lips. "Since when have you ever taken my advice? But if you want it now, then yes, I think you should take it."

"And if that means that I'm not fighting anymore, that I'm accepting this?"

"There's no reason it would mean that. The pill won't make this any more just. It won't make you forget that you're here."

"If I take the pill, I'm not fighting anymore, Cath."

"It's been a long day."

For the remainder of the week, Cath didn't press, didn't mention letters or phone calls or injustice, and the following week she drew the night shift. In that time, Nasim threw away the paper and envelopes and pens and shredded the list and threw away the scraps of it, too. When Delia suggested a walk, she went, the tar of her depression still clinging to her feet, weighing them down, sticking them to the ground; but she wrenched them free to take each step. When Peter suggested that they read, she forced her eyes over the letters, forced her hand to turn the page when she had run out of words.

She swallowed the blue pill each morning when she woke up, then got out of bed, forbade herself from languishing past nine o'clock. Forbade herself, too, from returning to bed once she had left it.

Several weeks into the routine she had forced on herself, Cath asked, "Do you want to write a letter today?"

"I'm not writing any more letters, Cath."

"You seem much better, though. Is it the pills, you think?"

"It's that I've given up."

"Nasim, you can't possibly-"

Nasim interrupted, "There's only futility in fighting."

SEVENTY-NINE

November 12, 2082

Delia was on duty, but Peter had appeared, too, just after the midwife but before the nurse arrived. The nurse had paused on entering, counting the number of people present and wondering if he had been summoned to the wrong coop, but Peter had silently waved him in.

The two handlers sat on either side of the bed, each offering Nasim a hand to hold. She squeezed them both, held them tight even when the pain ebbed.

The labor was quick. "Her twelfth," the nurse whispered to the midwife, who, of course, already knew that.

When she heard the cries of the baby, Nasim said, "I want to hold it."

The midwife was the one with the infant in her arms, with one hand unfurling the blanket to wrap the child in. She balked, but Peter said, "Don't be ridiculous. What could she possibly do to it?"

"It's just, we don't usually–" She wilted under Peter's disparaging look and handed the baby, still naked, to Nasim. It was a girl, hot and pink, eyes blue, head capped with a crop of blond fuzz. Nasim cradled her against her chest, put her pinky in the minuscule hand that curled around it. Then she ran her thumb down the tiny bridge of the child's nose and handed her back to the midwife.

The nurse was the first one to go, taking the child. Then the midwife, taking the afterbirth. Then Delia and Peter, after asking if she needed anything, and she was alone until the cat, who had been chased out by the midwife, sneaked back into the room. It was almost two in the morning. In the innumerable times that she had imagined this moment in the preceding years, Nasim had pictured herself getting out of bed and picking up the suitcase she would have already packed. She had imagined seizing freedom at the very first moment that it was hers, and now, in the middle of the night, minutes after her labor was finished, the thought of her impatience made her laugh. To no one, she said, "Where did I think that I was being prevented from going all these years? What destination was I hurrying towards? What's worth having at the end of that journey?"

And now the thought reminded her of something her mother had said, that she had been impatient even in birth. Her brother had taken sixteen hours and her sister, six, but Nasim had burst from the womb in a mere forty minutes. "My Nasim, always ready to get going," he father had teased her. She couldn't have been more than four or five when he had said it, and she couldn't dredge up any of the context. More than the memory itself, though, the sudden remembrance of her parents surprised her. She had thought so little about them since that period of anger, and her fear that the anger might return tempted her to cut the memory off.

But what do I have to fear? She stayed awhile in it. She groped for the details, the look of the place around her, the feeling of her father's laughter as his whole lap shook with it and the sandpaper of his cheek when he kissed her. Her mother was too far away to see with any clarity, a figure in the background but whose voice nevertheless came through, "Leave my little love be!"

Nasim looked for a trace of the anger she had once felt when she had thought of them, but it was gone. To the cat curled up beside her, she said, "Now we have everything, don't we?"

EIGHTY

It was the day Nasim received the phone call that the third insemination attempt had been successful. She had gone through the motions that she still forced every morning: wake, pill, shower, eat. Cath was on duty. She knew the likely content of the call when the phone rang, and Nasim confirmed it when she hung up.

"I can't stay, Nasim."

Nasim looked at her with uncertainty. "I can call Delia to come early. Or I'd be fine for the next few hours."

"Nasim." Cath was sitting on the couch, Nasim, still standing beside the phone. "That's not what I mean. I can't... I can't see you like this."

"Pregnant?"

"Defeated."

"But what...?" Nasim trailed off.

"I'm handing in my resignation this afternoon."

Nasim crossed her feet and sank to the floor. "You're leaving?" she clarified, hoping she might have misunderstood.

Cath nodded.

"But... what will I do...?"

"You'll be fine. You'll have Peter and Delia. And someone else. They'll arrange for someone else. Soon, I'm sure."

"But how can you leave when you said…"

The accusation lingered for a long time before Cath replied, "My staying isn't good for either of us. I can't help you heal any more than I can stand to see you broken."

"I'm not broken," Nasim whispered.

"All the more reason I shouldn't stay. If I can't even tell anymore…"

Cath hadn't told Peter or Delia, hadn't even been sure she would go through with it until she had written out the words earlier that morning. But when she had signed her name to the letter, the guilt of leaving had been but a shadow of the guilt she was leaving behind. That Nasim should resign herself to this injustice, that she should lose the will even to fight it, wasn't that the ultimate proof of inequity? If life began unfair, no effort could balance the scales to fairness. Cath looked at her feet when the director of the facility took the letter of resignation from her hand, studied the mud on the toe of her boot out of shame that even in this, the inequity played out: she hated this place and could leave; Nasim hated this place and couldn't.

When Delia came to relieve Cath, Cath said nothing about it, and Nasim kept silent, too, in the hopes that, unspoken, it might simply be untrue.

Peter received the call first, at his apartment. His hand lingered on the phone after he had hung up. He finally picked it up again to call Delia and work out a new schedule between the two of them, but he changed his mind before he dialed. They could talk when he relieved her at midnight and Nasim was sure to be asleep.

A moment later, the phone rang in the coop. "It's for you," Nasim said, handing the phone to Delia. For six years, Delia had always rushed to the phone when it rang, but the calls were always for Nasim, so she had given up lately. She took the receiver, held it to her ear. A voice on the other end spoke, and at the end, she hung up the phone without ever having said a word. She looked at Nasim uncertainly. "Do you…?"

"Yes, I know." Nasim forced the words out casually as she dug a few tears out of her eyes with her knuckles. Delia was saying something, but Nasim wasn't listening. The vertigo of the fall back into the dark, quiet space within - so quick this time, so far to go with such urgency - crowded out her other senses. Such safety in the numbness.

Delia touched her face, and the contact brought her back to the moment. "I'm so sorry, Nasim. But this pain will fade. It's not like being here. It's not a thing you'll live with every day."

"It's worse than being here."

"For now."

"Why did she go?" Nasim asked.

"I have no idea. She didn't tell you anything?"

"That it hurt her too much to see my pain. That it hurt too much that I'd given up. Does my pain hurt you?"

"Not too much to bear," Delia replied.

"You won't… leave?"

"Never," insisted Delia.

"But it hurts you?"

"Don't worry about me, Nasim."

"The darkness is so powerful, Delia." There was fear in Nasim's voice. "The emptiness inside me. What sucks me in. I can feel it again. In a moment it's swelled back up to its full power; it's ready to devour me again."

"It's a place you've been before. It's a place you've left before."

"I don't know that there will be any of me left to leave it this time."

"I promise you'll still be in there." If Nasim had been watching more closely, she would have seen the doubt in Delia's eyes. Nasim hadn't ever told her - hadn't told any of them - about how the darkness had come alive or about the nepenthe she had finally found somewhere deep inside. They hadn't known about the hours that she had spent with Abbas, hadn't known that they themselves had inhabited that space for a while, keeping her company in a world that was kinder than the one she was born into.

"You'll still be in there. I'll haul you out if need be."

EPILOGUE

Nasim stood at the gate, an ugly chain link thing that could be rolled shut but hadn't been in years. In her right hand, she held a suitcase, the same one she had packed when the men in suits had come to retrieve her from her apartment. She wore a black peacoat that was beaded with drops of mist or rain, she couldn't decide which. Her long, black hair was falling over her shoulders; a few strands worrying her face as the wind pushed them in front of her eyes. She didn't bother to brush them away; she was conscious instead of how her jeans didn't fit, of how tightly they stretched across the belly that was still there. But the suitcase was too small to fit much, and these were her favorite pair, so she had worn them anyhow. The moonstone that Delia had given her hung around her neck. In her fist she clutched that last note that Enzo had left. She had found it in one of her books years before - surely Peter had put it there, surely he had wanted her to be able to choose whether to keep it or discard it. It was crumpled and worn, the ink smudged from when she had first read it. In the last moment before she crossed the threshold of the campus, she let it slip through her fingers and fall into the mud.

334   *C. E. Rowland*

She thought one more time about what she had packed: clothes mostly. Her only compromise on pragmatism was the photo that Peter had given her of the lone surviving ash tree, now tucked into her copy of *Siddhartha*, the only book she had brought. Peter would keep the cat until she settled somewhere, and the remainder of her books and a few other possessions had gone into storage until then, too; but the rest she was leaving behind.

The guard at the gatehouse had told her that the nearest bus stop was a half mile down the road. "North," he had said, though he had pointed south, and she hadn't asked for clarification. There was only one road. She would come to a stop eventually. "And I don't know where it goes," he had called after her as her foot crossed the line between here and whatever lay beyond.

ACKNOWLEDGEMENTS

THANK YOU TO the people who have helped me, with great patience, find my way out of dark places: my parents, David, Emily, and Els; my siblings and friends, Susannah, Grace, Laura, Sarah, Agnieszka, Karolina, Beth, Aman, JC, Aidan, Charlie, Rita, Quyen, Catherine, Rich, YungChia, Nathan, Meredith, and Luca. But for your kindness and your wisdom, I don't know where I would be, but it certainly wouldn't be in the acknowledgments section of a novel.

Thank you, too, to all the strangers who made me mochas and lattes and poured me bourbon and to those who watched my computer for me while I hustled off to the restroom.

ABOUT THE AUTHOR

C. E. ROWLAND lives on a boat with her cats in Washington, DC. When she isn't working her day job as a scientist or her side hustle as a writer, she can be found adventuring through remote wilderness, plotting to take over the world, and picking up eclectic hobbies.

Rowland's previous works include *Transcending Limbo* and *The Watchmaker's New Order*.

www.ingramcontent.com/pod-product-compliance
Lightning Source LLC
Chambersburg PA
CBHW030409180626
46812CB00005B/1982